D0195039

MOMENTS OF TIME

Recent Titles by Gloria Cook

The Pengarron Series

PENGARRON LAND
PENGARRON PRIDE
PENGARRON'S CHLDREN
PENGARRON DYNASTY *

The Harvey Family Series

TOUCH THE SILENCE *
MOMENTS OF SILENCE *

KILGARTHEN
ROSCARROCK
ROSEMERRYN
TREVALLION

LISTENING TO THE QUIET *

* *available from Severn House*

MOMENTS OF TIME

Gloria Cook

This first world edition published in Great Britain 2003 by
SEVERN HOUSE PUBLISHERS LTD of
9–15 High Street, Sutton, Surrey SM1 1DF.
This first world edition published in the USA 2003 by
SEVERN HOUSE PUBLISHERS INC of
595 Madison Avenue, New York, N.Y. 10022.

British Library Cataloguing in Publication Data

Cook, Gloria
Moments of time
1. Cornwall (England) - Social life and customs - 20th century - Fiction
2. Domestic fiction
I. Title
823.9'14 [F]

ISBN 0-7278-5978-1

Except where actual historical events and characters are being described for the storyline of this novel, all situations in this publication are fictitious and any resemblance to living persons is purely coincidental.

Typeset by Palimpsest Book Production Ltd.,
Polmont, Stirlingshire, Scotland.
Printed and bound in Great Britain by
MPG Books Ltd., Bodmin, Cornwall.

To Ann and John Glinn, true friends.

One

Something was disturbing her sleep. The living and being world was breaking into Emilia Harvey's hazy drifting mind. Sharp noises. Loud voices. A scream. Her weary brain told her it was the boys playing a rowdy game in the back garden.

The intrusion persisted, denying her this precious time of peace in a place of soothing floating warmth. She longed to remain in the mesmerizing goldenness of her dream, for almost every day of her third pregnancy had been marked by insomnia, or nausea, or backache, or a lack of energy, as if the baby inside her was having problems forming and growing and was intent on sapping the goodness out of her.

She gave up resisting and opened her eyes. Blinked, and gazed up at the moulded ceiling of the bedroom. Tried for a second to remember the shimmering paradise she had been in, but it was already sinking into her subconscious where it would likely stay forgotten for ever. Will's and Tom's voices came again, and now her mother's, all screaming and steeped in fear and accompanying them were strange vicious noises.

'Mummy! Mummy!'

'Mummmmy!'

'Help us, someone!'

Emilia shot up and heaved herself off the bed, making her head spin. She recognized those snarling noises, and filled with guilt for wasting long, perhaps vital moments, she forced her legs to work and ran, terrified for her family, foolishly fast down the stairs before thrusting the front door open. 'Will, Tom, I'm coming! Mum, hold on, I'm coming!'

She raced round the house to the back lawn.

'Emilia, be careful!' Dolly Rowse shouted to her.

Now faced with the full reality of the horror, Emilia kept running. 'Stay there boys, don't move! Mummy's coming!' Both her little sons were cowering and crying, clasped together behind the swing, and her mother was trying to ward off an attacking Jack Russell. There was blood on the terrier's bared teeth and blood on Will's leg and on her mother's hand; the hem at the front of her skirt was in tatters.

'Pip, get down! Get down!' Emilia yelled as she made the last of the distance. On the way she picked up a cricket bat, ready to beat off the dog.

There was a sudden explosive noise. The garden seemed to shake and the little dog was sent hurtling away from Dolly, its middle a chaotic red, to land at the foot of a high privet hedge, contaminating a proud display of daffodils on the way. The shock made Emilia jolt in her run and only with an effort did she keep her balance.

'Jonny! Thank goodness.' Thank goodness Jonathan Harvey had been taught how to shoot by his uncle, Emilia's husband, Alec. Thank goodness his aim had been accurate or she might have just lost her mother.

Stunned and sprawled across the grass from the retort of the shotgun, the ten-year-old boy's face was set grave and serious. Panting, sweating, for he too had made a crazed run, his wide staring eyes were on the dog's remains. 'When I heard the uproar I knew there was only one thing for it. The gun's safe, Aunty Em, I only had time to load one cartridge. Poor Pip.'

'Never mind the darn dog, he came at us for no reason,' Dolly cried, rubbing her teeth-raked fingers down her skirt while anxiously studying her grandsons. She was shuddering, too shaky to go to them. 'See what it's done to us.'

'It's all right, Mum.' Emilia wanted to go to her but Will and Tom were her priority. Sobbing and gulping, clutching hands, they were running to her. Unaware she was trembling herself, she dropped down and gathered them in, hugging them tight, tighter. Ashamed and angry at herself for misinterpreting their first desperate cries for help, she pressed them to her, holding back her own tears of fright and shock. 'Don't worry, my loves, it's all over now. Everyone's safe. Tom, were you bitten too?'

Clinging to her neck, her younger son shook his head.

'Let's go inside. I'll send for the doctor to come and see to Will's and Granny's wounds.'

The shot would have been heard over every acre of Ford Farm. It was likely Alec, or Emilia's father, the farm manager, or one of the farmhands was hurrying to the farmstead to learn what had happened.

The housekeeper had already dashed from the wash house, and the general maid from the dairy. 'Heaven save us!' Her sleeves rolled up past her stout elbows, a starched tablecloth hanging from her hand and made dirty by being dragged along the ground, Tilda Lawry's shiny, freckled face turned a riot of crimson and white. 'Sara, help me get everyone indoors, then run to the village and summon Dr Holloway here urgently. Can you get up on your own, Master Jonny? Good, good. Come along, Mrs Em, up you get too. Shouldn't be down there like that with only three weeks to go.' She viewed the Jack Russell's body with disgust. 'Jim can bury that creature when he gets here.'

'No! Alec can do it.' Emilia had risen and was keeping her sons clamped to her. 'I've been telling him for weeks that Pip was getting more and more bad-tempered, growling and snapping at everyone and the beasts, that the other dogs were scared of him, but he insisted there was no danger, that it was just Pip's grumpy way. Will and Tom and my mother shouldn't have gone through this. I'm sorry you had to do what you did, Jonny. I know you were fond of Pip.'

It was a pathetic huddled group that crept its way to the kitchen. Jonny brought up the rear and went straight to the den to secure the shotgun back in its cabinet.

While Tilda bathed Dolly's hand and covered it with lint, Emilia sat Will on the end of the long scrubbed-white pine table. Will fought off her hands as she tried to tend to the dog bite.

'Come on, be brave and all that. It won't take long if you don't struggle.' Jonny had returned and he put his hands on his cousin's quivering little shoulders.

Will cried as the cooled boiled salt water stung his torn flesh, which would need a couple of stitches, at least. When Emilia had loosely bandaged his leg, she thanked Jonny for keeping him still. She had thanked Jonny on other occasions for his mature support.

She took her family to the settle, placing Will on the part of her lap her pregnancy still allowed and Tom at her side. Tom pressed his face against her arm and clutched her cardigan, his frightened brown eyes on his brother's pained face. Jonny sat next to Tom and gripped his hand. Emilia spread her arms around all three.

Dolly had collapsed on the huge carved chair at the head of the table.

'Will you be all right, Mum?'

Dolly nodded, tears grouping at the corners of her eyes. Emilia knew she was reliving the ordeal and she prayed the boys would be spared the same fate. 'Granny was brave and I'm proud of you boys,' she said, planting a kiss on each young, hung head. 'Your father will be proud of you too, Jonny.'

'This'll be something for him to tell his Army chums about,' Jonny replied, regaining some of his confidence.

Will, at only five years old, was trying to ignore the pain of the half-inch deep bite in his calf, although sniffing back tears. He was gazing at Jonny for reassurance; the tough, carefree and often reckless leader of the Harvey Gang. Emilia tried not to fret too much over Will, he hated being treated like a baby. She brushed back Tom's soft rich-brown hair – he was the only Harvey male not to bear coal-black locks. A year younger than Will, he was like her in looks and had her mix of resolute and thoughtful ways, which meant he sometimes displayed a quiet dignity, and was always friendly and sensible. Her dear loveable Tom, who, when sleepy and ready to snuggle up, seemed like a cuddly little field mouse. Pray God, he and Will would be able to sleep tonight.

Tilda had been busy with the teapot, plying the cups with generous helpings of sugar. 'Here, drink this, Mrs Rowse. You too, Mrs Em. What a thing to happen! One moment's all safe and well then 'tis like Armageddon all over again.' Tilda often referred in this way to the Great War. The Armistice had been signed five years ago, but after a short time of apparent prosperity, the country was again sinking into bad times, and Tilda was inclined to preach pessimism.

'We mustn't make a song and dance about it.' In control of herself again, patting her hairnet back into place, Dolly aimed her forbidding brow at Tilda. She was blunt, or candid, or jolly, depending on what an occasion called for, and stout-bodied and stout-hearted. She held up her bandaged hand and smiled at the children. 'It's not as bad as it looks. Only be sore for a few days and that don't matter. Who wants a big split with lashings of jam and cream?'

The children merely gazed at her. None had an appetite.

'It's infection I'm worried about,' Tilda said, eyeing Dolly's and Will's bandages.

'What's that?' Will's handsome grey eyes enlarged in panic.

'It's nothing to worry about, my love,' Emilia replied quickly, darting a 'please be more careful with your tongue' look at Tilda, who promptly coloured and apologized.

'But Aggie died of what Tilda just said!'

'I promise you, you'll be fine, old mate.' Jonny passed Will what Emilia knew to be a secret gang sign, probably something irreverent and aimed at Tilda. 'Aggie was an old goat, too weak to fight off the fever, but you're as strong as Hercules, remember? Besides, Dr Holloway will soon sort you out, and you'll have a brilliant scar.'

Emilia felt Will relax a little against her. His sniffing eased. His ordeal would heighten again when the doctor arrived and stitched his leg. She was picturing how the incident could have been much worse. Will and Tom had been running about, playing tag, so her mother had explained. If they had been sitting down, or had dropped down flat on the lawn in pretence of being shot in battle or something similar,

Pip might have got to their throats. She should have done something about Pip herself weeks ago.

She felt another flash of anger at Alec. He should have taken her fears over Pip seriously. Alec had a tendency to go off in his mind, to plan and occasionally scheme, but mostly, it seemed to her, he just daydreamed, drifted. Although shrewd in business matters he was content to let things jog along.

Her anger passed almost at once. Alec loved his family and he loved Jonny like a son. He had not recognized Pip's growing menace and would be horrified at the consequences. She hated to see Alec unhappy, as had been his unjust lot for so many years in the past. Now she reasoned it wasn't fair to leave the dog's body lying at the scene like an accusation against him. She was in no state to bury it herself, but the body should at least be covered up.

'Tilda, do you think you could find something to put over Pip's body? It isn't right to let it stay exposed.'

'Oh, I just couldn't!' Tilda's bristly ginger eyebrows shot up towards her old-fashioned frilled cap. She was organized and resourceful in her housekeeping duties, but her modest ways did not furnish her for such a task. 'Sorry, Mrs Em. Sara could do it. Should be back any minute.'

But Alec might arrive before Sara returned. Emilia gazed at Jonny, but the boy was staring down at the tiled floor. She couldn't ask him to do it. Pip had been his favourite of the many Jack Russells Alec had bred, his playmate when he had come to live at Ford Farm six years ago, after his now-dead mother had gone off with her lover. With his good height, broad build and above average intelligence, it was easy to forget Jonny was a child.

'I'll do it myself.' Will and Tom protested at her leaving them. 'I promise I'll only be a minute, you'll be fine with Granny and Tilda.'

Outside the back kitchen door Emilia was faced with two other Jack Russells, from the same litter as Pip. She froze, suspicious of them after the ordeal, but they wagged their tails and gazed up at her mournfully, as if conveying they were sad about what had happened, that they were no threat to her. 'Run along Bertie. You too Hope.' The black, tan and white pair scampered away and she sighed with relief. She carefully shut the door behind her and carried on to perform her grim task.

Keeping her eyes averted from the mess under the privet hedge she followed the path that cut through the hedge halfway along, and headed for the shed. There she picked up a hessian sack from a clean pile for storing vegetables, and steeled herself for what she must do. It was a warm spring day and the insects would already be investigating Pip's remains.

Before she could reach the doorway she was overcome by a peculiar forceful feeling. It shuddered painlessly down her lower back, spread rapidly to her sides, closed in at the top of the mound under her breasts, then swept down to the join of her inner thighs.

Dropping the sack, she grabbed the workbench with both hands. There was an old cider barrel nearby and she pushed off the things on it, and alarmed by the strange pulsation in her body she managed to sit down on it. This was different to when she had given birth to Will and Tom but she was in no doubt that her labour had begun.

She rested her arms over her bump. 'Not now, baby. Please wait, at least until we get over the fright your brothers and granny have just had.'

There were other sensations in her body now. Urgent. Unstoppable.

'Oh, help me! This can't be real.' Her baby was being born. Now. This minute. Instantaneous birth was rare in animals, surely it didn't happen to women? But it must do, for it was happening to her. Her waters broke and were wetting her and she felt the need to push the baby out of her body.

There was little chance of being heard if she shouted for help, tucked away as she was down at the bottom of the garden. Fighting back the panic she concentrated on what she must do to safely deliver her child. With the greatest effort she levered herself to her feet. The shed was large and had a wooden planked floor that was swept after each use. She scattered the pile of sacks to cover the biggest space. If she didn't get down on them straightaway her baby would fall out of her.

Manoeuvring herself into a half-lying position was the hardest thing she had ever done. Then arranging her clothes and with her knees raised she gave a mighty push, the only one that was necessary, and reached down for the pinkness emerging from her. Trembling, terrified she would drop the wet slippery child, she wrapped it in her skirt and brought it up to her chest. It had all happened so quickly yet each second had seemed an age spent in dread, consternation and disbelief.

The baby was floppy, its tiny, tiny face harsh shades of red and blue. 'Oh, God, oh God, help me. What do I do now? Get it breathing, yes, I must make it breathe.' With her smallest finger she gently eased open the little mouth and hooked out a blockage of mucus.

Nothing happened.

She gave the bundle in her hands a tremulous shake. 'Come on, baby, cry. Please cry!'

It seemed time had stopped dead. She wanted to close her eyes and wake up from the nightmare and find the day had only just begun. To find that Will and her mother had not been bitten and Tom terrified and her baby not yet born. Then as if something beyond her usual senses was taking control she brought the baby's face up close to her own, covered its nose and mouth with her own mouth and blew gently, giving it air. She did this again and again, had no idea how many times.

Then she was crying and didn't know why. Time had resumed its normal pattern and she was aware of her baby crying. The sound as soft and pathetic as the mewling of a weak kitten, but her baby was alive. A weightless, under-sized scrap; she had wispy hair, dark-brown like her own. Her beautiful baby, a daughter, whom twice she had generated life into.

The last stage of her labour was soon over. The cord had to be dealt with and somehow she must get the baby into the house or the dangers to her would outweigh those faced by Will and Tom today.

She heard a strong male voice calling her name.

'Alec!' Everything would be all right now. 'Alec, we're in here.'

Two

Together Emilia and Alec gazed down at their ten-day-old baby, the next to accommodate the boat-shaped rocker cradle of generations of Harveys. 'I've not long woken her for a feed, then as usual, she went straight back to sleep.' There was no need for Emilia to whisper. Few things caused tiny Jenna Harvey to stir.

Alec lifted Jenna up and she was engulfed in his solid, protective arms. 'She's our little angel. So beautiful, so perfect.' Then some of the strength and joy seeped out of him. 'She shouldn't have had to make such an awful entrance into the world. I'm sorry about your ordeal, darling. I should have listened to you about that wretched dog. At least we'll be able to get help quicker now we've had a telephone installed. Can't think why it never occurred to me before.'

'Don't keep punishing yourself, Alec. Jenna's fine, and the boys have forgotten about it now Will's stitches are out.' Emilia rested her face against Alec's shoulder and he included her in his embrace. Jenna's birth had made her family complete, rounded off her life with Alec. There had been fears over Jenna's low body weight and preliminary feeding problems, and they had even wondered if her christening should be rushed forward. When the doctor, only yesterday, had announced satisfaction with her progress, Alec had immediately planned a small party at the coming weekend to celebrate her birth.

Jenna did not have the roundness of chin common to babies. Emilia touched her daughter's peaceful, heart-shaped face. 'Jenna's so different to Will and Tom. I can't wait to see her tearing about with them.'

Alec kissed Jenna and rearranged the shawl that swamped her slumbering form. He would place her back in the cradle with reluctance. 'Can't see her being a tomboy as you were, darling, when you played here as a child with Ben and the others. I think we've bred a proper little lady.'

'I think you're right,' Emilia smiled. She couldn't think of many ladylike things about herself. Not for her the usual ten days of lying-in, resting and being waited on after Jenna's birth. Three days later she had dressed in trousers, shirt and boots and had gone back to work in the yard and dairy, which had been her jobs when an ordinary village girl, before her marriage. Her heart grew a little sad. Ben, whom Alec had referred to, was his youngest brother, and neither she nor Alec were on friendly terms with him now, and 'the others' were her brother, Billy, killed at Passchendaele in 1917, and her closest childhood friend, Honor Burrows, who, like Emilia herself, had once been briefly engaged to Ben, and was now married and living in Lincolnshire.

There was a tap on the nursery door and Tilda came in. 'Pardon me, Mr Harvey, Mrs Em. There's a lady downstairs, a Miss Bosweld, come here by bicycle, asking to see you, Mr Harvey. 'Tis about renting Captain Harvey's old place. I showed her into the sitting room.' The housekeeper cooed over Jenna even though she was deeply asleep, and even when awake was too young to respond.

'What impression did you get of her, Tilda?' Alec asked. Ford House, with four bedrooms, a stable and its own paddock was grand in comparison to his other properties in and around the village of Hennaford, and demanded a comparable rent. He had bought it off his brother, Tristan, Jonny's father, following the tragic death there of Tristan's wife, Ursula – this after being deserted by her lover and giving birth to his baby.

'She looks well-bred, a modern type, a bit full of herself, I thought, but I suppose she'd do.' Tilda made a face. She was content to be an 'old maid' and content to be in service, routinely working in a uniform of ankle-length, Puritan-grey dress, a pristine, starched, wrap-around white apron and a cap, even though Alec's relaxed views on just about everything meant his staff could choose to wear, as Sara did, what they liked.

'We might as well go down and talk to this Miss Bosweld together, darling,' Alec said to Emilia. He included Emilia in his every decision. She did all the paperwork for the farm owing to a strange condition of his, something which he found continually humiliating, which prevented him from reading and writing properly; his harrowing experiences at a top school in Truro had made him content to send Will to the village school. To Tilda, 'I don't suppose it would be asking too much of you to settle this young lady down for us?'

'Well, if you want to risk getting your supper late,' Tilda joked back, eagerly stretching out her doughty arms.

The woman introduced herself as Selina Bosweld. She was tall and in her early thirties. She was wearing a straightforward suit of dark blue, tailored but serviceable rather than stylish, and sturdy shoes that were well worn. In contrast a gold-coloured filmy scarf was tied round her bobbed tawny hair. She took the armchair offered to her at a quick, sinuous pace.

Emilia glanced at her ungloved hands. They were as used to manual work as her own, the nails cut short and clean.

Selina Bosweld saw her looking. 'I'm a nursing sister at the Infirmary, Mrs Harvey. I served at the Somme and Etaples. Niceties seem unimportant now.'

'Of course.' Emilia had heard how the impossible conditions of the field hospitals during the war had ruined many a fine pair of hands, and fine hands Miss Bosweld must have once had, for the rest of her was lithe and poised and in good symmetry. She exuded confidence in an autonomous way. 'The country's grateful to you, Miss Bosweld. My husband's brother was badly wounded and needed the dedicated care of the medical staff to bring him through.'

'Well, the country welcomed back its fighting heroes, but it wasn't quite so sure about women like myself.' Selina Bosweld's smile was short-lived, and Emilia took this to mean that her stance, like her own, was in opposition to the country's general viewpoint towards women. Despite the advances made in equality, including the right to vote in elections for those of thirty years or more, feeling broadly still held that women over a certain age, with the exception of those in service, should marry and raise a family.

Selina Bosweld's gaze, suddenly astute, officious and enquiring, fell upon Alec. 'Now, let's talk about the house. From the details at the estate agent it sounded just what we're looking for, that is my widowed brother, Perry, his child, and I. I rode on down past the farm just now to take a look at it and all appeared to be in good order. It was easy to find; across the ford, then up a hill by way of the right fork in the lane. The other direction leads to the village, a short distance, I understand?'

'That's correct,' Alec said. He was viewing the woman with his fingertips pressed together, wholly attentive.

'I saw two of your staff hard at work there, a girl inside the house and a youth stocking up the woodshed. We're fortunate to have good domestic help ourselves. My brother was in the Royal Army Medical Corps, a surgeon. He too served on the Western Front but was sadly crippled; was too near to an unexploded Mills bomb; lost a leg. It was dreadfully bad luck, the war was over and he was about to escort home one of the last groups of wounded and ill POWs. His hand was also injured, not too badly but seriously enough to prevent him from operating again. Now, would it be possible to turn one of the downstairs rooms into a bedroom for him? It would partly be an office for him. He now sits on the board of several charities for ex-service personnel.

'We're to sign the final papers on the sale of our house at Trispen, which is no longer suitable for our needs. Perry feels his daughter needs a larger garden; she wants a dog, that sort of thing. We thought it would be easier to rent something.' She gestured at Alec. 'You, as the landlord, would be responsible for the repairs and so on. As you can see, you'd have tenants of good standing for the foreseeable future. References to our characters can be provided, of course. I've brought a quarter's rent and the sum of security with me. We'd like to move in as soon as it's convenient. Mr Harvey?'

Alec had listened carefully throughout Selina Bosweld's account, for although due to a certain hawkishness she missed the definition of being beautiful, she had perfect deportment, a fascinating way of angling her head, of moving her smooth red lips. And her eyes, the colour of wild violets, had a magnetic quality. 'I can assure you, Miss Bosweld, that the house is in first-class condition, it was completely renovated after the last tenants left two months ago. There's a good-sized parlour and fully equipped kitchen. Of the two other downstairs rooms, one could easily be converted into a bedroom. I'd arrange that for you. Would you care to take a look inside the house before you make a final decision?'

Selina Bosweld glanced up at the skeletal clock above the fireplace, which showed it was late afternoon, but Emilia had the impression she had already made up her mind. 'I'm afraid I haven't the time. I'm on duty this evening and I must go home first. I'm sure there will be no problems. You see, before I ventured here I enquired about you, Mr Harvey. We have a mutual friend in Dr Reggie Rule, the paediatrician. You have a reputation for fairness and honesty.'

It amused Emilia to see Alec blush. She had the impression that Alec felt he was the one being interviewed. There was no doubt Selina Bosweld possessed drive and, so Emilia thought, powers to persuade, perhaps with an element of ruthlessness. Emilia had already mentally prepared a new rent book and terms of agreement for her.

'I hope you'll be happy and comfortable in Ford House, Miss Bosweld,' Emilia said, with a welcoming smile. She received a momentary puzzled frown. She had the impression the other woman was making an unfavourable comparison of her local accent to Alec's well-to-do deep tones. 'You'll be able to see the farm across the fields. The woods near the house run behind the farm. Would you like a cup of tea, or perhaps a sherry, while we go to the den to get the necessary papers for you?'

'I'd appreciate a glass of sherry, thank you, Mrs Harvey,

before I slip away. I'll settle with you when you return.' Selina Bosweld pulled a soft leather purse out of her jacket pocket.

Alec excused himself first. At the door, Emilia asked, friendly fashion, 'How old is your brother's daughter, Miss Bosweld?'

'Elizabeth's nearly five. We call her Libby.'

'Will she be attending the village school next term? It's got a good standard. I've not long fetched my eldest son from there.'

'My brother will instruct her until she's old enough for boarding school.'

Emilia was about to say something else but a queer glow came from behind the other woman's amazing eyes. The way she set her head, superior, aloof, left Emilia in no doubt what sort of Sister she was; no-nonsense with patients; no toleration of impertinence or low standards from junior staff. 'I saw your sons playing when I arrived, they were holding up one of your workmen. Your servant mentioned she had to fetch you down from the nursery. You are very young to have had three children already.'

'I just look young.' Emilia dampened down a sharper reply. 'The boys were talking to the farm manager, who happens to be my father, their grandfather. My parents live here, Miss Bosweld, so I have plenty of help with the children.'

Emilia closed the door behind her with a snap. 'Damned cheek!' She was cross at herself for offering so much explanation. If or when the disapproving, judgmental Miss Selina Bosweld went down into the village, she was likely to learn from some busybody that Emilia, at eighteen years old, had been expecting Will on her wedding day, and no doubt the nurse would form another opinion of her. It then occurred to her that Selina Bosweld's bluntness might have been a ruse to ward off more curiosity.

Smoking a slim cigar, whistling one of the latest jazz tunes, Ben Harvey, who owned properties on the other side of the main road that ran through Hennaford, approached Ford Farm on foot. Like Alec, he owned a stock of horses and ponies and a motor car – his, a fast tourer – but it was unthinkable to him to make the two miles distance in any other way. Before heading for the house he noticed the unfamiliar female's bicycle leant carefully against the inside of the perimeter hedge.

He sauntered round the side of the house with the intention of entering at the back and saw Alec and Emilia talking in the den while she was writing at the desk. Ben whizzed past the window, hoping they hadn't spotted him, but not before he noticed Emilia was looking grim. He took a satisfying puff on the cigar. Emilia had been his friend, his first love and he had adored her, but their break-up had been hostile, he blaming her for the partial blindness of his left eye, the result of their joint rescue of his late, senile grandmother one wet, dark afternoon from the garden, and Emilia claiming his belief was unjust. There was also bad history between him and Alec, of a business nature.

The farmyard, situated in the origins of the property, two centuries ago, was much like his own, well kept but twice as large. He stubbed out the cigar by the back kitchen door and scanned the dairy and the barn and each stone-walled, slate-roofed animal shed and storehouse, having to adjust the sight of his damaged eye as he did so. He was seeking signs of Sara Killigrew, hoping to creep up on her before she hid from him. The maid was the loveliest of the local girls, an innocent of nineteen years with dazzling white-blonde plaited hair, shy and meek from her workhouse background. She was the stuff of dreams, and Ben, who had been trying to get close to her for some time, was enjoying the slow intoxicating chase. He might have made progress by now if not for the sharp watch kept by her obnoxious twin brother against all suitors; he and Jim Killigrew maintained a reciprocal loathing. And now Sara was even less likely to succumb to his interest for she had recently become infatuated with someone else – Alec. It was a fact he alone seemed to have noticed, and one he could use to cause a lot of bother with if he chose to.

He listened through the unsynchronized cacophony of the

poultry and the penned-in animals for the sound of sweet singing – Sara's habitual and much celebrated pastime. Ducks were splashing in and out of the pond. A scraggy barn cat was scurrying off to chase an unseen prey. The host of well-trained Jack Russells, who were more settled now the aggressive Pip had been blasted out of their ranks, rambled up to him. He knew every one of them and bent to pat a head or two. There was lots of noise and movement but none relating to Sara Killigrew.

He went into the kitchen. Found it empty. Sara and Tilda were elsewhere, his brother and sister-in-law in the den, so where was the mystery owner of the bicycle? Probably shown into the sitting room. He carried on through the house, along the tiled passage, not caring that Alec and Emilia wouldn't approve of him wandering about as if he still lived here.

Ben found the stranger on her feet sipping sherry, studying the photographs of bygone and existing Harveys displayed on top of the piano. He viewed her with keen male appreciation. Her back was straight, her head casually aslant. In comparison to the chic, elegant women he mixed with in various select addresses, the finest hotels and the mayoral chambers in Truro, this woman was a touch shabby, but he was entranced. She was about a decade older than he was but he was used to older women. He acknowledged that he preferred them and dismissed the pursuit of Sara Killigrew as a waste of his time.

She turned her head without a glimmer of expression. 'You, sir, are obviously another Harvey. Another gentleman farmer by the evidence of your clothes.'

'You have the advantage of me, Miss, Mrs . . . ?'

'Miss. Selina Bosweld. I'm to rent Ford House off your brother, or cousin perhaps?'

'Alec's my brother. I'm Ben. I own Tremore Farm and Tremore House, also in this parish. The farm is smaller but the house is much grander. I've had much of it rebuilt and have added a balcony and a conservatory.'

'This is a fascinating house, though. It must have been your grandfather who was responsible for the fine Victorian extension we're in. A home with two very different characters, like your brother and your delightful sister-in-law, whom I was just talking to.' She flicked back to the photographs. 'There are a lot of studies of her.'

He moved up to her side. The photographs portrayed Emilia either by herself or with the children. He hated to admit it, but she made a striking figure with her lovely unsophisticated looks, natural warm smile and cloud of coppery hair. And despite bearing three children in quick succession she was still wholly desirable.

'Alec's taken up photography. He's got his own darkroom. The portrait nearest your arm is of my brother, Henry. He was killed in the war.'

'A tragedy common to nearly every family.' She pointed to a photograph of a Harvey in uniform in a prominent place up on the moulded mantelpiece. 'But he didn't suffer the same fate. That was taken recently.'

'My brother, Tristan. Alec snapped him on his last leave at Christmas. He survived the hell of the trenches and is currently serving on the Isle of Wight. I received a letter from him today informing me he's due home at the weekend. I've come to pass on the news to his son, Jonny, who lives here. He'll be cycling home from school in Truro about now.'

'Your brother did not write here directly?'

The woman moved until she was only a breath away from Ben. A thrill shot through him. He liked her musky perfume. He liked her being this close. 'Tris is the family peacemaker. Alec and I don't exactly rub along, it's Tris's way of making us get together and talk.'

Selina Bosweld's eyes traced a slow journey along the strongly honed contours of his face. 'You are the handsome one of the family.' Next instant, Ben's insides leapt in a mix of surprise and delight as he felt the featherlight touch of her forefinger at the side of his left eye. 'The war?'

Blood beat a furious path up from his neck to his hairline. His blindness was apparent in a pea-sized milky film and he was bitter about it. His voice emerged choked but he was eager to speak, to hold her interest. 'No. An accident.

It prevented me from taking up my place at officer training college. I wanted more than anything to fight for our country.'

'I'm sure you did, Ben. When we've moved into Ford House perhaps you'd like to visit us.'

Ben took no pains to hide his disappointment. 'Us? You're intending to marry?'

'Absolutely not.' She laughed with vigour but it was a graceful, beguiling sound. 'I'll be living there with my brother and niece. I should very much like to see your grand Tremore House, Ben.'

'Any time you care to choose, Miss Bosweld.' He was so mesmerized he wasn't sure if he had actually uttered the words.

'Selina. That's my name.' She glanced at the door. 'I can hear your brother and his wife coming back. I shall look forward to our next meeting.'

Emilia escorted the new tenant of Ford House to her bicycle. While Selina Bosweld wheeled her conveyance out into the lane, Emilia went with her and was not entirely sincere when she said, 'If there's anything we can do to help you move in, do say.'

'I'll arrange for a removal van. We'll be glad of as many strong pairs of arms as you can spare. Perry's hardly capable.' Selina Bosweld gave an unhurried smile as she mounted the bicycle. 'Mrs Harvey, I really must apologize for my remarks earlier. Mr Harvey is a few years older than you and I expected a wife of the same age. I'm afraid I've spent too many years giving orders and it's made me rather outspoken. We should be friends, call me Selina. Your boys and Libby must play together.'

Emilia watched her ride away. Upright in the saddle. In charge. Self-assured. Her apology and bright offer to be friends had not changed Emilia's opinion of her as being high-handed and domineering. Alec seemed to like her, but he would. Selina Bosweld was the sort of woman who endeared herself to men.

Ben was running down the front path.

'You've missed her. What a pity Jonny arrived home and kept you talking.'

'Shut up, Emilia.' He shoved past her and stared up the lane in time to see Selina Bosweld quickly putting distance between herself and the farm, her scarf adding a dash of brilliant colour between the wild daffodil and creamy-yellow primrose encrusted hedges, the heavily golden-flowered gorse bushes and the yellow celandines growing near the ditches.

Emilia followed the enthusiastic journey his eyes took until the bicycle and rider were out of sight. 'Don't you think you're being just a bit pathetic?'

Ben turned round to her. 'Not in the least.'

'What does Tris say in his letter?'

'Ask Jonny.'

'Don't be childish, Ben. Are you coming back in for something to eat? For Jonny's sake.'

'Got things to do. Why don't you like Selina Bosweld?'

'What makes you think I don't?'

'I know you. Your eyes are fiery.' He took all of her in, a habit of his, which he did because it annoyed her and because he enjoyed it in a carnal way. 'You look your best when you're fired up.'

'Ben, you get more like a tomcat every day. Doesn't Polly Hetherton appeal to you anymore?' Emilia had never liked his long-time snobbish war-widowed lover and she only made Polly Hetherton welcome in her house so she could see her adopted niece, Louisa, whom she had a special connection with. 'You'll get nowhere lusting after Sara, I'll make sure of that. And you're probably wasting your time drooling over our new tenant, she's a career woman.'

Alec appeared in the lane, having come out of the yard entrance. With him were Midge Roach, the cowman, and Jonny, who had changed out of his school uniform into old clothes and boots and gaiters. 'We're off to bring in the herd. Shouldn't you be doing the same, Ben?'

'I've got a large enough workforce to do exactly as I please. But don't worry, Alec, I don't intend to loiter about your property. Thanks for the invitation to the party you're giving for the baby. I'll come for her sake and because you've invited Polly and little Louisa, and, of course, hopefully, Tris will arrive in time.'

Jonny took no notice of the antagonism between the grown-ups. He was used to it. 'Uncle Ben, Dad's written to say he's got some exciting news to tell me when he arrives. Any idea what it is?

'Sorry, Jonny, not a clue.' Ben walked up to Alec. 'When are the Boswelds moving in?'

'On Saturday.' Alec raised a chary black brow. 'Why?'

'Would you mind if I helped out? I understand the brother's disabled.'

It was many years since Ben had asked something from Alec. Their estrangement had been caused over Ben's treachery at exploiting Alec's literary problem to gain the Tremore property, which Alec had been about to buy. Their uneasy reconciliation had been brought about by the heart-rending circumstances of the birth of Ursula Harvey's baby, the baby being the Louisa whom Ben had mentioned. All three Harvey brothers and Emilia were involved in a secret of sensitive proportions; Jonny had no idea he had a living half-sister.

Alec too had noticed Ben's reaction to Selina Bosweld. He knew his brother wasn't keeping himself exclusively to Polly Hetherton. Well, it was none of his business. 'Please yourself, but I'll be bringing Sara and Jim with me to help. I don't want any trouble.'

'You have my word there won't be any from me.'

Ben strutted past Emilia on his way home.

Three

Emilia paced the front path of Ford House while waiting for the Boswelds to arrive. Her hands were clenched at the sides of her sleeveless, loose and narrow dress, her mind on Jenna. Was it normal for a baby to sleep endlessly? And when awake to hardly be alert? And when it was feeding time to have to be coaxed to take the breast? Will and Tom had been ravenous feeders. All babies cried with wind, but occasionally Jenna became rigid, as if in spasm in every limb and she would howl as if in deep anguish. It had to be more than colic, the answer to every newly born infant distress. And afterward when her little body relaxed she'd fall asleep again, such a deep sleep where nothing disturbed her. Not her brothers' or cousin's noisy play, the sudden banging of a door, or light being let into the room. Was it natural? Was Jenna all right?

Dolly said she should be grateful to have a passive baby. She comforted herself with the thought that her mother knew best.

An arm was slipped around her waist, bringing her to a halt in front of a recently weeded border of azaleas, heathers and lavender. Alec looked up under her small-brimmed hat. 'They're not late, darling. Miss Bosweld sent word that they'd be here at eleven o'clock.'

'I know but it's going to be a busy day. I want to get back and help Tilda prepare for the party.' She positioned her hand over his, feeling the need to snuggle in against his body, making her aware just how worried she was about Jenna. This was silly. She must think of other things. 'Wonder why Tris hasn't let on what time his train is due in. The boys were hoping for the opportunity to do some train-spotting.'

'Obviously he didn't know exactly when he could get away,' Ben said, from where he was perched on the outer side of the drystone perimeter wall, his boots resting in the grassy verge. He was in work clothes, his shirt made of the usual stout, striped cotton and trousers of corduroy, but they were new. His boots were polished. His coal-black hair had been treated to a lick of oil and was neat and shiny. He smelled of a robust aftershave. His long tough fingers drew out a cigar from its wrappings and he looked at it with pleasure. It was the best that Havana could provide and cost a mint, but he could afford it. He had two more in his breast pocket, and although Alec and Jim smoked he would not ask either to join him.

Woman-bait. Done up as woman-bait, Emilia thought drily, as she watched him light the cigar in the manner of a movie star. He was gifted at narrowing his eyes to look sultry, lordly, central to the scene, while producing an instant flame from his single diamond-studded gold lighter, and drawing in, snapping the lighter shut and returning it to his breast pocket. All in an applaudable unbroken performance, done with the arrogance of a first-born son, which annoyed Emilia all the more. He thought himself a member of the county's elite, but the swanky clique he mixed with was too vulgar to be seriously considered as such. A business associate of his was a dubious character, Emilia suspected.

If Ben succeeded with the keen-tongued Selina Bosweld it would make an interesting pairing. He could be in for a shock. As beguiling as the woman was, there was also something predatory, intolerant and wilful about her, and while he thought himself stylish, sophisticated and discerning he still had a lot of immature youth in him. He thought himself superior to Alec in every way but he didn't even begin to make a match. Alec was more of an everyday man, home loving, content to visit the village pub on a Friday night, but he was the greater of the two brothers. He measured far above Ben in integrity and kindness, and although he did not have Ben's sort of classic good looks, his face showed a noble strength and he possessed a potent, enticing sensuality.

It had not passed Emilia by that after a brief hello to Sara, Ben was ignoring her. He never spoke to Jim – currently whirling a penknife between work-grimed forefinger and thumb, a cigarette dangling from his plentiful lips – unless with an insult or a warning. Thank goodness, Ben had never showed his interest in Sara in front of Jim or there would have been another of their clashes; in the past, one had even involved a public fist fight.

Ben chanced a glance at Sara but only to see where her concentration was focussed. Sweet and extraordinarily lovely, naive and pure, she had so far spurned all the avid male interest shown in her as if unsettled by it. She had a rolled-up apron in her hands and was periodically staring round the garden – and at Alec. Ben couldn't resist a private smirk. Alec aspired to nothing more than he already had and with his habit of daydreaming he would never realize the girl was besotted with him, and if he were told, he probably wouldn't believe it. Yes, Alec had everything, wealth, position, respect in the county, children, and a happy second marriage to Emilia. Not everyone realized how subtle and cunning Alec could be. Six years ago he had watched, wanting Emilia for himself, hoping for the chance to make a play for her, then taking advantage of her broken engagement with audacious speed.

There was no point in going over that again, Ben decided. A new, more exciting woman was about to come his way. Sometimes, though, he wished Emilia had moved out of his life completely. He hated to be reminded of a failure and he hated to see her subsequent happiness. She had never been punished for blinding him, for neglecting his grandmother for such a length of time that she had wandered outside and fallen in the garden in terrible weather, and had, in her fright, smashed an earthy fist into his face. That night, when he had asked Emilia to wash the grit out of his eyes she had done so without due care. His sight could have been saved, so the consultant whom he had seen later had stressed, if the particle stabbing into the left eye had been removed skilfully.

Sometimes he wished something as terrible would happen to her so she would understand how he felt.

His eyes descended on Emilia and she sucked in her breath at the bitterness in their tremendous grey depths. So, he was going over old scores again. Forgetting that it wasn't her fault the front door had been left unlocked and dear old Lottie Harvey had wandered out of the house. He never took into consideration how understaffed the farm had been with the war raging, how she had been trying to cope alone with all the household, the dairy and yard work, as well as caring for his grandmother. He didn't care about how much she had loved Lottie, how devastated she had felt at discovering her dead in her bed last autumn. She would never have done a thing to hurt Lottie and she had not deliberately hurt him and caused his blindness.

'Did I mention to you, Ben, that I've recently had a letter from Honor? She, Archie and their son are in all good form.' The lift of her mocking curved eyebrow was deceptive. Fire sparked in her, she was equal to any attack.

'No, and I'm not interested.' He hurled the cigar to the dusty ground; like all public thoroughfares through and around Hennaford it had recently been rough-paved, mainly by ex-servicemen, paid by the Government to give the unemployed useful work. He hated to be reminded how after gallantly offering marriage to Honor, now Honor Rothwell, to save her from poverty, she had been snatched away from him by another man. He chose to forget that he had started his affair with Polly Hetherton before Honor had forsaken him. He swore that no woman would ever make a fool of him again. He hated to be taunted over the fact that he had been engaged twice, at the ridiculously young age of eighteen.

Emilia and Alec watched the cigar roll down the hill until it disappeared in the ditch. They shared a secret smile.

Ben's eyes blazed in their direction. *Damn you both for laughing at me. I hope something happens to rock your cosy little world, and soon.*

The sound of horses and then a slowly moving motor-van brought every eye to gaze expectantly down the hill. Emilia and Alec moved outside the gate. Ben straightened up and smoothed at his hair. A trap drawn by a stocky pair of ponies rounded the bend and Selina Bosweld was waving to them. Her brother, presumably, was driving. Wearing a jazzy hat, he was waving too, and before they got up close it could be seen that here was the male equivalent of Sara in looks, a creature of unblemished beauty, although his colouring was not of the snow but the night. His smile was gorgeous, friendly, captivating.

'What do we have here?' Alec blew out through his lips. He had expected someone frail-looking, perhaps a little bent and crushed, perhaps hard and bitter because he was disabled and no longer able to practise his skill, but Perry Bosweld glowed with vigour and his upper body was as generously muscled as Alec's own. The trap was pulled up and only then did he notice a third person, a wafer-thin old woman wearing black and a high-crowned cloche hat on the seat behind.

'Should make a bob or two out of him for our trouble here today, I'm thinking,' Jim whispered to Sara, whipping his hands out of the pockets of his leather jerkin. A resourceful youth, he had suggested a ramp be made for each outside door to help the cripple pass in and out of the house. Mr Perry Bosweld looked as if he might be a grateful sort of bloke.

'What?' With the attention fixed on the newcomers, Sara had taken the opportunity to familiarize herself with Alec's body. She liked the way he moved, like some great splendid animal. His face was in profile, and she had studied its every approach and angle, so often she had it emblazoned on her heart. If Jim had not nudged her she would have become giddy with excitement. As it was, her palms were hot and sticky, her legs weak and quivery.

'I think he'll be a generous tipper,' Jim explained, then was off to help the gentleman in question to alight. He did not care what the conceited snob, Ben Harvey, did today – as long as he stayed out of his way and kept his stupid mouth shut.

Ben had gone round to the other side of the trap. Selina Bosweld accepted his hand down. She was wearing her yellow scarf and pulled it off and shook out her thick tawny hair. 'Hello, Ben. Thanks for being here, and you Alec and Emilia. For convenience of direction, we've led the motor-van since leaving the main road. I think we caused quite a stir in the part of the village we passed through. This is my brother, Perry.'

'Pleased to meet you, Perry,' Alec said, taking up the use of first names. 'Welcome to Ford House. I hope you'll find everything to your needs. Emilia and I will be glad to invite you and Selina to dinner once you're settled in. I hope you'll excuse us both for we'll soon have to leave. We have much to do at the farm. We've brought along Jim and Sara Killigrew, two of our staff, to help you move in.'

'We greatly appreciate that, Alec,' Selina smiled, tilting her head just a little at him. 'I see you've also brought us a box of vegetables and dairy produce. How kind. Thank you.'

'And Ben is your brother, so I understand,' Perry said in his cheerful pleasant voice. He shook Ben's elevated hand, and then looked down on the patiently waiting Jim. 'I can shuffle myself to the ground. Could you lift my crutches down, dear chap? That would be splendid. And then my wheeled chair? I'll need it for convenience later. It's folded up next to Mirelle.' He thumbed behind him and the woman lifted her head and smiled toothlessly, vacantly, anciently. Perry addressed the whole company. 'She's our maid, by the way. She's French. Selina brought her back with her from Paris-Plage in 1919. Afraid there's not much point in trying to communicate with her, apart from a smile or two. The poor old girl was too near an exploding shell while fleeing from her village and lost her hearing. She's a positive gem, we're lucky to have her, eh, Selina?'

'Absolutely true,' Selina answered in similar bright tones. 'Don't any of you trouble yourselves with anything in the kitchen, she's terribly territorial in that respect.'

Emilia took to Perry Bosweld's jollity. She watched, somehow fascinated, as he leaned against the trap while inserting the crutches in under his armpits before moving off effortlessly. The trouser leg on the right was pinned up from the knee. His sister pushed the wheeled chair, which had a central steering handle at the front, up to the front door. 'Have you arranged for your daughter to be brought along later, Perry?'

'Oh, she's in the cab of the van.' Perry's smile sparkled and shone. 'Simply begged to be allowed to travel in it. The two chaps said they didn't mind. I'm afraid I spoil her, Emilia. You probably wouldn't approve but when you've lost so much, when you've seen so many fields of suffering, well, loving those you care about is all that seems important. Ah, here she comes now. Libby, darling, come and meet our new friends.'

Elizabeth Bosweld was a disappointingly plain child after witnessing the excellence of her father and her aunt's alluring appeal – an appeal that was winning her frequent admiring looks from Ben and Jim, and, Emilia noticed, no defection into contemplation from Alec.

Emilia looked for the striking violet hue of Selina's eyes in Perry and Elizabeth, but only Selina boasted that particular gift from nature. Father and daughter had eyes of deep blue, a helpful compensation to Elizabeth, as was her beribboned curly hair – which was the same shade as her aunt's – and her lace-trimmed clothes and patent leather shoes. She giggled as she skipped over every inch of ground until she reached her father and flung her arms round his good leg.

Perry leaned down and kissed her. 'Libby, say hello to Mr and Mrs Harvey. This fellow here you must call Mr Ben, and we mustn't forget Jim and Sara. Perhaps Sara will unpack your things when Aunt Selina has chosen your room. Eh, Sara?'

'I'd be pleased to, sir.' Sara grew flushed and self-conscious for Selina Bosweld had turned what seemed a critical eye on her.

With a little cheerful ceremony the front door was unlocked, the keys handed over to Perry, then Alec and Emilia took the trap round the back to stable the ponies.

'Pleasant family,' he remarked. 'Seem to feel at home already. Hope they get involved in village life. Perry could brighten things up round here.'

'He has already. Libby seems a dear little thing.'

'You don't like Selina, do you?'

Emilia looked over the neck of the pony she was unharnessing. 'Why shouldn't I? I hardly know her.'

Alec came to her and wrapped his arms round her from behind. 'You might think I'm a bit of a wool-gatherer, angel, but I know when you don't like someone. What's she done that you object to?'

'I find her overbearing and I think she's the kind who changes her moods as quickly as it suits her. I suppose I'm wrong to make such early judgements, but there it is. Well, it hardly matters, as long as she doesn't interfere with us, the rent is paid, and she doesn't turn out to be a . . .'

'A what?' Alec was bemused.

'Oh, I don't know, Alec.' Emilia shrugged him away, suddenly impatient to leave here. 'Let's get this finished. We've got people coming and I want to get back to Jenna.'

Stunned by her sudden bout of irritability and the fact she had never pushed him away before, Alec strode back to the pony he had been working on.

Something caught his eye and he looked up. He was being watched, from the main bedroom, where Ursula had died and where, as locals would have it, while they had gathered kindling or played in the woods, her ghost had gazed out at them from the window. A legend had quickly built up around Ursula's tragedy – pining for the lover who had abandoned her just hours before her death, is how it went. Those of a more flourishing imagination declared she held up her dead baby to the glass and that her appearance always foreshadowed a death. A dead baby, of course, could play no part in a bona fide haunting, but level-headed people, including Dolly Rowse, had sworn they had seen Ursula's ghost. Two days after Dolly's sighting, his grandmother had died unexpectedly in her sleep.

The figure above caused a chill to ride up his spine and he muttered a quick prayer to ward off trouble, but almost at once he was breathing out in relief. It was Selina Bosweld who was looking down on him. At him and then Emilia, and her expression was ponderous and strange.

Tristan Harvey was closing in on Ford Farm in a sporty black Citroën, something he had been planning to own for a long time. He'd collected it from the dealer on getting off the boat two days earlier at Portsmouth. With him was his cousin, Winifred Stockley, and sandwiched in between them was her daughter, of Jonny's age, Vera Rose. Unknown to the rest of his family Winifred was now his fiancée. He had spent last night at her house, on the Cornish north coast.

He had the top down to enjoy both the dozy heat and the scintillating breeze, and was amused that despite the reduced speed for safe navigation through the narrow lanes, Winifred was hanging on to her wide-brimmed, voluminously scarved hat. It was what he liked about her, her touch of old-fashionedness, and the comfortable familiarity built up from their childhood years.

'Jonny's going to love this,' he referred to the motor car. 'Can't wait for the chance to take her touring again. Would you like to do that for a honeymoon, Winnie? I thoroughly enjoyed bringing her down. Followed the coast as much as possible, would never have seen those fascinating little places where I stopped off otherwise. We could go to Torquay, it has many fine hotels.'

'It's a lovely thought, Tris, but I think we should be careful about money, well, your money.'

'Stop worrying, dear girl. I've made a few successful investments with the money Alec paid me for the house and my bank wasn't exactly empty before that. We'll be able to jog along nicely for a year or two until I've worked out what I'd like to do now that I've resigned. I've thought about writing, although I don't see myself as the new Joseph Conrad. Might set up in a little business. I don't want you thinking of it as being my money only, Winnie. You'll be providing me with everything I need just at the right time.'

The wreath of knots marring Winifred's refined brow did

not shift. 'Great-Aunt Clara gave me to understand she would leave me a tidy sum after her death. It was a terrible shock to learn she was penniless. I was thinking I'd have to turn Roskerne into a guesthouse or sell it and move into something smaller. We could keep both options in mind, Tris.'

'Don't give it another thought. You'd hate to leave Roskerne and I'd hate to have lots of demanding people around me. Why don't we just see how things turn out? You've got me to look after you and Vera Rose now, so no more worrying.' Tristan smiled in his calm caring way. He was not handsome like Ben nor did he have Alec's imposing stature. He was pale and on the thin side and bore scars on his face and body from shrapnel wounds, but his quiet considerate manner made him everyone's friend and confidant. 'That's an order. No, scratch that, I don't give orders anymore. I'm just plain Mr Harvey from now on, and this time next week you will be Mrs Harvey. There'll be no more loneliness for either of us, we'll grow old contentedly together.'

At last Winifred let go of her hat and leaned back against the buttoned upholstery. She gazed at the hedgerows bursting with wild flowers, of pink, white and yellow. Bluebells swept along them and through the wooded areas. She caught the glorious scent of wild violets. At intervals, through sturdy five-bar gates, she saw Alec's thriving fields; a four-horse plough team was busy in one of them. In another were some of his cattle, and another his ewes and lambs. 'What's Alec going to say about us getting married? More to the point, what's Jonny going to say? Perhaps you should have mentioned it in your last letter to him, Tris. He would have had time to take it in by now.'

'Jonny will be delighted with me coming home for good and the prospect of living at Roskerne. He's always loved his summer and Easter stays with you. Eh, Vera Rose? More fun for you and Jonny on the beach from now on.'

'Can't wait. It'll be brilliant, Mummy,' Vera Rose enthused. She was concentrating on the steering wheel, longing to drive the Citroën herself.

Tristan was fond of the fun-loving, sporty girl, who was

confident in her school lessons, and who, like himself, had a great reserve of patience. She was the ideal companion for Jonny to grow up with for the remainder of his childhood. A childhood Tristan was grieved to have missed for so many years, but the catastrophe of the war and personal tragedy, then the need for the country to try to build itself up for the next generation had kept him away from home.

'Well, you two may be feeling confident,' Winifred said, 'but no one else has the slightest notion that this has been on our minds for quite some time.'

Before Tristan could offer another avowal, there came a bloodcurdling yell. It seemed to echo all around them, bouncing off the ground and hitting the trees. Tristan stalled the car, suddenly chilled to his bones. He knew it was silly, it was only an animal, likely a dog fox, but they had reached a hill closed in by tall bare hedges and covered over by overhanging branches, a place Ben had named Devil's Arch. A dark place Tristan had the occasional nightmare about, of dead faceless soldiers once under his command, marching into nothingness, and always preceded by Corporal Billy Rowse, Emilia's dead brother.

There was a loud swooshing, another unnerving ejaculation, then a rupturing and splintering of wood. Those in the car watched in horror as a figure hurtled into sight from high up in front of them and plummeted into the muddy ditch.

Tristan only just managed to suppress a soldier's oath. Fright made him petrify then he was dashing out of the motor car. The figure, a boy in clothes fit only for the rag-and-bone man, lay still, dishevelled and dirty. Down on his haunches, Tristan felt rapidly for broken bones along the arm that was covering the casualty's face. All seemed sound, so he moved the dirty limb aside, hoping he wouldn't be presented with a terrible head wound.

'Jonny? Dear God! Jonny!'

Jonny stirred, opened his eyes. 'Owahh. Oh, heck.' He did not realize it was his father helping him to sit up.

'Oh, heck indeed, Jonathan Harvey! What on earth do you

think you were doing? You could have been killed. Do you think you can stand up?'

Jonny blinked up into the alarmed, concerned face. 'Dad?'

'Here, Tris, take my handkerchief,' Winifred said from behind him, pushing the scrap of cloth into his hand. 'His ear's bleeding.'

'It's nothing,' Vera Rose, who had joined her mother, muttered with gleeful scorn. 'He was only stunned for a minute. Last hols he nearly chopped his arm off while pretending to be a musketeer.'

'What?' Tristan followed Winifred's suggestion, and from an upward glance he found himself surrounded by a crowd of urchins, all boys, all as grubby as tramps. Will was among them.

'Is he gonna die, mister?' a boy asked, sounding as if for the drama of it he was hoping to be told, 'Yes, and very soon.'

'Home, sonny!' Tristan boomed. 'And the rest of you. Will, where's Tom? You haven't left him behind somewhere, have you?'

'Mum says he's too young to come this far,' Will explained, contrite and respectful, until gaining a particular crossed-fingered signal from the leader of the Harvey Gang, then a stubborn gleam filtered through his eyes. 'We were only playing highwaymen, Uncle Tris. You were our victims.'

'You should have been loyal to your brother and not left him to play alone, Will. Get into the motor car.'

'Whose car is it, Dad?' Jonny's injuries, which to him would amount to a pleasing collection of bumps and bruises, were forgotten. He peered over his father's shoulder.

'It's mine, son.'

'Wizard! How fast does it go?'

'Not fast enough for you, I'll be bound,' Tristan said crossly, hauling the boy up gently in case he had a serious injury not yet apparent. 'Into the back with your cousin, and don't you dare get mud and filth on my new upholstery. When you're cleaned up, young man, you and I are going to have a serious talk.'

As the car continued up the hill, Will turned to Jonny to

share an impertinent grin and to poke playful fun at the silly moustache his Uncle Tristan was now sporting, but his leader was staring at the back of his father's head.

Despite his modest years Jonny had the sharpest mind in the Harvey family. Why was his father out of uniform? The running boards of the car had an unusual amount of luggage strapped to them. His eyes veered to his second cousin, who for reasons of respect he called Aunt Winifred. She had removed her glove to pass his father the handkerchief; a new ring with stones in it had replaced her wedding ring. She was getting married again, that was obvious, and to his father going by the familiar way he had handed her into the car just now. Jonny loved the lanes, the fields, the meadows and the moorland here, and especially the farm the motor car was now pulling up to. He was suddenly afraid for the future.

Selina thanked Ben and Jim for carrying a heavy trunk upstairs to the main bedroom, her bedroom. She was unaware of the underlying friction between the two men, so restrained towards each other had been their behaviour. Jim was eager to get a good tip. Ben wanted only to impress her.

'The only thing left to do now is to dispose of those few items out on the landing that we won't be needing. Would you mind taking them up to the attic for me, Jim? Then you must be given something for all the hard work you've done, your sister too. Perry and I insist.'

'I'll have it up there quick as pore, Miss Selina.' Jim left the bedroom at the same pace as his boast.

It was late afternoon. Selina had sent Sara home as soon as she'd unpacked Libby's belongings in a small front bedroom, explaining, 'Mirelle will know where everything else is to go.'

'It's all worked out well for Perry and I,' Selina said to Ben, when Jim could be heard pulling the attic ladder down. 'We sold most of our furniture to the couple who bought our house and we like what's here; good solid mahogany and pretty rosewood. I shall enjoy displaying our mother's Royal

Worcester.' She leaned back against the marble washstand, her hips jutting forward. She was wearing a loose flowing skirt and a fitted blouse, which accentuated her large rounded breasts. Not fashionable, but attractive because it was easy to wear and gilded her supple movements. 'Gosh Ben, look at you. You're quite grimy.'

'It's worth it if you're happy, Selina,' he smiled, rubbing his hands down the front of his shirt. He had smiled at her throughout the whole operation of moving her in and every smile had been reciprocated, without coquettish flirting or feigned coyness. Here was a woman proud of who she was, radiating self-assurance. She was, no doubt, unmarried because she had no wish to tie herself down to one man and domesticity. She was a woman of this post-war age. Ben found her qualities intoxicating. The excitement he felt about her outstripped anything he had ever known for a woman before.

'I won't insult you, Ben, by thanking you with an offer of money. You must come to lunch tomorrow. I'd like that very much. Perry too.'

'What time shall I come?' He was looking at her lips. Her eyes had dropped to his a moment earlier.

'When you like. We never stick to conventional times unless I'm on duty. We'll probably eat about one o'clock.' She had a way of suddenly coming towards a person and she did this now to Ben.

'I'll come at ten.' With her this close, it didn't feel he was being forward to reach for her hand.

She returned his firm grip. 'We have a special connection, Ben. I felt it that day at your brother's farm. You did too, didn't you?'

His heart leapt: she was going to kiss him. There was no build up of passion. She kissed him ardently from the start. Moving her lips against his with a power that was both draining and arousing, while using such a discriminating control his senses were pitched high and sent reeling.

They only stopped kissing when they heard Jim pushing the attic ladder back up in place. Ben was left fighting to regain his wits lest Jim see the evidence of the intense physical effect on him.

Selina wiped moisture off his mouth with gentle thumbs. 'We'll spend some time alone tomorrow, Ben.'

She led the way downstairs and asked Jim to wait outside the front door. She took Ben into the parlour to say goodbye to Perry and Libby, then she saw him off at the gate. 'Enjoy your family gathering this evening, Ben. Tell Emilia I'll be calling on her soon.'

When Ben had got round the bend in the lane he made to light a cigar but failed because his hands were trembling. His insides were churning; his head felt as if it was somewhere up high in the clear blue sky, floating with the cottony clouds. He broke into a run, leapt into the air, flinging his fist up victoriously. 'Yes! She's gorgeous!'

Selina surveyed Jim where he was waiting for his promised tip, his cap not yet replaced on his fair head. She ushered him back inside, took him into the parlour to Perry, who was now in the wheeled chair, and setting up a doll's house with Libby. Most of the toys had been placed in this room. Libby would spend most of her time with her father and only go upstairs to bed. Paintings of sailing ships in battle on dramatic seas, and elephants and tigers had replaced those formerly on the picture rail. A gramophone, ornaments of fairies, a collection of glass paperweights and a pair of stuffed owls had also been unpacked.

'Have you anything else for Jim to do, Perry?' Selina winked at Jim. 'We mustn't let you escape until every last little job is done. Awful, aren't we?'

'I don't mind at all, miss. Mr Harvey said to stay at your disposal for as long as it takes.' Jim was not the sort of youth to blush easily and become bashful. He wanted to make money, to save, in case he and Sara ever found themselves in need. His early years in the workhouse had left him wary of fate.

'No, no, you get along, young man. Thank you for all you did. Let me see.' Perry leaned back and felt about in his trouser pocket. Selina took the money he produced.

Out in the hall, Jim was pleased with the two half-crowns given him, one for himself and one for Sara.

'Oh, drat,' Selina exclaimed. 'I didn't see that box before in the corner. It's full of books and quite heavy. Would you mind, Jim?'

'Course not, Miss Selina.' Jim was calculating how extra jobs here might prove profitable towards his nest egg. He hefted the box up in his ample arms. 'Where to?'

'Up to my room please. I enjoy a read before I retire.'

Selina followed Jim into the bedroom and pointed to where he was to put the box down. 'Just a minute, there should be some magazines inside that I've finished with. You can take them home to Sara.'

'Thanks, Miss. She'd 'ppreciate that.' Jim hovered, unsure how to behave when alone with a lady in her bedroom.

Selina began placing books on the deep window sill. 'Do you live in the village, Jim?'

'Um, no, miss. At the farm. Both Sara and me. Been there nearly six years now. Was in Truro before that.'

'Do you miss town life? This is a quiet spot, isn't it?'

'Don't make no never mind to me where I live so long as me and Sara have a decent roof over our heads and good food to eat. Hennaford is quiet, but everyone knows everybody else's business, of course. Mr Harvey's the squire here.'

'I hate busybodies. Put this one on the table beside the bed, will you?' Other books she ordered to be placed on the mantelshelf. 'Here's a couple of magazines. Place them on the bed. There are more. Do you have a girlfriend, Jim?'

'No, miss.' He reddened, glued to where he was beside the rug waiting for the next order. Miss Selina Bosweld was as bossy as a schoolmistress, the sort who seemed able to read minds. Even though she had her back to him, if he fluffed this she might be able to tell that although he boasted of conquests, he had, in truth, got no further than flirting. 'Well, I'm sweet on someone. She'll be at the party tonight. Her father's the Methodist minister, he don't approve of me.'

Selina turned round, dropped a handful of magazines on top of the others. 'Don't let that stop you, Jim. I never let anything stop me from going after what I want. You have to believe you're good enough for anyone.'

'I-I do.'

'So I should think so. You are a sweet boy. You have a good face and, no doubt, a good mind. When you want to take a wife, I'm sure Alec Harvey will set you up in a cosy little tied cottage. You see, you already have a lot to offer a woman.'

Jim stared, his limbs frozen as she came closer and closer to him. Her beautiful violet eyes were boring into him.

'Have you ever had a woman, Jim?'

An age passed for Jim. He could only shake his head.

He was in a dream, wasn't he? She was running her fingers up over his chest. Her eyes . . . her eyes had him. Not that he wanted to flee from them. From her.

'I like your hair, Jim. It's the fairest I've ever seen on a man.'

He felt her touching his shirt. She was undoing the buttons! Her hot palms were sliding up in under his vest. She was breeding something in him. Feelings. Of shame and desire and fear. Shame of the sort he knew three or four times a week when alone in his little room after dark. And she was breeding spirals of desire in him. The kind of desire that tormented him. Because the completion of each shameful event had left him wanting, discouraged, fearful of discovery and swearing to never succumb to the shame again. But he did. The fear intensified. His shame was obvious now. It seemed to please her.

'Do you like this, Jim? And this? And this?'

He could only nod, and he forgot to breathe until the sense for survival locked in and the sudden intake of oxygen made him giddy. The shame was over but this time he was not left wanting. He felt embarrassment of the worst kind but it did not stop him meeting her eyes.

'We'll do something else now.'

The pressure of her hands was back on his flame-hot skin and she pushed him down on the bed. He was vaguely aware of the magazines tumbling to the floor. The twin orbs of burning violet were coming closer again. She put hard open kisses all over his young lips, put them under a barrage, and she moved his frozen juvenile limbs wherever it took her fancy.

'Don't shut your eyes, Jim. Look, see and learn.'

In a rush of panic he tried to sit up. 'Your brother! The maid!'

'Perry will think you've left by the back door. Mirelle won't come upstairs. Not another word.' Her hands crushed his face. It hurt.

Then came knowledge he should never have learned in the way he did. Of unimaginable pleasures coupled with intense pain.

A manhood was born, exploited and enslaved.

Four

Leaving the twisting ribbon of Ford Lane, Selina and Libby Bosweld stepped out on to the main thoroughfare that ran through the middle of Hennaford.

'How charming it all seems,' Selina said, while Libby looked about for any of the local children, who in the last three days, had turned up at the house with their curious, welcoming mothers.

Set back in a deep cobbled courtyard was the public house, the Ploughshare. It was whitewashed, with dark and sleepy small windows. A whistling deliveryman was unloading heavy barrels of ale from a dray. Almost opposite was the sturdy grey Wesleyan chapel.

They followed the road, which ran in a roughly straight line before climbing gently uphill, and which after leaving Hennaford behind passed through many a hamlet, then depending which turn was made, led on to Truro or Redruth. The opposite direction eventually led out of the county, which the locals referred to as 'up-country'. 'Oh, this is so quaint, Libby.'

Straggling either side of the road, without forethought for conformity or symmetry, was a range of homes and businesses. Cottages of stone or cob, some white or cream, others grey from neglect. Some were charmingly knobbly and uneven. Some had slate roofs that were slightly sunken, yet looked resilient enough to last another decade or two. Other roofs, like the Ploughshare and the ironmongers were thatched. The little front gardens were overrun with crocuses and pansies. Selina was sure the back gardens would be planted with vegetables, and perhaps there would be hens or a pig or a goat.

Across from them was the little Anglican mission church, a late-Victorian addition to compensate for the parish church being over two miles away, in almost secretive isolation down the lanes, past Ford Farm. The forge was halfway up the hill, glowing devilishly from within and sending out loud echoes of clangs and bangs. Selina wondered if the blacksmith was young and brawny, gorgeously sweaty and grimy, with blackened, clever hands the size of dinner plates.

At the end of a row of cottages was Hennaford's stores and post office. The place, apparently, that was the centre of the community. Over the road Selina and Libby went, then up the shop's four wide mismatched granite steps, sidling carefully past a sleeping tabby cat to open the broad low door, its glass smothered with faded advertisements. The doorbell tinkled merrily and they paused on the threshold to see what they could see, but Selina felt at once within these astonishing cavernous confines the atmosphere of calm, solidity and camaraderie. And newcomers were welcome to join in. If only one could bottle up this invigorating yet soothing mix and keep it close at hand for the dark, lonely times.

And so they wandered about, woman and child, eyes never so wide and bright, under the low ceiling, up and down the packed shelves, delving into all the enchanting nooks and crannies. Peaceful. Inspired.

Selina waited in the disorderly queue to be served with the patience she didn't usually have, introducing herself and Libby to the shoppers and the loafers, content to chat and learn a little of each individual's history, while still looking over the surprisingly, tantalizingly diverse wares. Her nose was gloriously assailed by the smells of wax candles, fishy glue, nippy paraffin, sealing wax, lamp oil, harsh soap, scented soap, cocoa, succulent ham. And toffee. Golden, ruby and dark brown toffee, shiny and inviting in the slabs. Perry must try each seductive taste.

''Tis a honour and a pleasure to meet you, Miss Bosweld, and the little miss,' Gilbert and Myrna Eathorne, the middle-aged, cheerily red-faced, comfy-plump owners told her with gusto when finally she was next to be served. She declined the offer to sit on a strategically placed hoop-backed chair. A young, pink-faced, heavily pregnant housewife, her cloth bag already packed with her shopping, wearing a small straw hat and still in her pinny, was sitting on the second chair; silent, listening, almost half asleep, she seemed. Selina knew everything she was about to say would be spread all over Hennaford before midday, and she liked that thought very much. She squeezed Libby's hand, felt her throbbing with the anticipation of receiving some of the divine sweets on offer; knowing her aunt would spoil her shamelessly.

'Likewise, Mr and Mrs Eathorne. We've enjoyed every minute we've been here, haven't we, Libby, darling? People have been so kind. Yes, that's the brand of flour we like. Granulated sugar, please, and baking powder. Do you deliver? Excellent. I'll place a regular order and one of us or the maid will pop along for extras.'

'Most of us get on round here,' Myrna Eathorne said. She nodded at the young housewife, who was content to lounge and beam. 'This is my brother's maid, Maisie, by the way. Her man, Jack – he was one of the few young men what came back safely from the Front – works for Mr Ben Harvey. Can plough a furrow as straight as corduroy cloth, he can, can't he Maisie? She lives on top the hill, near the school. Got three younguns going there. Mr Frayne's a good 'master. Squire Harvey, now he's a good man and no mistake, he's not above sending his boys there.'

Myrna winked at Libby and reached into a glass jar and plucked out a fat purple violet-flavoured sweet and plonked it into Libby's grasping little hand. 'The blacksmith's dog just had puppies. He'd be glad to show 'em you, my luvver. You only have to ask.'

'Thank you, Mrs Eathorne,' Libby said, always polite, always as interested in news as any grown-up. 'How many puppies?'

'Five or six, wasn't it, Gilbert?'

'Yes, my handsome.' Grinning a wide toothy grin, Gilbert sipped the tea Myrna had put three heaped spoonsful of sugar in, and then he got ready to fetch the next item on Selina's list. Washing soda. Selina accepted a cup of tea; pleasantly strong. She automatically went into nurse mode on spying Maisie's swollen ankles. 'You really should keep your feet up as much as possible, you know, Maisie.'

Before leaving the shining sweetness and cosiness of the Aladdin's cave, Selina and Libby were told, 'We're chapel, by the way, most of us folk in the village. Maisie here chars at the Manse. If you ever need extra help about the house, after she's had her next little blessing, of course, she won't mind. Will you, Maisie?' And finally, 'Yes, we're mainly a close, happy lot round here, aren't we, Gilbert?'

Gilbert agreed.

Selina left thinking that if Myrna and Gilbert Eathorne weren't two of the happiest people in the world then they deserved an immediate horribly painful death.

Outside on top the steps Libby peeped longingly into the wicker basket over her aunt's arm.

'Go on, then,' Selina stooped and kissed the little girl's petite nose. 'You can have the sweets I've bought you now. I'll keep the peppermints Daddy said you can have for after lunch.'

'Thanks heaps.' Libby united with Selina in a conspiratorial smile then proceeded to jump down each individual step, making the tabby cat, obviously used to comings and goings, open one eye then close it lazily again.

'Don't let your face get sticky, Libby, or it will be a giveaway to Daddy over our little deceit and he'll scold us both, particularly me. Oh, look, there's some people drawing water from the pump, let's go over and introduce ourselves.'

Libby wasn't interested in the small group of villagers queuing in the court with pitchers and buckets round the decorative pump; another village meeting place. 'It's not a good thing though to have deceit, is it, Aunt Selina?' Libby squinted back up at her. She was an inquisitive child and she never forgot anything her father taught her.

'Not usually, darling, but we get so little time to ourselves because Daddy monopolizes you, so a little deceit won't hurt for today.'

'What does mono-polize mean?'

'Well, it's—'

Selina's explanation was broken off by a sudden commotion at the pump. Her alert eyes took in what was happening. The voices were raised, pleading, quickly turning into angry demands over a huddled figure in the centre of the group, and the figure started up a high-pitched wail.

Taking Libby's hand, Selina went across the road. Others were gathering in the court. As if sensing a drama was about to unfold, people were suddenly appearing at their doors and windows. Keeping Libby slightly behind her, Selina asked a housewife what was going on.

The woman, wearing a dress gone a rusty shade of black under her pinny, answered with the glee of a telltale, ''Tis poor Wilfie Chellow. He come back from the Front mazed in the head and his poor mother do have some trouble with him. He scares all of we with his antics at times, this being one of 'em. My boy, who was with him back then was killed,' she tagged on hastily and mournfully, as if she was the mother who deserved the most concern.

Selina peered over shoulders and past bobbing heads and saw a near-hysterical woman trying to prise the huddled man, presumably poor Wilfie Chellow, away from the pump. Wilfie Chellow, short and slight, was clinging on to it, shrieking and spitting, his feet scrabbling as if he was running for his life. The few words he was screaming out were indecipherable.

Glancing behind, Selina saw Myrna and Gilbert Eathorne were now on their top step, with Maisie and another shopper, all watching the drama with alarm. More spectators were fast approaching for a closer look or to join in with the struggle at the pump.

'Time that boy was put away somewhere 'fore he hurts someone,' the housewife whom Selina had consulted remarked indignantly to a newcomer.

'Has he hurt someone before?' Selina demanded to no one in particular.

'No,' a wizened old man in a cloth cap that looked too

large for his shrivelled head, croaked in reply. 'But he ought to be locked away in his room for his own sake, if you ask me. He's got a thing about the pump, only the Lord knows why, and if the mood takes him wrong he won't let nobody get any water. What good's that to the rest of us?' Selina recognized the whine of helplessness.

Selina edged Libby to the outskirts of the gathering, where she could not witness any more of the grim spectacle. A quiet young woman was there, hanging back but watching anxiously. 'Take my niece's hand, would you, please? I think I know how to deal with this.'

'Yes, of course,' the young woman complied eagerly.

'Aunt Selina, don't be long.' Reluctantly, Libby allowed herself to be relinquished to this new stranger, who gave her a friendly smile.

'Don't worry, darling. I'll soon sort this out.' Selina took a sherbet fizzer out of Libby's sweet packet, then swept through the people with such decisiveness they immediately gave way to her authoritative bearing.

Someone shouted, 'Pump the handle. A shock of cold water will sort the bugger out.'

She boomed back, 'Don't you dare!'

There was only Wilfie Chellow, muttering and gibbering, and his distraught, haggard mother left at the pump now. Selina took a position where she could see Wilfie's face, pressed, almost crushed, against the hard iron. With feather-light fingertips she eased off his tattered cap and stroked his exposed cheek, bruised where someone had slapped him. 'It's all right, Wilfie, dear. No one's going to hurt you.'

'You're wasting your time, miss,' Mrs Chellow said in a choked voice with much sniffing, wiping tears from her prematurely wrinkled eyes. 'He don't understand nothing since he was brought back. He don't even know who I am.'

Selina ran a gentle finger down the ragged, livid-red scar on Wilfie's temple. It stretched a long way back over his scalp and his hair no longer grew there. Like his gawping, fearful eyes, which Selina was sure were vacant at other times, it was a cruel reminder of the damage inflicted on his brain. 'He understands kindness. Don't you, Wilfie?'

Lowering her voice to encourage him towards calmness, she put her mouth closer to Wilfie's ear and she stroked the remaining rough dark hair at the back of his head, and slowly, carefully, instinctively knowing when it was the right moment she brought the sherbet fizzer up to his lips.

It seemed the spectators were holding their breath. All were frozen in amazement as Wilfie stuck out his tongue and the white-furred tip tasted the sweet. There was an immediate retreat but after an instant, in which the rest of his body stopped jerking, he licked the sherbet. Selina knew his limited perception had already robbed him of the hazy instinct of where he was and why, and she also knew that the slightest untoward word, touch or gesture would plunge him into panic again. Keeping up the soothing words she caressed each one of his white knuckles clenching on to the pump. She ran her fingers from each of his dirty broken nails on to the backs of his hands, following the paths of bulging purplish veins to his taut wrists where she could feel his pulse still thundering from the fright. When the dreadful beat had at last eased, she was able to peel away one finger at a time off the pump.

By the time Wilfie had eaten the sweet out of her hand, Selina had got both his hands off the pump. His eyes went completely blank and expressionless. He had poor balance: one of his arms was curled up awkwardly and the leg on that side was twisted in at the knee. This was the shambles of what was left of a young man not yet twenty-five. Supporting him, she put on his cap and motioned to his mother to come and claim him. 'Do you live in one of these cottages, Mrs Chellow?'

Mrs Chellow wrapped one arm round Wilfie's waist and he was safe in their double embrace. 'Just behind us, miss.'

'Let's take him home.'

To sentences of wonder and congratulation and then a spontaneous outbreak of clapping, they got Wilfie inside the front door, which led directly into the one living room of an end dwelling.

'Thanks, miss. Well, I know you to be Miss Bosweld, newly come among us, and thank God for it,' Mrs Chellow said, her eyes wet from a different emotion now. Some of the haggardness seemed to have dropped off her. 'I can see to Wilfie now he's in.'

Selina rested a hand on the woman's stooping shoulder. 'I know how hard it must be for you to see your son like this, to have him as not man or child. To think about what might have been for him if there had never been a war. All you can do is to love him, Mrs Chellow, and be proud of the sacrifice he made.'

'All I've ever wanted since he was brought back was for some round here to show him respect, to treat him with dignity. God bless you, Miss Bosweld. I'll never forget what you've done this day.'

Perry Bosweld was in the back garden of Ford House. His family's belongings were arranged satisfactorily inside, he had brought his charity work up to date and now it was time for leisure. To indulge in the sport denied him for several weeks due to packing up and moving house.

The lawn was perfect to set an archery lane up on, shooting south to north, the second distance for male competitors of fifty-six yards. He looked with pleasure at the canvas-faced target, up on a buttress of firm straw-packed sacking, a low buttress owing to him being in his wheeled chair, the central steering handle folded down, the quiver slung from the side of the chair. In quick, easy succession, well inside the maximum tournament time of four minutes, he shot an 'end' of six arrows, all marked with his initials and light blue markings from his longbow.

'Bravo!' he congratulated himself. Four arrows were in the inner-red scoring zone, the zone nearest to the gold centre of the target, the other two arrows were in the gold centre, giving him a score of fifty-six out of a possible sixty. His elation was blemished by disappointment. It would have been more of a triumph if there had been someone to witness the feat.

He made to start another 'end'. He laid aside the longbow

and peeled off his finger protectors, exposing his long sensitive fingers. He stared at his smooth pale right hand as if he had never seen it before, flexed it and turned it round, and round again. It looked as steady as iron. He had taken up archery after recovering from the explosion that had caused so much destruction to his body, and there had been no weakness in operating a longbow and shooting the arrows. Hours and hours of slavish practice had raised him to peak standard. He had won many competitions. So why could he no longer wield a scalpel or stitch up a wound? He turned his hand side on, brought it up close to his eyes. There it was. The long thin white line, the scar that told of the tiny injury that had robbed him of absolute steadiness, that made it just a little bit difficult to hold his fountain pen. It took him twice as long to produce a letter now. So why go on pretending it didn't? And hoping that some day the steadiness would return and he'd be able to practise his skill again? The only profession he had ever wanted to be in. It didn't matter if he missed a target, but it would if he made a fatal mistake while venturing inside a patient's body. Stupid optimist! Stupid pretence! Stupid hope.

'We're back!' Selina's cheery voice reached him and he heard Libby running round the side of the house. 'The shop's a delight, Perry, and one can just about order anything there. It has steep steps, so you'll have to be careful whenever you venture up them.'

'Glad you've had a good first excursion,' he called back. Never one to make others suffer his regrets and discontents he dampened down his frustration and manoeuvred the wheeled chair on to the lawn, all smiles. 'Oh, good, you've brought a visitor with you.'

'This is Miss Elena Rawley. We met outside the shop,' Selina said, while Libby skipped up to him. 'Her father's the Methodist minister. Miss Rawley kindly invited us to tea one day, Perry, but I said, why wait? So I brought her along to meet you.'

'I'm pleased you came, Miss Rawley.' He lightly shook her

small, gloved hand. 'We've had villagers call on us every day. It's what we were hoping for – friendly natives. They came bearing gifts too. We've been inundated with jars of jam, apple pies and butter and eggs. It'll be putting Mrs Harvey, our landlady out, but I suppose most of the produce comes from her dairy and hens anyway.'

'Yes, I suppose it does. I'm pleased to hear you're settling into village life, Mr Bosweld.' Elena Rawley had taken charge of Libby a short while ago; she was sociable in a modest way and although in her early twenties, appeared intent on good, old-fashioned spinsterhood. Small-boned, the sort who could easily be overlooked, her figure was hidden by shapeless clothes of stout tweed and hand-knitted wool; her hair, glossy and mid-brown, was rolled up in an unflattering bun. There was something sweet and appealing about her politesse, and Selina could see how the awkward youthful side of Jim Killigrew – *the way he had been* – could be attracted to her. 'You practise archery, how fascinating. I must say, I've just witnessed Miss Bosweld practically performing a miracle.'

'Oh? I'd be intrigued to hear about that.'

'It was nothing,' Selina said, but she was pleased with the outcome of Miss Rawley's tale regarding Wilfie Chellow. She knew the details would be greatly exaggerated when word was passed on about what she had done for another tenant of the fascinating Alec Harvey. 'I can't bear to see former servicemen treated like that. People don't understand what it was like for them.'

'Well, it's a jolly good thing you happened to be there,' Miss Rawley said, with an element of hero-worship. 'It was brave of you to nurse at the Front, Miss Bosweld, in fact, brave of you to nurse at all. I don't think I could do it.'

Perry smiled at his sister. 'Good for you, Selina. I'll take the liberty of calling on this Wilfie Chellow. If he isn't already benefiting from an agency like the Royal British Legion, perhaps his mother will allow me to get in touch on his behalf. Ah, Mirelle's spied you, Miss Rawley,' he went on even more jovially. Open and gregarious, hating loneliness, he was pleased with the number of people he had already met, pleased that Libby had made new playmates. The two young daughters of one of Alec Harvey's labourers had been invited back to play with Libby this afternoon. 'The kettle will soon be singing. Mirelle doesn't like to mix but she's quite a one for hospitality. We've lots of goodies to offer you to go with a cup of coffee – we nearly always have coffee because Mirelle prefers it. She thinks the way the English make tea is pretty awful. The schoolmaster's wife brought us some delicious saffron cake, my favourite. Mrs Frayne, wasn't it, Selina?'

'Yes, my dear. You will learn, Miss Rawley, that my brother does like to prattle on, bless him.' Selina was gazing down at her flat brown shoes. They were tied with coloured laces. Perhaps she wasn't quite the mouse she seemed, but she was definitely dead in the romantic and sensual department. She was completely unmoved by Perry's good looks. This, and his having a disability usually bred a desire in a woman to protect and serve him, to want to nurture his motherless child. A powerful draw. She didn't even seem curious about him, and she must have heard his circumstances from the steady stream of visitors.

'My father likes a good chat too, and they say it's us women who talk the most.' Elena Rawley gave a small unsure laugh. Unsettled by Selina's attention to her shoes she studied them to see if they were animal-fouled.

Libby, who had been sitting on her father's lap, patiently waiting for a break in the grown-ups' conversation, posed her simple little face up at him. 'When can I have a puppy, Daddy? The blacksmith's dog's just had some, the lady in the shop said so. I could have one of those. Please say I can, please, please, please. It'll be fun.'

On her way to fetch two garden chairs, Selina lingered to listen. Perry glanced up at her. 'What do you think, dear? Know anything about these puppies?'

'Mrs Eathorne mentioned they were Labrador-cross, and should be quiet and obedient.' Selina wagged a finger at her excited niece. 'You mustn't forget, Libby, that a dog must be trained properly and kept in order at all times in case it pitches Daddy over when he's using his crutches. Daddy will take you to look at the litter and if he thinks they're suitable you may choose one.'

Libby squeaked with joy. She kissed her father twice, then she ran to her aunt. 'Thanks for ever. I love you, Aunt Selina.'

'I love you too, ragamuffin.' Selina lifted her up and whirled her round in a circle. 'Off you go now and play and make yourself all grubby.' Seeing Elena Rawley's astonished expression and gauging correctly that if the boring young miss ever did have children they would not be encouraged to do likewise, she added in a wicked tone, 'Those farm boys aren't the only ones who know how to play at rough and tumble. The three Harvey boys were showing off, walking on our wall yesterday and making idiotic noises,' she explained.

Libby went to perch cross-legged on the rug her toys were spread out on. She chattered to her dolls, all of which had been given French names, telling them in accomplished French – the language was included in the lessons her father was teaching her – about the puppy, asking them to help her choose its name.

'She's adorable,' Elena Rawley said. 'She's very welcome to join the Sunday School.'

'Does Emilia Harvey send her children there?' Selina asked, carrying a pair of heavy wooden, folding chairs from the shed as if they were weightless. She placed them down either side of Perry. Cushions were tucked in under her armpits and she flung them down on the seats with gusto, making Elena blink.

'They go to the church Sunday School.'

Selina hastened up the path to meet Mirelle, who was hobbling along with a large lap tray of refreshments, obviously too heavy for her bony black-clad arms. 'Café au lait, mademoiselle.'

Selina took the tray from her and set it down on its short legs. She thanked the maid with copious nodding. Mirelle bobbed to the guest and left.

Selina poured the coffee and cream. 'Libby, come and get your milk and biscuits. Sugar, Miss Rawley? Do you see much of the family? The Harveys?'

'Two lumps please. Oh, yes, I call at the farm quite often. The Harveys are involved with every aspect of village life. The Boxing Day Hunt always starts off on their land and one of the village's favourite events, the summer sports day, is held in Higher Cross field, behind the school, immediately after the haymaking.'

'Indeed. What does Ben Harvey do?' Selina stretched out in her chair, kicked off her shoes and wriggled her toes about in the grass. Amused that this seemed to shock Miss Rawley, she pushed the plate of cake in front of her. Mirelle had cut the cake into chunks; no respectable dainty manse-sized slices here.

'Thank you.' Elena Rawley accepted a chunk. 'He doesn't organize anything, well, not as yet. He recently mentioned to my father that he's thinking of starting annual fêtes in the grounds of his house, with all benefits to go to the village. My father's going to suggest the school would appreciate some new equipment.'

'We'd be pleased to support anything like that, wouldn't we, Selina?' Perry said.

'We'd love to.' Selina fixed a penetrating gaze on her guest. 'Ben and Alec don't get on, do they?' She knew the story behind the brothers' uneasy relationship. Ben had told her and Perry about it over lunch the day after they had moved in, but she wanted to learn more.

'I don't really know a lot,' Elena ducked her head.

'Of course you have to be diplomatic. I understand.'

A bird's call echoed in from the field adjacent to the low natural, primrose-scattered hedge at the bottom of the garden. A much-admired cluster of white violets grew amid them. 'How marvellous,' Selina said. 'Are we the first to hear a cuckoo hereabouts, Elena?'

Elena Rawley was too stunned at being hailed by her first name without invitation or a longstanding acquaintance with the other woman to respond immediately. 'Um, no, one of

Mr Ben Harvey's employees, a woman called Eliza Shore actually had that distinction two days ago.'

'Much rejoicing on the Tremore property then.' Selina lifted one leg, rested the ankle on the opposite knee and proceeded to massage her foot. She heard Elena Rawley's heavy snatch of breath at her lack of decorum. 'Ah, there it is again, but no, it's an answering call from the woods. I do admire the cuckoo. It's such a clever creature to use others to do the hard work of hatching and feeding its young. I love the woods, don't you, Elena? I can still hardly believe our luck at living with one just a stone's throw away. All the gorgeous bluebells, and the kingcups down by the stream, the wonderful smell of bark and moss, the fascinating species of fungi. The stream is so pretty here and so restful. I love the feel of cold water running over my bare feet. Have you the time to take a little stroll with me now, Elena?'

'No, I don't think I have. I mean I . . .' Her cup rattling on its saucer, Miss Rawley put the crockery down on the tray. 'Actually, I have to be going. There's a Social coming up, just a small one, but I have a lot of organizing to do. If you'll excuse me . . . Thank you so much for the coffee. Don't get up, I'll see myself out.'

'You're incorrigible, Selina,' Perry said, the second the minister's daughter was heard closing the front gate. He helped himself to another chunk of cake. 'She's not likely to come here again after all that. I rather liked her.'

'That's the idea. She'd bore us silly if she called here often. She asked me if I'd like to join the Sewing Guild or attend a revival meeting! Definitely not my type, although she is rather . . . no, forget it. Anyway, I was just having a little fun before I return to the daily grind.' Selina threw her head back so the sun could caress her face. She loved warmth and fresh air on her bare skin. It spoke of freedom, and freedom of all kinds is what she craved.

'You really shouldn't mock people in front of Libby. I don't want her thinking it's all right to do the same.'

'Oh, she wouldn't have understood any of that even though she is growing up so quickly, bless her.'

'Selina, you know you don't have to go on working. Living simply as we do means I've got enough to support both of us for the rest of our lives and to see to Libby's education.'

'I won't be kept by anyone and you know I couldn't bear to stay at home all the time. I know nursing still isn't seen as a suitable occupation for a lady, but I enjoy its application and challenge.' She bent over to retrieve her shoes. 'I'm going to put you through a tough exercise regime this afternoon. It's time you persevered with the prosthesis again.'

'Must I? I'm quite happy with an empty space below my knee.'

'Well I'm not, and yes, you must. Think of Libby, it'll be better for her seeing her father wearing a pair of shoes.'

'Libby's used to the way I am. It's years before I'll need to walk her down the aisle.'

'I hope you want more out of life for her than that! What I want is for her to see what can be achieved with hard work and determination. She could follow my career or aim for something higher. No more arguments, no more laziness from you. Right, I'm off for a little walk.'

'Anywhere particular?'

'The woods. I'm meeting Jim.'

'Can't think what you see in that boy.'

'Oh, he makes a welcome change from older experienced men and handsome young bucks like Ben. Ben's champing at the bit, it's such fun keeping him at arm's length.'

'Be careful with your games, Selina. Where you seek gratification. I believe Ben was hoping to see you again before the arrangement for dinner at his house next week. There's a sadness about him, don't you think?'

'Is there? He's going to fetch us in his motor car, by the way.' Selina was disappearing down the garden. 'I'm off to pick bluebells,' she laughed uproariously. 'If I'm not back in time for lunch, keep it warm for me.'

Five

Tristan was in the grounds of his new home, Winifred's house, Roskerne, which overlooked the coast at Watergate Bay, near the fishing town of Newquay. It was a fine square house, evocative of Victorian confidence, an uncompromising tribute to the classical, with a verandah, stained glass in some windows and lancet-shaped doorways. A lot of the brickwork had deteriorated with age and weather, the gutters and downpipes were leaky. He would put his attention to the repairs in the coming weeks.

With the formalities of the wedding over, which by mutual choice had been a small affair, there was now only the immediate family left and while the children were tearing about somewhere he and the other adults were lolling in deckchairs on the terrace.

He was not as settled as he looked. It had taken a lot of persuasion to prevent Winifred from calling off the wedding, for Jonny had taken the news of the marriage badly, going off in an uncharacteristic huff and sulking for hours. He had been surly and uncooperative since, refusing to be best man, which Tristan thought he would have been both amused and honoured by.

'Why must you change everything?' Jonny had shouted at him. 'I don't want to leave the farm. I don't want to switch schools. I'll miss Will and Tom and Aunty Em and Uncle Alec and everyone here.' Tristan knew that most of all he would miss Alec, and it had saddened him to realize just how much his brother had taken his place during his absence.

In an exchange of roles for the brothers, Alec had counselled him. 'You need to give Jonny time to get used to his new life, to make new friends. He'll settle down.' But Alec had been unable to hide his own hurt at Jonny moving out, and although at only a distance of fourteen miles it did not make for frequent visiting.

The children suddenly went quiet, pointing to Jonny's heart not being in high spirits today. They had probably gone up to the attic, where, Jonny had written to him once during a stay here, he liked to 'poke about' in the things once belonging to departed Stockleys. Tristan looked up at the high roof of rounded tiles, picturing Jonny inside, quiet, morose, wishing the other children would go away. Alec had often been like that as a boy, when their father had thrashed him over a poor school report, or when he'd been unable to read out an address on a letter or a label on some goods. It grieved Tristan to think of his son feeling so despondent.

He swept his eyes to Winifred, who was facing him, her back to the sun, holding up a parasol, her feet up on a stool because her new shoes were pinching. She had been watching him, seeking reassurance yet again that they had done the right thing. In his smile he tried to convey a contented anticipation for the future.

Winifred, who had a swan-like grace, was transformed into the typical glowing loveliness of a bride and looked younger than her thirty-four years. She smiled back then glanced down shyly. She had been thinking about the difference in their ages. What had her guests, specially the women she played bridge with weekly, thought of her marrying someone younger? It was only a couple of years but, bearing in mind one usually married a man a few years older, it didn't seem right. And she was trying to get used to the strangeness of one of her cousins now being her husband. She was worried about Jonny. He had hardly eaten a morsel at the reception.

To forget her worries Winifred watched while Alec cradled Jenna to his shoulder and Emilia leaned across and wiped dribble from around her tiny mouth. 'The pair of you do fuss over her. You never gave the boys so much attention.'

'She's our precious little princess,' Alec replied, unashamed of the pride and the emotion he displayed. He kissed Jenna's fairy-like face. 'Aren't you, darling angel?'

'I thought Emilia was your angel,' Ben pouted, starting on his umpteenth glass of champagne. Despite his misgivings about the marriage, believing his brother and cousin had acted hastily out of fear of loneliness, he had behaved impeccably as best man in the church, but now the guests had gone he had dropped his scintillating charm and was planning to get drunk. Pixillated. Red-nosed, leg-reelingly drunk. He was bored and wished he had not agreed, like his overconfident brother and insufferable sister-in-law, to stay overnight.

'I'm fortunate enough to have two angels in my life.' Alec's tone carried a hint of superiority.

Ben gazed at Emilia. Why did she have to be so damned lovely in her outfit? It was a dress of ice-blue silk crêpe, with appliqued circles at the dropped waist and wrists and a softly-brimmed floaty hat and double T-bar, fashionably low-heeled blue shoes. Three rows of pearls hung from her graceful neck, the longest reaching down to where he thought her navel to be. Recalling how he had seen that delicious little part of her, he stirred awkwardly. Not surprisingly, she had received far more compliments than Winifred in her mushroom-coloured effort. Alec, damn him, had received compliments all day about her from women who had admired her and men who had desired her. She was that sort of woman.

He had stared at her only two minutes ago, when Winifred had asked her how she'd managed to keep her slim figure, while lamenting over the few extra pounds she had put on in all the unflattering places. Emilia had no unflattering places on her body nor was she ever likely to. Everything about her was in perfect proportion. She hadn't favoured yet the short fashionable hairstyles. How cunning of her to know men usually preferred a wealth of beautiful hair. Cunning and desirable, damn her.

Hell and damnation! Why did he keep putting her on a pedestal of physical beauty? Why did he still feel attached to her? Why did he still enjoy the relish when he considered he had some riveting secret he thought she would like to know?

She had no idea he had been hoping to take another woman in the same bed in Ford House where he had made love to her, their first and only time together.

Get out of my head, Emilia! I have designs on Selina Bosweld now. She's more fascinating than you.

No, she wasn't. Her feet are big and she moves her hands in a mannish way and she was messing with him. All over him one day, brushing him off the next. A quickly bored sort.

He was smarting over her treatment of him at the lunch in Ford House. He might as well have been the rector, the distance she had kept from him. If Perry hadn't kept up a lively conversation, he could easily have fallen asleep from boredom himself.

Damn you, Emilia! You were perfect for me all that time ago. Only you didn't love me enough to stay loyal.

He was still spying on her, and as always when their eyes met, they clashed. She lifted her chin a little and made to stare him out. Damn it, would he never get the better of her? And she was so besotted with Alec she wouldn't care if he bedded Selina Bosweld and every other woman in Hennaford. Except for Sara. Now that was an interesting thought. No, it wasn't, he couldn't be bothered. The girl could stay clinging on to her virginity.

He needed a smoke. Couldn't indulge this close to the baby, so he excused himself, taking a fresh bottle of champagne with him. Tottering down the seven stone steps from the terrace, he shunned the paved path in preference for the lawn and headed towards the fence that was set well back from the edge of the fifty foot cliff.

'Poor Ben doesn't know what to do with himself.' Winifred thought it a shame he had not found the right woman for himself yet.

'Stupid young fool,' Alec shook his head as he watched his youngest brother spill some of the precious drink. 'Should find himself something worthwhile to do.' Both he and Ben had a surfeit of workers now, with the downfall of the national economy and with so many unfortunate ex-servicemen desperately seeking employment. It meant they were both true gentlemen farmers and could please themselves when and if they worked on their land. They both pitched in manually nearly every day, both knew every mark on every beast in their herds, but while he spent time nurturing his family and calling on his tenants, Ben wasted too much time on dubious pleasures.

'No rancour on my wedding day, please,' Tristan chided light-heartedly, coming to sit at Emilia's side. 'Tell your husband to relinquish Jenna for once. I haven't had the chance to hold the baby yet.'

'Might be doing this for yourself next year,' Alec winked while passing his daughter across to him. Emilia was pleased that Jenna was staying awake and active for an unprecedented length of time today. She made sure Tristan's grip on her was secure.

'Oh, I don't know about that,' Tristan laughed, glancing at Winifred. 'More children are hardly on our agenda, are they, my dear?'

Winifred blushed. She and Tristan had only spoken about their marriage in terms of security for them both and Vera Rose and Jonny. 'Mind your own business, Alec.'

'You're looking good, Tris,' Emilia changed the subject to take the heat out of Winifred's embarrassment. The bride had confided in her that she was dreading the wedding night. 'It would feel strange sharing a bed with any man again after seven years of widowhood, but it's even harder to think of Tris in that way. Emilia, I hope we've not made a huge mistake.'

'Winnie, it's Tris we're talking about here, remember?' Emilia had said. 'He's the kindest and most sensitive of men. Just give a little time for you and he to get to know each other in a different way, and for him and Jonny to bond again. It will happen. Trust me.' Looking at Winifred now, she could see her advice was unheeded.

'Now I've shaved off the 'tache, you mean?' Tristan wriggled his top lip. 'No one liked it, and there was me thinking it gave me a certain something.' He cooed to Jenna. 'Oh well, you'll grow up loving your uncle whatever I look like, won't you, poppet? She's gorgeous. There's something special about little girls, isn't there? Mmmmm, perhaps a little sister for Jonny and Vera Rose would be nice.'

'Are you sure about that, Tris? You wouldn't go anywhere near Polly Hetherton's little adopted girl at Jenna's party, and Louisa's a sweet thing.' Winifred had meant it as a joke, but her husband's sudden extraordinary dark expression told her she had made a mistake. And both Emilia and Alec were looking away. 'What have I said?'

'I'll tell you sometime,' Tristan replied, hiding his face behind Jenna's soft body.

Ben glanced back at his brothers and their wives. He couldn't stand the sight of so much matrimonial cosiness. They looked middle-aged and smug in companionship already. Alec was preparing to take another round of boring photographs.

He stabbed a cigar between his lips, lit it and inhaled a deep lung-clogging puff. When he took the next long draught of champagne, the rim of the bottle clanked against his teeth. He set off to get away from everyone. Trying to make a steady passage to show his self-satisfied eldest brother that he was in fact in control of himself, he ploughed along the length of the fence and carried on until there was a sizeable distance between himself and Roskerne.

He plunged on over the spongy grass of the cliff top, swingeing through spatterings of short-stemmed primroses, allowing heather and prickly golden gorse to snatch at his trousers. He lobbed the butt of the cigar over the cliff edge. Gulping with care out of the champagne bottle, so as not to lose any of the sweet nectar, he was hoping to finish off the last pockets of soberness.

When he reached his intended spot, a dip in the cliff top which offered shelter and privacy, he flung himself down, leaning his back against the bank of coarse pale-green and straw-coloured grasses and wild plants. Lots of plants here – a botanist's dream – none of which were doing his suit any good. This was a place he had relaxed in on school holidays, eaten picnics after playing rowdy games with some local brats whose parents worked a little further downcoast at the Watergate Bay Hotel – there had been no children his age living at Roskerne then. Well, Jonny had taken over the crown of gang leader; he was hero-worshipped. And Alec, damn him, had taken over Emilia. Damn her.

He may have no longer wanted her for himself after their bitter quarrel over his running away at the news of her brother's death, but Alec should have allowed time to see if they'd make things up. Alec, the sly, underhanded lover-in-waiting. He had wanted a hard-working, tough-minded, loyal brood mare for his next wife instead of risking another upper-middle-class, tormenting bitch. And Alec had then had the cheek to accuse him of treachery over Tremore! He'd only taken what was rightly his, his inheritance. So what if he'd reworded a couple of documents so he could get his five thousand pounds before he was twenty-one? Alec shouldn't have been so bloody damned superior in allowing him only five hundred. And what had Alec wanted Tremore for anyway? He'd already had a lot of property in the parish. He wanted to own everything, have everyone.

He emptied the champagne bottle and let it fall from his hand, then cursed loudly and heartily because he needed another cigar but his pocket was empty.

He saw the sky, high and free and blamelessly blue. The clouds looked as if God had daubed the celestial canvas with white and swirled it here and there with a blithe fingertip. A sparrowhawk zipped into sight, close overhead. Ben leaned up on his elbows and watched the bird of prey, a male by its grey colouring and barred breast and underparts, swoop to near ground level, hunting along the long expanse of shrubbery, bramble and gorse that topped the bank. A sudden pounce, a sharp shriek, and it was off and away with its reward of a young rabbit. Ben wished he could do that. Yearn, ensnare and fly away in triumph. So far all he had done with his life was to build up a rundown farm, renovate and extend an old house, raise the yields in a few fields to Ministry satisfaction and buy in healthy stock. Some might find that fulfilling. Not him. Not with his brother always having more.

He saw the sea, the great and terrible Atlantic Ocean, reaching out in indigo and emerald green, shimmering with white crests, going on and on in an everlasting expedition, leaving the shore to go far, far away, proceeding unendingly with its ambition and purpose. That's what he should be doing. His horizons ended in 186 acres within the boundaries of an insignificant rural parish.

But what did he really want? Not Polly Hetherton, his regular bed partner, not anymore. She was fair in every way, witty and creative, but although she wasn't seeking an end of her war-widowhood by marriage to him, she did see him as exclusively hers. She had monopolized him throughout the party held for Jenna, talking as if he was substitute father to Louisa, and not Julian, her brother. Louisa was a lovely, even-tempered child and he adored her, but he didn't want to feel suffocated by her existence. Trouble was, he and Polly had grown so used to each other they weren't far removed from the homely pair of couples he had not long forsaken.

He lay back and shut his eyes, not wanting to witness nature and its glories of promise and freedom anymore. Tomorrow he would go home and then what?

A face of incredible vitality and mystery came into his mind. And a pair of dazzling, piercing violet eyes; so intense was the vision it was almost as if those eyes were looking at him now. Selina Bosweld was the most amazing woman he'd ever known. No, she wasn't. It was all a façade. She was playing some sort of game with him and he was in no mood for the challenge. He wished he hadn't invited her to his house. But, let her come. Let her play her next hand and discover a surprise. He was not going to let himself be made a fool of.

He was smiling to himself when he drifted into sleep and did not wake when, as can often happen in April and especially here on the coast, there came a short sharp burst of rain.

Six

As the skies drew in and the sun sank slowly in a blaze of luminous reds, mauves, lemon and gold, Emilia crept into the summerhouse. Smiling happily, for she was looking forward to some company, she sat on a cushioned, wrought-iron bench and waited. Something warm touched her leg. She reached down to brush off what she thought was an insect. The warm thing came again. It seemed to be searching her flesh. It was a hand.

With a cry she jumped up and peered down behind the bench. 'Ben! So this is where you are.'

Having returned to Roskerne, but wanting to remain alone and feeling sick and heavy-headed, he had stretched out in here and slept again. Stiff and aching all over, he moaned while struggling to get up. He smoothed at his damp crumpled suit, looked about for his absent tie. 'There was a time when you would've helped me.'

'There was a time you would've been worth it. You've missed dinner, it was rude of you. Go in and apologize to Tris and Winnie.' She spotted the tie, tossed over the waxy dark-green leaves of a pot plant. 'Here.'

'Here what?' Lurching on unsteady feet he grabbed the bench for balance.

'This.' She pushed the tie, made of expensive silk, into his hand.

'Don't get shirty. I can't see properly, remember? Put it on for me.'

'There's no point now. You smell disgusting. Go in and take a bath.'

'Damn it, woman, you just can't resist giving orders, can

you?' Ben's blurred vision cleared and he had a good look at her. 'Mmmm, damned attractive evening dress.'

Emilia was too late in pulling up her fringed shawl to cover the upper swell of her breasts, which were more fulsome due to her motherhood. 'Be careful you don't fall down the steps on your way out.'

'What are you doing here like this? It takes a lot to drag you away from the baby.' He gave a wicked laugh. 'Good heavens! An assignation. Let me see, who are you waiting for? There could only be one candidate. Alec. Well, lucky old Alec. Is this a special place for you both?'

For once he had the upper hand. Emilia turned scarlet, glowing as brightly as the setting sun. 'Was it in here you and he first got down to a spot of clinch and grapple? And now you slip in here for old times' sake when you visit Winnie. How romantic. Bit soon after Jenna's birth though, isn't it?'

Emilia was not about to allow her hung-over, pathetic brother-in-law to defile her love life with Alec. 'We just want to spend a little time together, that's all. Ben, will you please go.'

'Well, I certainly don't want to stay and watch!'

As he moved his foot, he stumbled and fell into her. His weight sent them hurtling down on the bench. She cried out in shock and pain as her back hit the hard wrought iron.

Ben was suddenly hauled away from her, the next moment doubling over as Alec drove a fist deep into his gut. 'Stay away from my wife!'

'Alec, it was an accident.' Emilia leaned forward and grabbed him, fearing he would go after Ben again. 'He was just leaving, he fell.'

'I heard, I saw, but that doesn't excuse the way he was speaking to you. It's time he grew up.' Alec kept his fists balled. He was steady on his feet, ready for anything Ben might do.

Ben coughed and groaned. He uttered a stream of foul words. 'You had no need to thump me, you miserable rotten swine. I'll pay you back for this.'

'Think you're up to it, do you? You're a poor excuse for

a man. The way you strut about as if you're more important than anyone else is sickening. There was no need to get drunk so early and go off alone. You're not fit to be in this family, you're a poor excuse for a brother. Tris doesn't deserve to be concerned about you and your whereabouts on his wedding day. Now sober up and make recompense to him and Winnie. And never, ever, speak to Emilia with such disrespect again.'

Clutching the arm of the bench, panting, Ben levered himself upright. He glared at Alec. Emilia saw more than bitterness and resentment in him this time. He was emanating pure hatred. 'I bet it's you who's making more fuss about my conduct than Tris. You're jealous of everything that I do, admit it. You're the one who's selfish, Emilia will see that one day.' He groaned and held his stomach. It felt as if his insides were rearranging themselves. 'I swear, if something doesn't make you suffer, and I mean both of you, for this one day soon, then I'll do it myself.'

From his bedroom window Tristan was gazing out across the ocean, concentrating on its steady advance and retreat. Winnie's maid had closed the heavy swagged and valanced curtains, but he had swept them open as far as they would go. He'd ask Winnie if she wouldn't mind sleeping this way every night and, after a suitable time, if the lace curtains could be dispensed with. He always took pleasure in the fresh air, the light and the soothing rhythmic sounds.

'Tris . . .'

So at one with the sea was he, he had missed Winifred coming in from her dressing room and getting into bed.

'Sorry, Winnie, I was miles away.'

'I was beginning to think you were going to stand there all night.'

She was lying with the covers clutched up to her chin, a young-looking figure in the vast stump bed, an ornately carved oak relic from her late husband's family. He felt nervous and silly. He may have mentioned having a daughter in fun earlier, but the intimate side of married life, this next duty, hadn't actually occurred to him before this minute. In the last five years he had occasionally visited certain working women, as a soldier might, but regular lovemaking – it was an awesome and a pleasant thought. Poor Winnie though, she was dreading it from her strained expression. 'Well, I, um, had better get in then.'

'Turn out the lanterns first.'

'Of course.'

Winifred turned her face away while he slipped off his dressing gown and got in beside her.

He lay down. Kept himself to his side of the bed. 'Did you enjoy the day, my dear?'

'Yes,' she lied. 'Did you?'

'Yes. Pity Ben and Alec are at loggerheads yet again. Em doesn't help matters with her stroppy attitude towards Ben.'

'You're close to Emilia, aren't you? I've noticed how her friends usually call her Em.'

'Yes, I suppose I am. It's good to have her in the family.'

'It's Jonny I'm worried about. He was rude to Vera Rose just before bedtime. We're going to have problems with him.'

'Not if I can help it. I'll talk to him tomorrow after the others have left for home. I've been thinking about things from Jonny's point of view. It's been a terrible wrench for him to leave the farm, but he could spend time there in the holidays and the occasional weekend. Vera Rose too. Should please everyone. I'll see about getting him into the Cub Scouts. Take him to watch the fishermen unload their boats. Plenty of activity, that's what he needs.' Tristan turned on his side towards his bride.

Winifred was set on delaying the inevitable, but what she was about to say next was not a tactic in the cause. There was something she was burning to know. It was against Tristan's tolerant nature to take exception against anyone, particularly a child. 'Tris, will you tell me why you have a problem with Louisa Hetherton-Andrews?'

'Ah, yes, that's something you've got the right to know about. I'm afraid it's an unpalatable truth, Winnie. Just a minute.' He pushed his pillows up against the hard bedhead and leaned against them in the semi-darkness. He took a sip from the glass of water close by on an old military chest.

'It sounds serious,' she said, electing to stay lying still, keeping far enough away not to be touching him.

Tristan took a deep breath. 'It is. Because of that child's existence I agreed to something I've always regretted. There's much that happened in the past you don't know about, Winnie. You see, the girl is Ursula's child, her lover's child.'

Winifred forgot her modesty and sat up beside him. 'But the baby was stillborn!'

'She wasn't, though that was what Jonny was going to be told anyway. It was always meant that Ursula's child would be secretly adopted, to make it easier for the new start we were supposed to have, until Bruce Ashley turned up again. Emilia was there at the delivery. Ben was also in the house. They promised Ursula her dying wish, that if it was possible they would always look after her baby. While I sat alone with Ursula and watched her die, Alec noticed the child had a birthmark on her face and the district nurse said the intended adoptive parents wouldn't take her because of it. The next option was an orphanage, but Alec's always hated the thought of anyone being rejected, and . . .' Tristan expelled a heavy sigh and put a hand over his face. 'Dear God, this is awful.'

Winifred reached for his other hand – close cousins again.

He hung on to her warmth. 'When I came downstairs, Alec, Emilia and Ben were actually arguing whether she should go to Ford Farm or Tremore. They made my head spin, Winnie. It was unfair. I, as Ursula's husband, was responsible for the decision over what happened to the baby. Ben's young friend, Julian Andrews was also there. He suggested he and his sister adopt the baby. As you know, he's got a weak heart and isn't expected to live many more years, and Polly, apparently, had been told she could never conceive. They had always longed for what neither could have.

'I agreed, Winnie, and Andrews took the baby away. But if

I had been asked about it the next day, I would have refused. Now I have to live in fear that one day Jonny will find out that Louisa is his half-sister and that I lied to him. He might forgive the others for keeping the truth from him but not me, I'm his father.'

'I can see why you've never wanted to step inside Ford House again after all that happened there.' Winifred pulled away from him. 'Well, you've succeeded in getting Jonny away mostly from the farm, which is visited by Julian Andrews and Polly Hetherton and away from Truro where they live. He's not as likely to be exposed to Louisa now.'

Tristan touched her shoulder. She went rigid. 'Winnie, what is it? Are you disgusted by the whole affair? Do you think me heartless for wishing the girl had gone to an orphanage?'

'I know we've got a marriage of convenience, Tristan, but I didn't expect to be used.' She was shedding tears of humiliation. 'You've made me feel undervalued.'

'What are you saying, Winnie? Turn round to me. Please, my dear. I don't understand how I've upset you.'

She refused to budge, even when he put his arms around her from behind and rubbed the side of his face against her cheek. 'If it wasn't for Jonny you'd have sent me some money to help see me through and stayed in the Army until you'd retired, wouldn't you?'

'Oh, Winnie, please don't think that. Don't cry.' He sought to wipe away her tears. 'It isn't that at all. I promise you I resigned because I wanted to come home. I wanted family life again. I was lonely. I longed for a woman's company, all that she could give me. I had it in mind to ask you to marry me before I managed to wring it out of you that you had money worries. Yes, I won't deny that I feel better to have Jonny further away from that little girl, but I wouldn't have settled in or near to Truro anyway. Ursula's family live there. Jonny coped well when he learned his mother died bearing her lover's child – that couldn't have been kept from him, of course – but it hurts him being shunned by his grandparents. They're unforgiving, and I fear they'd throw Ursula's downfall in his face. I'm sorry, Winnie. I was a fool not to have told you all this before but there was a lot to do leading up till today. Say you forgive me, Winnie. Please.'

She let herself fall back against his body, wrapping her arms over his. 'I'm such a silly, Tris. I forgot what Emilia reminded me of earlier today.'

He kissed her wet hot cheek. 'What was that?'

'That you're the most sensitive of men. I'm sorry for making a fuss.'

'Understandable. You'll have to pull me up sometimes, you know. I'm too used to being on my own.' He kissed her cheek again.

She moved her head so she could kiss him in the same way. She felt the slight roughness of stubble on his chin and her lips burned. She had forgotten how exciting the hardy qualities of a man felt. How a man smelled, somehow raw and unrefined. How, in the dark, a man's strength and dominance could take her to a place she could never admit to knowing. A place she missed.

Tristan was aware of her softness, the full supple contours of her body. The feel of her hair against his chest sent ripples of pleasure swirling down to his loins. 'Winnie, darling . . .'

She was too shy to respond in the way she wished to. As he kissed the back of her neck, nuzzling in that zone of exquisite sensitivity, she was too shy to let out moans of delight and anticipation and arousal. She simply closed her eyes and let him run his fingertips up and down her arms, making her tingle wonderfully under the lace-encrusted satin, pleased now not to have opted for a nightdress she would have felt sheltered in. She gave way to the pleasures as he took them to sink down on the bed.

The first taste of his lips on hers was fleeting. She caressed his face, his gentle pale thin face. She felt safe with Tristan. Her lips were ready when he brought his back again. He didn't progress in what she thought of as the usual way of a man. Hands on her breasts then a fast demanding journey to the lower regions. Instead he brought her hands up and kissed them, taking her fingertips inside his mouth one at a time. He made lingering feather-light voyages with the backs of his fingers, the sides of his hands, the curved flats of his hands all over her except where she was foremost a woman. He did the same with his mouth. It was like a form of worship. A gift. An honouring. And so it went on. Gaining in commitment and passion. Experiences new and exquisite and divine to her.

It seemed half the night had passed before he finally joined their bodies together. By this time her nightdress was heaped on top of his pyjamas on the floor and he had made her a pioneer in his quest.

Long after midnight, Alec lay watching Emilia. She was lingering over the cot brought into the room for Jenna, touching her, keeping a vigil by lantern light. Emilia had been in no mood to share kisses and loving embraces with him in the summerhouse after his furious interchange with Ben and she had stayed subdued all evening. Damn Ben! He had spoiled their special place. Ben was always in the background of their love. He had been her first lover and Emilia would probably be married to him now if not for that fateful rescue of his grandmother. But it was the first time Ben had tainted his and Emilia's passion and delight in each other. He wished his brother far away.

'Darling,' he whispered through the muggy gloom. 'Are you worried about Jenna? Or are you angry with me?'

Her attention stayed over the cot. 'Alec, there's something wrong with her.' Her voice was thick with tears, heavy with fright.

He rushed out of bed to Emilia's side. 'How do you know? She appears to be sleeping soundly. She took her last feed, didn't she?'

'Yes, but . . . oh, I don't know, Alec, there's something, I know there is. I'm her mother, I feel it.'

He felt Jenna's brow, it was warm and a little moist. 'She's not burning hot. Her breathing's not ragged or anything. Bring her into bed with us, hold her all night if it'll make you feel better, darling.'

'No, she's peaceful. It would be a shame to disturb her. I'm just being silly.' Even as the last words left her lips she knew she didn't believe them. As soon as she got home she would take Jenna to the doctor, just to be sure . . .

'Then come to bed, you'll wear yourself out. Do you want me to take a peek at Will and Tom?'

'No. Sorry, darling, I'm making you worry too.'

Jenna suddenly opened her eyes. 'Hello, sweetheart, did naughty Mummy and Daddy wake you?' Emilia crooned, caressing her soft downy cheek.

Alec put his finger in her tiny fist. She didn't grip it, but next instant her whole body went into spasm and she was crying in pain, first shrilly, then a loud pitiful wail.

Emilia picked her up and cradled her to her breast and rubbed her back. 'She must have wind. Shush, shush, sweetheart, Mummy will make it go away.' Usually when babies had wind they drew up their knees and bawled. Jenna was suddenly limp in her arms.

'Never heard her make a noise like that before. Or Will or Tom.' Alec held his hands out helplessly. 'What can we do?'

'I'll walk about with her for a bit. That might do it.' Emilia paced once up and down, then up again on the Wilton carpet. As suddenly as it had started Jenna's crying ceased. 'There, that's better. Let's get into bed with Daddy and we'll all snuggle up together.'

Emilia kissed her daughter's forehead. 'Jenna? Jenna? Oh, my God, she's stopped breathing. Alec! Alec! Do something!'

He raced across the room. He was trembling. 'Breathe into her mouth like you did the day she was born.'

In her panic Emilia couldn't function. She thrust the baby into Alec's hands. He laid the little inert body over his arm and while supporting her head on the palm of his other hand he breathed into her.

Emilia didn't realize she was crying for help, dancing a dance of fear on the spot. When others rushed into the room, bringing more light with them and making outlandish noises, she fought against the strong hands that were trying to give her comfort. 'My baby, my baby! Save her.'

To add to the living nightmare, Tom wrapped his arms around her legs and Jonny tried to pull him away, but Tom clung on and screamed that he wouldn't let go. Emilia saw Will standing back ashen-faced, and then Winifred got in the way of her view of what Alec was doing to Jenna. 'What's happening? Let me see!'

Tristan grabbed her and this time he held on tight. 'Stop it, Em. Listen, Jenna's crying. She's going to be all right.'

Winifred stepped away. With tears streaming down his gaunt terrified face, Alec was holding Jenna with the side of her face against his neck and Jenna was crying loudly, lustily. Tom finally allowed Jonny to draw him back. Emilia felt herself collapse with relief and Tristan had to support her. 'Thank God, thank God,' she sobbed over and over.

'Let's get everyone up on the bed,' Tristan said. 'We'll send the maid for Winnie's doctor to take a look at Jenna.'

When Emilia was sitting beside Alec, he gave Jenna to her then gathered his whole family in to him. 'Dear God, Alec, I didn't know what to do this time.'

Jonny was standing close to Alec and wound his arm round his neck. 'Uncle Alec always knows what to do. He's the bravest man in all the world.'

Tristan and Winnie exchanged rueful looks.

Ben appeared in the doorway. He had got drunk again and only the maid clumping down the stairs to fetch the doctor had woken him. He leaned stupidly against the doorjamb. 'Something going on, is there?'

Alec eased himself away from the bed then shot across the room. 'Get out! This is all your doing. You ill-wished us earlier tonight and brought us near to tragedy. You've gone too far this time. I'll never forgive you and I no longer consider you my brother. If you ever step on my land again, and that includes Ford House, I'll take a gun and hunt you down like a dog.'

Seven

It was market day. Two of the farmhands had taken the calves by cart into Truro at daybreak, but Alec had decided not to follow on after breakfast to observe the auction or conduct his other business there. Instead he lined up more of his farm vehicles in the outer yard.

'Jim! Jim!' Taking an impatient puff on a cigarette, he peered about for the youth who should have been on his way to him with paint, axle grease and tools. 'Jim! Where the bloody hell are you?'

'Time you had another word with he, Alec.' Edwin Rowse was about to leave for town, deputizing for his son-in-law. 'Lazy young bugger's slipping off all the time, he's getting tired to the bone and as cantankerous as Pip was. No one can say a right word to him.'

'Do you think he's sickening for something?' Alec snatched at the opportunity to consider someone else in his household might be ailing rather than his beloved daughter.

Edwin guffawed and grinned. 'Aye, spring fever! Got himself a maid, he has. Haven't you seen the silly look on his face when he goes out? Or gotten the smell of him when he finally gets back?' The farm manager tapped his weather-raddled neck. 'Got marks here he have and that's not the only place.'

'Don't tell me he's actually gone that far?'

'Bound to happen one day. He's always been one for casting his eye round.'

'Sounds like he's seeing someone experienced, so it can't be Elena Rawley.' Alec sighed, rumbling like a steam engine. 'I'll speak to him, before we get some outraged father turning up with a shotgun.'

'He's always gone a long time so whomever 'tis must live yonder. Put the ruddy bull to shame, he will.' Edwin hoped a spot of wicked humour would lessen Alec's moroseness. He was another one who looked as if he needed a good night's sleep.

'Well, he'd better not spend any more time with this girl when he's supposed to be working. Market cart's hitched up for you, Edwin. The pig is on board for the butcher. We'll put away one for ourselves in a fortnight; Emilia says the pig meat's getting low. Did you pick up the money I left on the desk for your lunch? Take my usual table at the Red Lion.'

'Dolly's made me a pasty and I'm taking a flask, never catch me in a posh hotel.' Edwin did not take his elevated state all that seriously. The cowman here before his daughter married his boss, he was ordinary, small in build, middle aged but looked much older. He took simple enjoyment from his and Dolly's extra comforts since leaving their tied cottage five years ago, and quiet delight in the close proximity of his three grandchildren. Shortly before this he had been showing Will and Tom how to make sailing boats from corks, twigs and triangles of canvas. When he got back, they were to float them together on the pond.

'At least have a pint somewhere.'

'I might.' Edwin took out his tobacco tin and started a slow deliberate filling up of his ancient charred pipe. 'What's the matter? Why're you finding so much work close to the house? The carts are usually only cleaned up one at a time, and anyway none of 'em needs nothing urgent done. Why're you so unsettled today then? I know you don't like change. Cap'n Tristan getting married and Jonny leaving here's disturbed you, and you always do say that change and change about's usually followed by some disaster.'

Alec lit another smoke from the butt between his lips. 'I'm afraid, Edwin.'

Edwin lifted his flat cap and scratched his donkey-grey hair. 'Afraid's a strong word. Can't see what you got to be afraid about.'

'I can't get this feeling out of my mind that something terrible is about to happen.'

'Sometimes I think you're a mite too superstitious. Never seen the old folk sniff the wind as often as you do, or buy so many trinkets from the gypsies. What's on your mind this time?'

Alec watched Edwin's stubby leathery forefinger work the tobacco into the pipe bowl in precise circular and prodding movements. He had a lot of respect for Edwin's unruffled nature and common sense, but nothing could shift the unease icing up his guts. He didn't want to feel this way. Have this insistent foreboding. This touch of insight, foresight, whatever it was. On these occasions he had been proved right or wrong in equal numbers, which pointed to it all being coincidence. But he was a deep thinker – it was a longstanding habit of his. It was useful at times, a retreat. Or like now, a curse.

'I'm afraid because Emilia's afraid for Jenna. She hasn't left her for a second since she stopped breathing at Roskerne and she sat up with her again all last night.'

'She's her mother. She's bound to be worried after a terrible fright like that. Women usually fuss more over their children than us men. The little maid's all right. The new Mrs Harvey's doctor said so, didn't he? He said she's a bit of a weakling but should thrive, given time.'

'He wasn't there when it happened. The man's a god-damned, incompetent fool!' Alec shuddered as he relived the biting fear of losing Jenna. He shook in anger as he recalled the humiliation of being dressed down by Winifred's condescending, aging doctor who had accused him of foolishness, of being likely to have done Jenna more harm than good with his actions. 'He was wrong, Edwin. Emilia did not panic for no good reason and cause me to panic too. Emilia's too strong, too sensible for that, and I'd never, ever do anything to risk the welfare of one of my children. I've delivered enough animal young to know when one of them needed assistance to start breathing. That Newquay quack was furious at being hauled out of his warm bed. He might have been satisfied with Jenna's breathing and heartbeat, her colour and even the way she cried while he manhandled her, but he didn't explain why for a few revolting seconds she was dead. She was, Edwin, I swear she was.'

Edwin had never seen Alec so intense, so anxious, consumed by fear. He was worried himself now. Jenna had been taken to Hennaford's Dr Holloway the day after the return from Roskerne. He had agreed with the Newquay doctor's diagnosis, but Dr Holloway was becoming increasingly absentminded and dithery, had even been known to contradict himself during a consultation. Few locals had faith in him anymore. 'What're you going to do?'

'Emilia's suggested we give it a week. If Jenna's not put on any weight by the end we'll seek specialist advice.' Alec had someone in mind, his lawyer's son, Doctor Reggie Rule, the paediatrician Selina Bosweld had consulted about his character.

Sara approached them on her way to the dairy to scald the morning's milk to begin the process of producing trays of thick, golden cream which would find its way into many of the county's shops, hotels and guesthouses, and much further afield. 'Jim's holding the pony for you, Mr Rowse. He says, she's getting skittish.'

'So that's where he is. I thought Midge had harnessed the market cart.' Alec massaged his temples. His head was aching so much it felt about to explode.

'He did but left for the fields, not thinking Mr Rowse would be so long,' Sara replied, hoping her remark would not be considered disrespectful. She was eager for Jim not to get into any more trouble. Since he had taken up with this mysterious girl, whose identity he was refusing, unusually, to share with her, he was even more bigheaded and his tiredness was making him grouchy and uncooperative.

'I'd better be off then.' Edwin made haste away, his head down. Always a little bent over, the smoke from his pipe drifted back from an even lower level today.

'Mrs Em's taken the baby out for a walk in the pram,' Sara

said quickly, before Alec moved off or got lost in thought. 'She said it would do her good.'

'It will. Was Jenna wakeful?'

'No, fast asleep.'

'Was she pale?'

His eyes were boring into her, demanding answers. Making Sara both timid and rapt to be receiving such close scrutiny. 'Um, she had lots of colour, I thought, when I took a peep at her.'

'That's good.' It was something to cling to, but not enough. 'Tell Jim to make a start here on his own scraping down the wagon. Tell him also that he's not to leave the yard today.' Alec needed to be alone, with no distractions. He needed to concentrate harder than he ever had done before. To will Jenna better. To pray good health into her. In a drawer of his desk he had a growing collection of good luck charms. He would take them to the church, to call on any and all powers, to plead for a safe and happy future for his child.

'You don't look well, Alec. Can I get you something?'

'What?' He had half turned away and the silvery-sweet voice had broken through his urgent strategy like a violation.

Sara leapt back. Her moment of bravery in keeping him with her a little longer had gone horribly wrong. Her remark and her question had been personal. Although her master usually insisted everyone call him by his first name, having no time for what he called petty convention, she had never done so before. She had breached propriety and was in for a well-deserved reprimand. Her heart dropped like a stone. He would never see her as anything but a lower-class servant who should remember her place. Worse still, he might now think her a nuisance.

'My goodness, Sara, did I snap?' His hand came to rest on her shoulder. 'You look shaken. I didn't mean to frighten you.'

'No, I . . . I, um, just thought you looked a bit poorly, that's all.'

'I'm sorry, sweetheart. You were being kind and here's

me barking the wits out of you. I do have a headache. I'm going to take a breath of air. You run along.'

Although he was dejected, Alec's long athletic strides took him quickly out of her sight. Rooted to the ground, Sara rubbed a hand where he had touched her. She turned her head and sniffed that sacred place, her excitement making her believe she could detect the smell of him there. Her tummy did crazy somersaults. Her head soared up to the sky and she broke into a joyful version of 'You Made Me Love You'. How she wished she could make him love her, and keep the sensation of his touch, his wonderful masculine essence on her for ever. She had an idea where he was going. Long Meadow was one of his favourite places when he wanted to be alone. How she wished she could run on ahead of him, find herself a little hiding place there and curl up and watch him.

A lonely half a mile on from Devil's Arch, the church offered Alec the privacy and isolation he desired. He sat at the end of a pew beyond the north aisle, the oldest and darkest part of the echoing, cold building and spread his lucky charms – cheap tin animal shapes, silver horseshoes, dry and disintegrated sprays of heather – along the hymn book ledge in front of him. He called on each talisman separately to do its work. He had also brought the gold cross, that had once been his grandmother's, from Emilia's jewellery box. Gripping the cross so tightly its holy shape was impressed upon his flesh he stared ahead, imploring the half life-size crucified Christ fashioned from polished mahogany up on the wall near the altar for His divine intervention.

'Please,' he whispered. 'It wasn't your Father's will for my first child to survive when Lucy sought to purposely destroy it inside her, nor for my brother, Henry, to come through the war. Please don't let my little Jenna be taken away from Emilia and I. I'm sorry for being weak, but I don't think I could bear it.'

It was closing in on midday when his leaden feet were crunching back down the gravelled, weed-strewn path outside. He felt as cold as ice and the earnest warmth of the sun did nothing to give him ease or comfort. He didn't hear the rooks cawing from tree to tree or notice the glorious yellow and pink primroses and the bright blue speedwell spilling over the banks and graves.

The rectory was only a few hundred yards away, hiding behind a tall hedge and trees of sycamore and ash. He and Emilia had only been there two days ago to arrange Jenna's christening, which was to be held on Sunday afternoon. He could go there now and ask the staid, but kindly, rector to pray with him for Jenna. But he couldn't bear it if he was told he was probably worrying over nothing, or that God's will was God's will and was not to be questioned, or that whatever Jenna's fate might be God knew what was best for her. He didn't want to be reminded of one of the rector's favourite expositions: that whatever happened in life, God gave those who called on Him the strength to see it through.

Alec fell down on the churchyard steps and wept. 'It's not strength I'm asking for, Lord. I just want my little girl to be all right.'

Eight

Holding Jenna in her arms Emilia knocked on the door of Ford House. She was surprised by who answered it.

'Doctor Rule! Reggie.'

'Mrs Harvey. Emilia. How good to see you. So this is the latest addition to your family? It's a pity you're arriving the very same instant I'm leaving. Got a clinic in an hour, you see.' Reggie Rule had dull hair parted in the centre and a full moustache that overwhelmed his small, boyish face. He was dressed in a long leather coat and boots suitable to his mode of transport, an adventurous motorcycle. He was carrying a medical bag and a leather helmet; a pair of goggles was hanging round his neck. His father often lamented that Reggie was wasting his highly attained skills by not setting himself up in Harley Street, in the capital. He was a pleasant fellow who lived alone, reserved and bookish, kind and obliging, content to practise his profession in the place of his birth.

'I'm so glad you're here, Reggie. You're the very person I wish to see. Please don't go yet, I promise I won't keep you long.' Emilia wasn't usually so forthright, so demanding, but after spending another night agonizing over Jenna, when she had been forced from time to time to labour to hear her breathing, she was desperate.

'Really? Do go into the parlour. I'll follow on after you. I'm afraid that Selina's not long left for duty at the hospital, but Perry's there. We've had a late night at cards. I hear they're off to Ben's for dinner tonight. Are you and Alec going?'

'No, we're not.' The last thing Emilia wanted was to get into a conversation involving Ben. While Alec had been putting the overnight cases into the motor car at Roskerne,

Ben had blustered outside to him and there had been another heated exchange, ending with Ben shouting, 'To hell with you then!' and speeding off in his own vehicle. She did not share Alec's belief about Ben ill-wishing them, of being responsible for Jenna's distress, but she had suffered enough of his loutish behaviour.

She burst into the parlour. 'Good morning, Perry. Sorry to drop in unannounced.'

Perry smiled from where he was leaning on his crutches while spreading a small square table with sheets of newspaper. 'Not at all, Emilia. You're welcome at any time. How wonderful, you've brought the baby. Selina will be sorry to have missed you both.' On the sideboard was a tin tray loaded with pots of paint and glue, scraps of cloth and other oddments. 'This is for Libby, for when she and Mirelle get back from viewing the blacksmith's puppies again, can't keep Libby away from them. You know Reggie, of course. Have you come about the school concert next week? Miss Rawley declined any help from us. I'm afraid she didn't take to Selina. Selina does have an unfortunate way of putting some people off. Can I get you some coffee? Or tea? I manage very well in the kitchen when Mirelle's not there to chase me out, you know.'

'I think Emilia's here on a serious matter, Perry,' Reggie said, discarding his travelling appendages and removing his coat.

'I'm sorry for taking advantage of you both like this. I came here for help. The thing is, I'm so worried about Jenna. Could I call on your professional skills? Specially yours Reggie, you know all about children's diseases.' Her brow creasing more and more in anxiety, Emilia looked persuasively from former surgeon to doctor. Both were interested in what she had to say and seemed so intent on helping her it made her eyes fill with tears. She told them the details of Jenna's birth and her brief medical history, about the nightmare event at Roskerne and Dr Holloway's terse agreement with the diagnosis given by Winifred's doctor.

'You'll think me an over-anxious mother too, but I know

there's something wrong with Jenna. I feel it right here.' She pressed a hand over her heart. 'Would either or both of you take a look at her, please? I'll pay for the consultation.'

Perry and Reggie exchanged a look of understanding and Emilia was heartened.

Perry said, 'We would be happy to examine your little girl and we wouldn't dream of accepting payment for it. Bring her into my bedroom, Emilia, and lay her on the bed. Reggie, would you fetch my bag? You'll find it at the bottom of the wardrobe.'

It was a high double bed covered with an oatmeal-coloured, textured counterpane and when Emilia laid Jenna down on it she looked like a little lost soul on a sea of grain. She was drowsy and not making a sound, and she was pink, a vivid unnatural pink, her lips and chin a pallid white, tinged with greyish-blue. After resting his crutches beside the shiny mahogany headboard, Perry sat down on the bed close to Jenna. Emilia was aware of the two men studying Jenna as she undressed her, then, with a horrid feeling that she was somehow abandoning her baby, she stood back and watched anxiously as they took turns to apply their gentle-handed skills on her.

In addition to the usual observations, again and again they shone a light into Jenna's eyes and tried her reflexes and listened to her chest with their stethoscopes. At one point, Perry clapped his hands together close beside her ears. Jenna was not the least bit startled but Emilia cried out in alarm. During one moment it seemed Reggie was staring down at Jenna, while holding his breath and massaging her chest. Every now and then throughout the meticulous examination the two men glanced at each other. There was a certain nod, a soft drawn-out sigh, a tightening of mouths, as if conveying some secret code.

Finally, the medical instruments were put away. Perry repinned Jenna's nappy. He wrapped her in her shawl and lifted her into his arms. He cradled her and kissed her forehead.

It had all happened in about fifteen minutes but those

minutes had crawled by for Emilia. A long agonizing time and a horribly short time in which to have her fears confirmed, as she was sure they would be, for she believed firmly, absolutely, that Jenna was unhealthy, or abnormal, or was never likely to thrive.

'Well?' Without knowing it she took a step backwards.

Reggie was gazing down at the floor, expressionless but not guarded. He looked up at Emilia and smiled. It was a feeble smile, as if it held a forlorn meaning.

Emilia was jigging on her feet. Fear was cramping her heart. 'What is it?'

Reggie shot a look at Perry.

'You go ahead, Reggie. You're the expert,' Perry said. He patted the bed beside him. 'Why don't you sit here, Emilia?'

She had been expecting bad news and now she was about to get it. She shouldn't have come. This terrible moment could have been delayed. All she could do was to shake her head.

'Emilia,' Reggie began in a way that was soft and soothing, and chilling. 'I think we should all go up to the farm and get someone to fetch Alec. He should hear this too.'

'No! I can't wait that long and you don't know Alec. He doesn't know I'm here. It's better you tell me first. He'll take any bad news hard. It's very bad, isn't it?'

'I'm going to insist you sit down, Emilia.' Reggie touched her arm and she jolted forward, regaining that lonely retreating step she had taken a minute ago. On legs of ice she obeyed him, perching on the edge of the monstrous bed where she had laid down her little girl, where for a few moments of time she had given up control of her and placed her fate in the hands of others.

Reggie joined her and took her hand. She was sandwiched between the two men. They were seeking to protect her but were only adding to her misery. She kept her eyes on her baby. Her Jenna. Her precious little daughter. The first girl born into the Harvey family in four generations. She was wanted and loved so much. And she was so tiny, so comfortable in Perry's tender arms.

Reggie drew in a soft breath. Emilia crushed his hand, not wanting to hear, yet needing to know his expert opinion. His voice travelled down her ear like a thundering storm, each word an affront, a cruel affliction. 'Emilia, as you've noticed for yourself, your little girl has few of the correct reflexes. I don't need to make further investigations as to the reason why. I am convinced she has cerebral palsy. She's a spastic. It may have been caused at her birth, when she may have been starved of oxygen for a little too long, but it's my belief she didn't form properly in the womb.'

Numb, as if in a dreadful dream, knowing the tide of dreadful tears would come later, Emilia reached out a hand and touched Jenna's slumbering face. She whispered, 'I knew it was something . . .'

'And—'

'And? No ands. We'll love her just the same. Now we know we'll do our very best for her. We have two healthy boys and she's our special baby.'

'Yes, she is your special baby and she always will be. I'm very sorry to add to your misery, Emilia, but I have to tell you that Jenna is also blind and deaf. Perry has intimated his agreement to me on all these matters. We are both so very sorry. I can't tell you how much we feel for you.'

Emilia stared all round the room. She noticed the addition of weightlifting equipment to the usual bedroom furniture. It was odd, peculiar here. No, she wasn't really here, learning all these terrible things about her daughter, being told that nature had played cruel tricks on her baby, the most vulnerable person in her life. The walls closed in on her. The pattern on the wallpaper, of sunflowers, turned into grotesque mocking shapes.

She was weeping, as soundlessly as Jenna usually did. She stretched out her arms to her. 'My poor little girl. Give her to me, please.'

Reggie restrained her and was suddenly holding her by the shoulders. Tightly. 'Emilia, you'll need to be very strong.'

'Of course I'll be strong! Jenna won't be able to see or hear us and she'll need lots of attention as she grows up, but she'll know she has a family who loves her and will always protect her. She'll know that all of us think she's worth it. Let me go, Reggie. Let go of me. I want my baby. You're behaving as if there's something worse. What could be worse than what you've already told me?'

She stared into each male face. Still and gaunt they were, and so full of understanding and so sorry for her. She hated them just for that moment. Then her whole world became distorted and collapsed all around her. No! What these two men were trying to tell her was worse than her direst imaginings.

This was crazy. It couldn't be right. It just couldn't be. She was here, with none of her family or friends to support her, being told her baby was more than a weakling, that she was malformed and hopelessly damaged and had no future. That she was dying! That her Jenna was going to die.

She heard Perry's voice above the appalling confusion in her mind, the crushing pain in her soul. 'It's her heart, Emilia. If the two GPs had been a little more conscientious they would have heard the abnormal echoes in the chambers of her heart and sent you to someone like Reggie for a proper diagnosis.'

'I'm afraid there's nothing that can be done in Jenna's case, Emilia,' Reggie said. 'She actually stopped breathing for several seconds while I was listening to her heart. It's very weak. All I can do now is to assure you that she's not suffering. She won't suffer.'

While Reggie kept holding her, Perry put Jenna into her arms.

Hugging Jenna into her body, Emilia cried over her. 'Wh-when . . . ? How long?'

Someone was stroking her hair. She didn't know who it was out of these two kind gentle men. She didn't know which one of them whispered, 'At any time now.'

'Oh, God! Oh, my God! She's only three and a half weeks old! Oh, Jenna, Mummy's sorry. Don't die. Please don't leave me.'

'You can cry, Emilia. Cry for as long as you want,' Perry said. 'Then we'll see about taking you home.'

'Home? That's where I have to be,' she sobbed. 'But how am I going to tell him? How am I going to tell Alec?'

Nine

Ben sent his foreman over to fetch the Boswelds and got his housekeeper to open the door to them. He had set an earlier time of arrival for Polly Hetherton and Julian Andrews and they were already ensconced in the drawing room, having unpacked for an overnight stay. Not wanting to entertain at all he kept the company waiting, listening at the door.

As he expected, Julian, who was of an amiable nature, was at ease with Perry and they were chatting, laughing occasionally. He could just make out the low voices of the two women. He pictured them. Polly, fair and refined, would be in a prominent chair near the fireplace, her back straight, her neat ankles crossed. Selina would be standing up, perhaps prowling about, commanding the greater presence in the room. There would be frostiness between them. Likely, they were weighing each other up as rivals for his interest.

He lingered another minute or two then went in, head up, handsome in his dinner suit, determined to stay in charge of the occasion. 'Please forgive me for the delay. Had something urgent to attend to,' he said in the polite way of a host. 'Hope you've introduced yourselves.'

A glance at the women showed him his first mistake for the night. Figures of class in fashionably flat, tubular dresses Polly and Selina were sitting side by side on a sofa, sharing in a serious tone their approval of the move in parliament to allow women to divorce unfaithful husbands.

Selina gave him a moment's attention. 'We've hardly been aware of your absence, Ben.'

She seemed calm but Ben saw the sparks in her extraordinary violet eyes, enhanced almost magically tonight by the same colour shadow on the lids. She was offended by his rudeness at not greeting her, at not fawning over her as he had done during the lunch at her house, and she was probably angry at the addition of the other guests. She was behaving as if she had never desired him. But she had been on heat that day in her bedroom and only Jim Killigrew's presence had stopped them moving on quickly to full intimacy. Well, if a cat and mouse game was to be played it would be played on both sides and if they did finally end up in bed it might make it all the more pleasurable. Her only attraction was sexual, but it was a strong compelling attraction.

'Well, it's time for cocktails. What would you like, Selina?' Ben said at the drinks table.

'I only drink champagne. Polly's going to show me over the house after we've eaten, if that's all right with you, Ben.'

So one of her tactics was to ignore him and befriend Polly? 'Feel free. Polly's responsible for much of the decor. I often lean on her for that sort of advice.'

'All wise and excellent choices,' Selina congratulated Polly. 'No clutter, nothing dark. The blend of Moorcroft pottery and modern furniture goes well with the antique Brussels tapestries.' Back to Ben. 'I adore those internally decorated vases. No flowers in them – don't you like flowers? There's a tantalizing use of mirrors in the room, and out in the hall too, I noticed. I like mirrors, the broader and longer the better.'

'I noticed that you brought nothing modern with you to Ford House.' Ben had poured the champagne and was mixing a dry Martini for Polly.

Selina got up and came towards him. 'I've never bothered with possessions or the latest fad. I'd wear the same frock every day if Perry didn't, very sweetly, arrange for someone to run up a few things for me.' She met Ben midway on the brick-red Tabriz carpet and curled her crude fingers over his hand that was carrying the drinks on a small silver tray. 'Tell me, are all your staff stupid or ugly?'

He was unprepared for the swift change of subject. 'I beg your pardon?'

'Your driver looked shifty and took several attempts at his name before we could understand what it was. He didn't have a clue how to cope with Perry's crutches. He smelled of the farmyard and kept telling us that's where he usually works. He told us he has an imbecile brother, who also works for you. He was off to the pub, he said, so I don't want him driving us home. And I've seen more flesh on a cadaver than the woman who let us in. And the other day in the village I saw one of your farm workers and was amazed to learn it was a woman. She looks and dresses like a man.'

For one horrible second Ben felt he could hit her for her offensiveness and he got the uneasy feeling she wouldn't mind if he did. 'Cyril Trewin and his brother Albie, and Agnes and Eliza are good, honest workers. It's all that matters to me.'

The lights in her eyes leaping, Selina picked an imaginary speck of fluff off the shiny lapel of Ben's jacket. 'Oh, I'm not insulting you, Ben. All the ugliness around you only serves to make you look more handsome.'

'Can I have my drink, Ben?' Polly demanded, growing huffy at the delay.

'Take no notice of Selina, Ben. Nor you, Polly,' Perry said, grinning at Polly, who was glaring at his sister. 'She's a terrible tease.'

Suddenly Selina was throwing up her arms in a giveaway gesture. 'You shouldn't take anything I say seriously, Ben.'

Perry's words and her gaiety worked together to take some of the steel out of Ben's mood. He had allowed the miserable events at Roskerne to colour how he felt about everything, especially Selina. Looking at her now, confident and arresting, amusing and flippant, drinking down his expensive champagne, he felt she was worth going after, but only when it suited him.

As if reading his mind, Selina lifted an eyebrow and inclined her head at him in her perky, beguiling manner. At an angle that only he could see she ran the tip of her tongue along her lower lip.

Then she took Polly's Martini and dawdled back to her. 'I

do so admire your hair, Polly. Perhaps you'd be good enough to let me have the name of your stylist. Mine's usually a mess and I can't get it anywhere near as sleek as yours.'

There seemed something sincere and confidential in the way she was speaking to Polly, and Ben watched amazed as his lover, not realizing the other woman had just propositioned him, fell again under her spell. Their heads close together, they discussed the fashion merits of the Duchess of York's wedding dress – the royal nuptials a recent event – and Ben wondered if this was a ploy on Selina's part to put Polly off guard or whether she simply enjoyed the sisterhood of modern women. Selina was a diverse mixture. Fascinating and alluring she may be, but she was also a little rough at the edges and, he sensed, merciless with men.

Polly reached for her sequinned, fringed evening bag and jotted down the details of her hairdresser for Selina. Ben could see Polly had relaxed now she was re-established as the lady of the house, even though she did not live here. She was usually sharp and he had not thought of her as being gullible before, but she was exactly that if she thought Selina meant to be her friend.

So why did he want a woman like Selina? Was casual sex with her really a worthwhile goal? A few years ago his greatest longing was to fight for King, country and Empire. He had been prepared to sacrifice his life. Now his life held little meaning. Confusion and melancholy got a grip on him again. He had upset all of his family. Some of his family had rejected him. He had outgrown his passion and need for Polly. And no matter how electrifying the other woman in his drawing room was, there had to be something more to life than looking forward to bedding her, which was a foregone conclusion.

He wished the evening was over but he must go on acting the perfect host. Perry asked for whisky and soda, being no cocktail drinker. Julian only drank mineral water owing to his heart condition. Ben mixed a Martini for himself and joined the men, struck at how vital and healthy Perry looked and how macabre and deathlike Julian was. Julian was tired, having travelled back from London after consulting a heart specialist, a journey that had taken four days up and back by motor car, his frailness requiring his chauffeur to make several stops. His paper-thin skin seemed translucent, highlighting rivers of indigo veins, his pale eyes were darkly under-shadowed and his lips were an odd mauve colour. He looked like a ghoul in a silent motion picture, old and wizened, and it was hard for Ben to think of him being the same age as himself. He had recently become perpetually breathless, and like Perry, required a bed downstairs.

Ben felt guilty at not making himself available for the Boswelds' arrival – Julian would have felt obliged to explain about his condition to them. 'The London trip's knocked the stuffing out of you. Are you sure you're up to this?' he whispered in Julian's ear.

Julian's character was such that there was little he minded. 'Could do with a snooze soon, actually. Think I'll have to retire as soon as we've eaten.'

'What was the name of the chap you saw?' Perry asked.

'Beatty. An American. He knows his stuff. I asked him to give it to me straight.'

'What did he say?' Ben was dreading the answer, dreading the inevitability of Julian's fate. He might be weak in the body but his strength of mind and caring disposition had rescued Ben from his misery and subsequent humiliation of being in a drunken state after learning of his permanent partial blindness.

Julian replied matter-of-factly. 'Said he was amazed I'd lived this long. Don't be sad for me, Ben. I didn't travel up expecting to learn of some new medical breakthrough. Only did it for Polly's sake. I've had a good life. Have managed a few years more than many an unfortunate fellow who perished on the battlefields. I've had the pleasure of dear Louisa these past five years and I've the comfort of knowing Polly will have her for company after I'm gone.'

'You're a brave man,' Perry said, too much of a realist, too insightful to offer insensitive platitudes.

'He is,' Ben's voice surfaced, choked and throaty.

'If I may be permitted to move on to something different but not entirely unconnected,' Perry said, shifting to an angle where he could look straight into Ben's face. 'Ben, have you seen anyone or had word from Ford Farm today?'

At this, Selina halted in mid-sentence and gazed at the group of men. Sensing her gravity, Polly did likewise.

'No, and I'm not likely to. The last time I was spoken to by Alec it was accompanied with a repeat of a threat to blow my head off. Let's talk of other things.'

'You really ought to go there, Ben,' Perry persisted.

'Why? Nothing would induce me to.'

'Take Perry's word for it please, Ben,' Selina said. For the first time it seemed she was pleading rather than issuing an order or being suggestive.

'Why? Tell me what's going on? Has something happened?'

'It's not for us to say anymore.' Perry was grave, unshakable. 'You must go there. Go tomorrow. Or you may regret it for the rest of your life.'

Ben stared from the Bosweld brother to the sister, then at Julian and Polly, as if they might somehow supply the answer to this puzzle. Julian gave a weak shrug of his scrawny shoulders and Polly shook her head.

Getting up, Ben stalked about the room, thinking hard. Hurt at Alec's ludicrous accusation that he had ill-wished – an ancient superstitious belief – harm on his family, consequently causing Jenna to be taken ill, and outraged at Alec's bloody-minded unforgivingness, he had left Roskerne swearing to never make things up with his eldest brother again. The situation Perry and Selina were hinting at now could only concern Jenna, which had come up immediately after talk about Julian's heart condition.

'It's the baby, isn't it? My God, don't tell me she really did stop breathing that night.' He gazed at Julian's waxen face and sunken wedge-thin body. Was this what Jenna had in store? 'Oh, bloody hell! Jenna! Poor Emilia.'

Selina was there, wrapping an arm round his waist. 'All grievances should be put aside on occasions like these, Ben.'

'But Alec's unlikely to agree to that. I'll telephone, ask if I can see Jenna.'

'No, don't do that. Just go there. Your other brother's been sent for.'

'What?' Ben rubbed a hand down his face, pulling his good looks out of shape. 'But she can't be . . . ? No! Oh, my God.'

'They'll need you, Ben.' As tears glittered in his eyes, Selina wound her other arm round his neck and brought his head down on her shoulder. She whispered, 'And you have us now. You have me.'

Ten

Emilia was outside alone in the front garden, in the dark. She was feeling numb and deadened inside, in such a state of anguish and disbelief that when someone suddenly loomed up in front of her she was barely startled, unable to comprehend who it was until he spoke.

'Emilia, please don't send me away. I had to come. How are you?'

'Oh, it's you, Ben. I thought I'd imagined a motor car stopping in the lane.' Her voice was low and dull, then high pitched and frantic for Ben's presence at this late hour reinforced the terrible truth she had learned today. 'Perry's told you about Jenna?'

'He mentioned something. I guessed how serious things are. He said I should come tomorrow but I couldn't wait till then. I got dinner over with as quickly as I could and drove the Boswelds home. What's happening?'

From the glow of lights thrown out from the upstairs and sitting-room windows Emilia saw his hair was messed up, speaking of his hurry here. 'It won't be long. I've come outside to give Alec a couple of minutes with her alone then I'll go in and we'll stay together until it's over. She looks so peaceful, as if she never really belonged in this world. She's like a little clock winding down. I can't . . . can't believe it's happening.'

'Is Tris here?'

'Yes. He and Winnie are taking care of the boys.'

'Can I go in to say goodbye to Jenna? Would you mind?'

'I'm glad you can put aside your bitter feelings, Ben, but Alec's taking it hard. You'd better go. I must go in. I'll send word . . .' Her voice loaded with tears she turned to leave him.

He grabbed her arm. 'Have you had Jenna christened?'

She nodded. 'The rector came this afternoon.'

'And he's inside now?'

'Yes. Waiting with my parents. They're very upset.'

'Everyone's there but me. Alec never will forgive me, will he?' The pressure he had on her arm became insistent. 'Emilia, Em, you have to believe me. What I said in Winnie's summerhouse was never meant to harm your baby. I'd never think that way. Never! I was just expressing my hope that Alec, and you too, I admit, would be taken down a peg or two, that's all, I swear. You do believe me, don't you?'

She gazed up at him, his face half in shadow, half in golden light, and saw him as handsome as a mythological hero and as fraught as a small friendless boy. 'It's horrible when you're accused of something you haven't done, isn't it, Ben? Something that should never have been thought of, let alone said.'

'You're talking about me accusing you of causing my blindness, aren't you? Oh, God, Em, how ever did we get to this? We used to be so close.'

'I can't deal with your feelings now, Ben. Maybe one day we'll talk about it.' She pulled away from him and ran towards the door. Stopped and turned round. Ben had followed her part of the way. He paused on the lawn, stooped, forlorn and dejected. He was holding out his hands to her, quite helpless.

Despite her heartbreak and what she still had to face, she sensed his aching loneliness. That he had been feeling this way for years and it was even worse for him now, shut out of his old family home, misunderstood, shunned, unforgiven. 'Stay here if you want, Ben. You'll know when she's gone, the windows will be darkened.'

'Thanks, Em. It means a lot. And, Em, I'm sorry about Jenna. Sorry for the way I acted towards you all that time ago.'

Emilia nodded.

Then she went inside and upstairs to the room where Jenna had been conceived, where she and Alec would soon have to endure saying goodbye to her.

Ben's eyes never left their bedroom window until an hour later when the lanterns were turned down low.

Eleven

Louisa Hetherton-Andrews was pushing a doll's pram down the winding garden path at her adopted aunt's house, in Kenwyn Church Road, at Truro. Tripping over the long clothes she was dressed up in, tottering precariously in a pair of ladies' high heels, she halted every few steps, not to recover her balance but to fuss with the covers in the carriage-built pram and keep her reluctant 'baby' imprisoned inside.

'Stay in there, Kitty! I'm getting very cross. You have to go to sleep. I'll not tell you again.'

Polly was watching her, proud and doting, through the open door of the conservatory while she worked on a piece of tapestry. 'Be careful with the kitten, Louisa, darling. Perhaps you should let her out and take one of your dolls for a walk instead.'

'She likes it.' Louisa looked back over her shoulder, her defiant smile and shiny blonde curls hidden by the large picture hat she had donned.

'You may keep her in there only a little longer,' Polly wagged a finger.

'Mrs Hetherton,' the housemaid's voice broke through the balmy quietness of the summer afternoon. 'It's Mr Harvey for you, ma'am.'

Polly put her tapestry aside. 'Alec, how good to see you. I take it you've time for a cold drink? Ivy, bring some iced mint tea, and lemonade for Miss Louisa, please.'

'Won't be a tick.' A lanky girl with a willing demeanour, the housemaid scuttled away.

'Your new girl seems to have a nice manner,' Alec

remarked, coming to sit on another of the Regency cast-iron, cushioned seats, where he was closest to the fresh air. The sultry environment with its exotic plants rearing up everywhere, including a copious vine, was too stifling for him. He stretched out his long legs.

'Ivy's a treasure, Alec. Can't tell you how pleased I am to have her. She's mature for her fifteen years and is bright and hard working. Her mother's just got herself remarried to a man with a brood of small children and there wasn't any room for poor Ivy, but I'll see she's all right. I'm paying her an extra shilling a week so she'll not be tempted out of service.' Polly found Alec wasn't listening to her tale of domestic arrangements. His attention had veered to Louisa, as it always did on the numerous occasions he had called here in the past three months.

'Hey, little lady down the garden,' he called out. 'Aren't you coming to say hello to me?'

Louisa staggered on the hem of her trailing organza, righted herself – while Polly gasped in relief – and twirled round and waved to the man she knew as Uncle Alec. 'Come on, Kitty.' She hauled the kitten out of the pram and scraped her high heels back up the path. 'See what I've got, Uncle Alec.'

'He's cute, Louisa.' Alec circled a finger on top of the kitten's smoky-grey head. 'But isn't Kitty a female's name?'

'It's a she anyway and her name's not Kitty, it's Myrtle. Don't you know every cat's called Kitty, Uncle Alec?' Louisa shook her head as if astonished by his ignorance and her hat fell off. It brought into view the ragged pink birthmark on her right cheek, which was the size of a half-crown. It didn't do a lot to mar her looks but she was self-conscious about it owing to the stares of adults and the teasing of some children, and she preferred to play only with those she could trust not to mention it, like Jonny, Vera Rose, Will and Tom.

'Well, that's told me,' Alec grinned, smoothing at Louisa's ruffled tresses. 'I've brought something for you, if your Aunt Polly will allow you to have it.'

'I believe there's a conspiracy going on between you two,' Polly laughed. 'You know very well, Alec, I can hardly refuse when you mention whatever it is in front of the little madam here.'

'I'm not a madam, Aunt Polly,' Louisa widened her cheeky blue eyes. 'I've told you, today I'm a grand-duchess.'

'A beautiful grand-duchess,' Alec said. Since bonding with her shortly after her birth he was eager for Louisa to disregard her birthmark and grow up feeling positive and full of self-worth. He was delighted to see her little pink mouth sagging open in eagerness as he handed over a small gift-wrapped box.

Polly had expected fudge or chocolates as on other occasions. 'What on earth is it? Alec, what have you done?'

Alec coloured and cleared his throat. 'I'm sorry, Polly. I didn't think.'

Louisa tore the ribbon away from the box and pulled off the lid. Inside, a tiny silver locket and chain lay nestled on a platform of silk.

'That's some pretty.' Ivy had brought the tray of drinks.

'Alec, you shouldn't have.' Polly's tone was vexed, compromised.

'Well, I just slipped into Parkin's to get something for Emilia and there it was. Ah, Ivy, you're a life-saver, I'm parched.'

A short time later, with Louisa allowed to wear the locket until teatime, and off playing with her dolls now Myrtle the kitten had escaped her overwhelming mothering, Alec tried a smile on Polly. 'Don't be angry with me, Polly.'

'Alec, I'm pleased that your seeing Louisa more often than before is helping you to cope with dear Jenna's loss, but you must promise me you'll never do something like that again. You will tell Emilia that you've bought the locket for her? Or you'll put me in an awful position.'

'Of course I'll tell Emilia,' he sighed. 'I'm sorry. I can't seem to get to grips with things these days. I'm glad you don't mind me coming so often. Strange, isn't it? Emilia finds comfort in taking Will and Tom to play with Libby Bosweld, and I need to come here and see Louisa. I feel . . . oh, I don't know, Polly, I just feel . . . misplaced. I know it's a strange word, but I feel more than just being at a loss. I hope I help you in some way too, with you losing Julian shortly afterwards.' His thoughts jolted back to the terrible, precious moments when Jenna had slipped away from him for ever. He blinked on wet eyes.

Polly pressed a hand over his. 'Alec, you're more than welcome here, and it does help me having your sympathetic friendship, especially now Ben's gone away and I'm missing one of my closest companions.'

'That's typical of Ben's selfishness.'

Polly took her hand away. 'I don't see it like that, Alec. He was here every minute of every day while Julian was fading away and he stayed with me for as long as Louisa and I needed him. He's a good friend.'

Alec kept the smirk on his brooding face. 'But he's more than that to you, Polly, and he hasn't even told you where he is. Or have you heard from him at last? He would only tell Tris before he headed off that he needed to get away.'

'He did need to, desperately. Ben and I had many serious talks and I understood him completely. Things have changed between us. I always knew deep down that our closer relationship wouldn't last for ever; after all, Ben will want his own family one day and I'd never leave the town for village life. It was hard for me to accept at first but I had to let him go. We'll always remain friends and he is a doting uncle towards Louisa. You shouldn't continue being so beastly towards him, Alec. It's not fair. In fact, it's cruel.'

'I've offended you.' He put his drink down. He hadn't taken a sip of it and probably wouldn't have done, nor touched the biscuits Ivy had brought. His lack of appetite meant he had lost a lot of weight since Jenna's death. 'I think I'd better go.'

'Alec, you spend a lot of time thinking but it seems to me that it's often one-sided. Don't stay away, for Louisa's sake.'

Polly had her head down and would not meet his gaze. Alec had made cutting remarks about Ben every time he had come here, now he had gone too far. Why all this sympathy for Ben? It wasn't he who had lost a child. 'I apologize to you, Polly. I did allow Ben to go to the funeral.'

Polly lifted her regal fair head and met his uncompromising grey gaze. 'Only because Emilia insisted he should go. She and Ben want to bury the past. They want to move on. Don't you think it's time you did too?'

'We're all different, Polly. You're very upset. Is there something you're not telling me?'

'No, Alec. Our talk has made me realize just how lonely I am, that's all.' She dropped her eyes once more.

Alec wasn't sure if she was dismissing him or if she was about to cry. Perhaps he had reopened her grief over Julian. Either way, he had to go, and he knew it was his fault he would leave today even lonelier than when he had arrived. 'I'm sorry,' he whispered. 'I'll come next week, if that's all right. Say goodbye to Louisa for me.'

He longed to receive an understanding smile, a kind word. Polly only nodded, as if weighed down by sorrow.

He could have followed the tiled path round to the front of the house but went back through the house to the hall, where he had left the particulars of a monumental stonemason; Jenna's headstone was ready to be put in place. Looking at the folder on the side table he didn't feel he could bear to pick it up. He leaned his back against the wall and stared ahead, into the drawing room, and saw photographs of Louisa at various ages, some of which he had taken himself. Jenna would have been nearly four months now. He went into the room and searched for a photograph of Louisa at about that age.

Is this how she would have looked if she was still alive? Smaller and not so chubby, of course, but . . . The image in his hands swam as burning hot tears came. He put the photograph back and wiped his eyes. Polly was there. 'I can't stop the pain, Polly. How do I make it go away?'

'You don't have to try, Alec. The way I coped with my husband's death in the war and now with Julian's is to make it mean something.'

'How do I do that?'

'By reaching out from here and not hiding away up here, where you see things all wrong.' She touched her heart and then her head to illustrate her point.

'I don't know if I can change, Polly. Will you help me?'

'Emilia will do that if you let her.'

'Yes. Of course. I'm sorry, I've behaved badly towards you today but we're still friends, aren't we?'

Polly glanced at other photographs dotted about the room in their classy Art Nouveau frames. There was one of Julian and Ben, arms round waists, laughing together. She no longer had Julian at all and Ben was somewhere far away. She gave in to the tears that had been building up in her since becoming cross with Alec. 'Of course . . .'

At the same moment their hands reached out to offer comfort but they wrapped their arms round each other instead.

Twelve

Emilia left Ford House through the little brown-painted gate at the bottom of the garden. She had spent nearly half an hour chatting to Perry, weeding the strongly scented roses and Madonna lilies that grew against a sunny wall with him, keeping busy – it was vital to keep busy nowadays.

She had left Will and Tom playing a noisy game of double-dare with Libby. Her dear boys, missing Jonny's passion for adventure and entertaining leadership and unable to grasp the swift coming and going of their tiny sister, had been eager to stay behind and have fun with Libby and her puppy, Casper.

Trudging over the coarse sun-baked ground of the adjoining field, Emilia formed a half-hearted smile at the squeals of delight coming from behind her. Perry had joined in with the children. He would have become the Big Bad Wolf or a wicked wizard, the children daring each other to creep up behind his wheeled chair and dodge his quick hands before ending up as his 'little pig dinner' or being turned to stone from a tap of his 'evil-doing' wand.

She could have willingly stayed in Perry's undemanding company, when he would have patiently explained to her yet again about Jenna's condition and why, in her case, she had only had a few weeks to live rather than months or years. He would have reassured her that Jenna's fate had not been due to anything she had or had not done. He had invited her to drink lemon tea with him and she had been tempted, but Selina was due home soon from some mysterious appointment to put Perry through a physiotherapy session; he had confided that he wasn't looking forward to it. Selina had been sympathetic too over Jenna, kind even, but Emilia always came under close scrutiny from her nowadays, as if the nursing sister was waiting for her to confide her deepest emotions, but those were private, even from Alec at the moment.

'I'm not far off mastering the use of an artificial leg again, you know, Emilia,' Perry had said, with one of his gorgeous smiles when escorting her to the gate. 'Had one before, hated the thing, got round much easier with crutches. Selina insists that I get used to the new leg. She's right, of course. It will encourage other ex-servicemen. She got it specially made up for me but it still rubs and she accuses me of being a coward, says I don't hold my balance right, hence all these wretched exercises. She can be quite a bully. I do want to keep in good shape, of course. You'll be seeing me walk with just a stick one day soon, Emilia.'

She told herself now that she was looking forward to seeing his triumph. Perry was such a good man and he deserved all the success that came his way. And she was tentatively looking forward to returning to village life again. She and Alec had recently agreed to a shy suggestion of Elena Rawley's that the sports day, in a few weeks time, be held as a memorial event to Jenna. Then it felt as if something was clamping her insides in a vice. It was the first time in weeks she had looked forward to anything and she felt guilty, as if it somehow pointed to her deserting Jenna's memory. The numbness of her grief had worn off, but sometimes her anger over what felt like the meaninglessness of Jenna's short life frightened her. Would her heart always feel this bruised? Her arms this empty?

Yet a moment ago she had managed a smile. Her moods hopped about out of her control and her mind was in confusion. She couldn't bring herself to go home yet. She needed peace and solitude.

So into the woods she went, in under the canopy of oak, ash and beech. Her sandals made a listless passage along the light-dappled mossy floor of one wide corridor of her old playground. She hoped none of the village children would be here today for games and make-believe. If she was going to find solace, it would be here among the sorrel, wood anemone, sweet violet and many varieties of fern; near the stream that tinkled a short distance away; and surrounded by the carpets of wild flowers where the hawthorn, hazel and willow had been cut down for sticks and poles, allowing in extra light.

Leaning against the heavily fissured bark of a towering oak, she closed her eyes, but inside her eyelids she could see patterns of light and shadow – the sun sparkling through the leaves overhead. She allowed herself a moment of peace in a magic land, away from painful reality. But only a moment. She wanted her grief more than anything: she wasn't ready to leave her baby behind yet.

She was so still a wood mouse appeared on a tree root and she was able to trace its runway system from the root to a fallen branch, a hop on to a large stone then along the ridge of a low bank. The wood mouse stopped to nibble on a snack of seeds, small snails and a caterpillar. Such an appealing creature, its tail the same length as its warm-brown and sandy body, its ears large and eyes round. It was sweet and cute, like her Tom, now her baby again. 'Run away, before a weasel or one of the farm cats gets you,' she whispered. As if heeding her warning the wood mouse scurried away.

The sound of voices and laughter intruded on her sanctity and she sighed, annoyed and beleaguered. The trespassers were adults, a male and a female, and their risqué tone suggested they weren't here to gather wood. She put her hands over her ears to shut them out but also so as not to recognize whose they were. Even so, she thought the male voice belonged to Jim.

Leaving the cooling shade of the trees, she went out once more into the field, moving further on, seeking a new haven on the bank of the stream. She flopped down with her back to the sun, wrapping her bare arms over her raised knees and letting her head fall down on them. Apart from the steady burbling of the water over the stony bed, there was silence. Not a breath of wind stirred the reeds in the water, nor the sweeps of nettle, meadowsweet and buttercups spreading all around her. She became aware of the drone of a hundred species of insect. She didn't mind this natural sound, or the bleat of a sheep in a nearby field.

Drowsy and mesmerized, she concentrated to conjure up the sound of Jenna's soft baby cry. And her low gurglings and gentle sighs. When she had her tiny voice captured inside her head, she kept it there and gloried in it. She would never, ever, let it go.

A tender touch was on the back of her neck. 'Emilia, you must move. You're getting sunburned.'

'I don't care. Go away.'

She refused to lift her head in response to the well-wisher. Why must there always be someone making sure she didn't spend too much time alone? Why did others believe they knew best how she should mourn? Her mother and father fretted about her daily visits to the nursery, telling her it was time to dismantle the things in there. Tilda talked continually, trying to 'brighten her up'. Sara only sang songs with a light theme instead of the sorrowful ballads she excelled at. Jim had even stopped being difficult in her presence. Why couldn't everyone behave normally? It's what she wanted. After all, it was normal for children to die – the mortality rate from the usual childhood diseases, measles, diphtheria and so on was still disturbingly high; every churchyard in the country bore witness to that. There was an old saying: 'You're not a mother until you've lost one.' Emilia's musings were so deep she had forgotten someone was there.

A cold wet cloth suddenly landed on her neck, making her shriek and throw her head up.

'Sorry, old thing, but I can't stand by and let you get sunstroke.'

'Oh, Selina, it's you. Ouch, I'm burning.'

Selina was kneeling at her side. She skirled her handkerchief again in the cold soothing stream and began bathing Emilia's arms. 'This will help. Then you'd better put my cardy over you to stop you burning any more. Don't worry. I'm not about to lecture you. I understand, and all that.'

Keeping quiet, Emilia allowed Selina to take care of her.

'I haven't lost anyone as close to me as you have, Emilia, but I'm serious about all the roles I undertake as a nurse and I think I do understand what most people undergo in bereavement. You're going to feel dizzy when you get up. I'll walk you back to the farm.'

'Thanks.' The top of Selina's dress fell down off her shoulder. From their close proxity, Emilia couldn't help noticing she wasn't wearing any underwear and there was a vivid red mark on one breast. The sort of mark made from union of the passionate kind. It was Selina she had heard laughing with Jim in the woods. She wished she didn't know this.

She caught Selina grinning at her. 'Don't look so shocked. Making love is a perfectly natural act whether one is married or not.'

'It's none of my business really but your choice of partner isn't a good one for many reasons,' Emilia said, as Selina helped her to rise. She closed her eyes against a sudden rush of giddiness. With Selina supporting her waist, they began a slow ascent up and across the field behind the farm, picking a path through thistles and dried cowpats.

'It won't last for ever. I never keep on with anyone for long.'

'You don't intend to settle down and have children then?'

'No, never, but please don't think I belittle any woman if it's what she wants out of life. It's my choice to live my life to the full.'

'Ohh, my head's aching. I was foolish to stay like that for so long. I've got a lot to do at home.'

'Never mind that. You need to drink plenty of water, then take a couple of aspirin and lie down in a darkened room. Have you got some calamine?'

Emilia nodded, grimacing in pain where Selina's cardigan rubbed her scorched skin.

'Good. I'll apply it to your burned areas.'

'Thanks. The boys are with Libby, I'll send Sara down to collect them.'

When Emilia's burns had been soothed and cooled by a

liberal wash of calamine lotion, Selina arranged her pillows so there would be no painful contact, then she wrung a cloth soaked in cold water and spread it across her brow. 'This should help.'

'I should have stayed talking to Perry.'

'You get on well with him, don't you?'

'He's the sensitive sort, like my brother-in-law, Tristan. And Perry was the one I turned to, with Reggie Rule about Jenna, so talking to him helps me to keep connected to her. Selina . . . ?'

'Yes?'

'I can't help being curious about Perry's wife. How did she die? He never mentions her and I don't like to ask.'

Selina made a vague face. 'Her name was Ada. There's not a lot to tell about her. I never met her. Perry married her shortly before going on active service.'

Weariness was coming over Emilia and she let her eyelids fall. Then snapped them open again. 'I was lying here when my boys were attacked by one of the dogs, and soon afterwards Jenna was born.'

'Don't run away from bad memories then they can't haunt you.' Selina smoothed at her hair.

'Do you really think that's true?'

'Mostly. It always helps if you share your fears, your feelings.'

'Thank you, Selina. You've been very kind.'

Selina stroked her hand. 'I've enjoyed talking to you, Emilia. I'd like us to be friends. Sleep now. I'll stay a while.'

When Emilia closed her eyes again, she felt the other woman giving her a gentle kiss on the cheek.

Outside the bedroom door, Selina met Alec rushing down the long corridor. She put her finger to her lips to silence an outburst of concern. 'She's resting at last. Make sure your servants do all the tasks she usually does for the next few days. Emilia needs space and comfort. I'll call back tomorrow and see how she is.'

'I'll see she's not disturbed.' Alec's brow was furrowed,

the few lines gathering at his eyes deepened. 'Tilda says she's burnt to a crisp. How come?'

Selina tugged at the black hair curling over his collar. 'It's not as bad as that but she'll be sore for a couple of days, so be careful when you touch her. Like you, she's not looking after herself. You're both getting woefully thin. Eat a good dinner tonight and coax her to as well.'

'Yes, I'll do that. Thanks for looking after her.' He glanced at the bedroom door, eager to get on the other side and see Emilia for himself.

'I'll see myself out. Let me know if there's ever anything I can do for you or Emilia, Alec.'

Alec entered the room on tiptoe, shut the door as softly as he could. He sat on the bed, leaning over Emilia, watching the tensing in her face as she dreamed. She had pushed the cloth off her brow in her sleep and it was wetting the pillow. He put it back in the washbowl, then using feather-light fingers caressed the damp hair away from her neck. 'Don't be sad, darling. Don't stay sad,' he whispered. 'I love you so much.'

There they stayed until the afternoon was over, she sleeping, calmer now after his tender touch, he in loving attendance.

'Oh,' she moaned, her head aching so much she could hardly lift it. 'The boys . . .'

'Sara's brought them home, don't worry about anything, darling. You need to sit up and drink, let me help you.' He pushed a careful arm in under her waist and raised her. She leaned against his strong body and sipped from a glass of water. He kissed the back of her head, heedful to avoid the lotion-pink areas on her neck and shoulders.

'You're good to me.' She sank back against his hard muscles, ignoring the sore areas that came into contact with his body. She raised his hand to her lips and kissed it.

'I've missed you, Emilia. You know what I mean . . .' His voice came husky.

'I do, Alec, and I've missed you too. Of course, the usual six weeks weren't up before Jenna died.'

'I suppose we haven't made love because it is more than us being together, it's the process that made her.'

He had been thinking, thinking about how losing Jenna had marred every part of their life together. It made Emilia cry and grip his hand, afraid to let it go. Afraid to let him go any further away from her, for they had chosen different routes and different friendships to cope with their tragedy, and soon they would be busy with the haymaking. 'Alec, I don't want another baby yet. Perhaps next year. You do understand?'

'Yes, of course. I'll see to it. By the time this sunburn's gone perhaps we'll both be ready to make love again.'

'I love you.'

'I love you, angel. Dolly is going to put the boys to bed. After we've kissed them goodnight, why don't we have a quiet meal up here? Just on our own?'

'I'd like that.'

The quiet meal did not happen. Tristan turned up to discuss a problem, which quickly led to trouble.

Thirteen

'Why don't you ask Jonny to help you do that, Tris?' Winifred crept into the spacious library-cum-study which Tristan had taken over as his own private space. Panelled in highly polished mahogany it was the usual sort of domain for relaxing, reading and working in. He was unpacking the last trunk of his belongings sent on from the Isle of Man.

Tidy even before his regimental training, he pressed out a crumpled sheet of newspaper used as wrapping, and smiled at her. 'I should have done this ages ago, quite forgot what interesting little gems I had in here. See these?' He held up a pair of tall metal vases. 'Any idea what they're made from? Artillery shell cases. The raised floral and leaf design was formed by hammering round it. Done by Belgian soldiers, these particular vases. I've got quite a collection of Trench Art, bought many a piece off other chaps, mostly from the ranks, when word got round I had a fascination for it. Ex-soldiers have approached me to buy from them. Sadly many needed the money. I thought I'd display it all in here.'

Winifred took one of the weighty vases from him to study it by a bay window, where it glinted in the sunlight. 'It's beautiful, but also rather grim, don't you think? I understand though why people should want such a souvenir, or as I should say, a memorial.'

'It gave the men something to do to take their mind off the horrors. I've got a brooch of Art Nouveau design painted on cloth somewhere. You must have it, darling. Wear it in tribute on Armistice Day. And there's some Ypres lace too, it's beautifully made.'

'Thank you, darling. It's all very fascinating and don't think I'm not interested, but what about Jonny?'

A shadow crossed Tristan's thin face, making the tan from his constantly being outdoors, helping the craftsmen with the repairs, appear darker. 'He'd be spellbound by the whole thing if it wasn't mine, Winnie. You know how things stand between us. I only made things worse by running to Alec yesterday.'

'You were asking Alec for his advice. I can't understand why he became so upset. Until this, I didn't realize just how unreasonable he can be. Poor Emilia. But what are you going to do about Jonny? We can't go on like this.'

'Whatever I do isn't going to be right for someone.'

Tristan drifted back to the day before. Having set out for Ford Farm in a furious mood he had arrived disturbed and offended by his son's latest misdemeanour.

'You can see what a fix the little beggar's put me in,' he had explained to Alec, who had come downstairs to him, in the den. 'Jonny sulks and is rude at every opportunity to Winnie, Vera Rose and the maids. He swears and has been disruptive at school. The final straw was a cruel practical joke he played on the newspaper delivery boy with a length of rope. The boy was sent clean over the handlebars of his bicycle and he was damned lucky not to have been seriously hurt. I'd confined Jonny to the house for a week. After lunch today he went up to the attic where he actually lit a cigarette and managed to set fire to an old couch. In fact, it was in perfect condition, only up there because it didn't fit in with some new decor a few years ago. Well, it's Winnie's house, he could have burned it down, and all this is making me feel like an intruder in my new home. Clearly, I've got to punish him severely for his misdeeds, so that's why I'm here, to tell you I've forbidden him to stay at the farm during the summer holiday.'

'What? You've done what?' Suddenly Alec, who had listened grimly from the start, was shouting as loudly as his voice would rise. 'For goodness sake! I've lost a child, yet you see fit to come and subject me to a lot of self-pitying complaints about a boy's natural behaviour. Yes, natural. Hasn't it occurred to you that Jonny's only trying to get attention because he feels it's he who's an intruder in the house? You're the one who ripped him up from his roots. Show him some understanding, for heaven's sake. You had no right to say Jonny couldn't come here, you'll also be punishing Will and Tom. Have you forgotten they've not long lost their sister? One minute she was here, the next she was gone. Just like Jonny. They miss him. I miss him. Or are you too bloody damn selfish to realize that?'

Tristan had backed away from his elder brother as if blown off course by the fury in his breath. He had shaken his head, unable to articulate the answers and justifications that had been forming inside his head throughout the vicious tirade.

Alarmed by Alec's bawling, Emilia had pulled on her dressing gown and come down to them. 'Alec, why on earth are you in such a rage?' Tristan could see she was feverish, holding her head, which was probably spinning, as she went to where Alec stood, red-faced and fuming beside the fireplace.

'Go back to bed, Emilia. This need not concern you.'

'Em,' Tristan had appealed to her. 'I'm sorry to have come like this while you're unwell.'

'What's going on?' she had demanded. 'Alec? Tris? Tell me.'

Alec had ignored her and stabbed a stiff finger at Tristan. 'I never had any trouble with Jonny. Never! If you can't cope with him then it would be better if he came back here to live, for good.'

'Alec, that's a terrible thing to say,' Emilia had shouted at him, clearly getting angry herself. 'I don't know what Jonny's done, but Tris has got the right to be concerned about him. Now apologize.'

'He's planning to keep Jonny away from me.' Alec had glared at her, then at Tristan. 'We're close, very close, as close as . . .'

'Father and son?' Tristan suggested, past a painful throat.

'Well, we're close. That's all I'm saying.'

Then Emilia had trembled and staggered as if about to faint, and Alec had carried her up to their room, leaving Tristan stranded alone.

'It was terrible, Winnie. Alec nearly crushed my soul. I can understand now why Ben felt the need to go off suddenly and why he hasn't been in touch.' Bringing a sigh from all the way up his body, he joined Winifred by the window. Gazed out to sea where he usually found inspiration and balm. 'What am I to do about my son? The son I hardly know after so many years absence in his young life? I don't want to allow him to go to the farm after what happened there, that's for sure, but if I don't, there might be some nasty consequences. Jonny's threatened as much. He says he hates me over the ban. He says I'm shiftless and useless because I haven't decided what to do yet with the rest of my life. He wouldn't listen when I tried to explain that I wanted us all to settle as a family first. Truth is, I simply don't know what to do about him. I had easier decisions to make in the war.'

Winnie put the vases down on the windowsill and looked up at the gaunt and worried face of the husband she had grown quickly to love.

He saw the way she was twisting her lips and he rested his hand on her shoulder in the caring, intimate way that, unknown to him, she loved. 'Is there something else? Don't be afraid to tell me, darling.'

She lowered her face and rubbed it against his fingers. 'I'm sorry, Tris but I'm afraid we may have another problem. You see, I'm pregnant.'

'What?' He let out an enormous puff of surprise. 'How did that happen? Well, I know how it happened, but a baby wasn't really on the cards, was it? A baby! But that's . . . that's brilliant, isn't it? You don't mind, do you? There'll be quite a few years between it and Vera Rose.'

She wrapped her arms round Tristan and reached up to kiss his lips. 'I'm delighted. It's what I've been secretly hoping for once I knew our marriage was working, and it is, Tris, it's working very well. We'll have to keep it to ourselves for a while, for poor Emilia's sake. She'll be glad for us, but a few more weeks between little Jenna's passing over would help before we break the news.'

'Yes, of course.'

Tristan was suddenly staring at the shell-case vases. 'I think I've got what could be a good idea. Where's Jonny now? It might just work . . .'

Fourteen

Ben set out on the journey he had been making daily for the last three weeks. To a silent city of the dead.

From a small friendly hotel in Ypres, he set himself on the Menin Road and then a north-east course to Passchendaele, marching on strong determined legs over ground that was flat in places and ridged in others. Over land that just a few short years ago had been battlefields. There was a church-silence now where once artillery and aircraft shells had screamed in destruction and thousands of young men had been killed instantly or died of wounds and diseases.

Nearly all the land and surrounding forests had been blasted into mires of mud, mud deep enough for men to drown in. *How terrible to drown in mud.* It was land left scarred and sacred for ever, once barely supporting miles and miles of trenches, some only yards from enemy lines, where men, living, breathing souls, husbands, fathers, brothers, sons, had huddled, cold, lonely and frightened, part of them still a child inside, wanting only to go home. Now the land was mercifully retrieved as roads or farmland, or honoured as military cemeteries. Several cemeteries. And there were the countless poor wretched souls who had been buried by shell blasts and would lie in their friendless secret places for ever.

He had lingered in the few remaining trenches and in the blasted-out woods, some well off the beaten track, and in German pill-boxes, the most solid of the unchanged features, until he'd got a feel of the pride and anguish and suffering. He had also experienced some fearsome vibrations from the past and chillingly felt and smelled the lingering aura and stench of death. Desolate and disturbed, he had acknowledged he would never be able to comprehend how it must have actually felt to endure those dreadful deprivations and the formidable terrifying battle conditions.

So much loss. So much suffering. And now with the Allies failing to agree on a moratorium on Germany's war reparations, and France and Belgium occupying the Ruhr and its coalfields, leading to more hatred and violence, and the German mark in desperate decline, and a vociferous little individual named Adolf Hitler, the leader of the small but extreme, anti-Semitic Nationalist Party stirring up more unrest, Ben wondered about the possibility of the world being threatened from the same quarter again.

It was hot and sunny, the sort of weather when it was wonderful to roll up shirt sleeves and leave neck buttons open and to amble along, but it was inappropriate here. He was wearing a dark suit and black tie and stopped every half mile to shake the dust off his trouser hems. As on every other day he was keeping a distance from the road to avoid travellers on the same quest, in horse-drawn or motorized vehicles, some on organized tours run by war veterans. All were here to remember their beloved dead and see their last resting place.

The road was busy. With the number of dead it was inevitable there would be a large number of pilgrims. The Ypres Salient was the most visited place on the Western Front, circled as it was by vast cemeteries, and nearly every visitor ended up at Passchendaele, the most poignant and the most terrible and the most important battlefield of the Great War.

An hour and a half later Ben arrived at Tyne Cot Cemetery, the largest of the British cemeteries, site of a former battlefield. Overheated and perspiring, he used his handkerchief to mop his brow, then to wipe the dust off his shoes, bringing them up to a military polish. Then he was moving through the forest of gravestones, rows upon rows of them, neat rows of regulation oblong memorial stones, repeating a trail he had left his footprints on many times before.

He passed black-clad, sorrowing mothers and wives, some with children of an age too young to have been born before their fathers were killed. There were elderly stooped fathers; sisters; brothers; cousins; old comrades and guides. When he reached his holy grail, his particular lozenge-shaped white marker, he took up guard there.

'Here I am again, Billy.'

There he stayed. And stayed.

Occasionally other mourners skirted round him, sympathetically allowing him his veneration. A guide pointed him out to a small family group and whispered, 'That's him.' Ben had no idea people were moving on with eyes filled with tears for him. That he had acquired the title in Ypres as the 'saddest pilgrim'.

Sometimes he continued his one-sided conversation aloud. Other times he spoke in his thoughts. And he listened. The listening was important. And he was receiving the voice of the six-years-dead Corporal William Rowse, 14th Infantry Battalion, more clearly each day. Billy – Emilia's brother, who had been just an ordinary bloke, cheerful, uncomplicated, honest, inoffensive and helpful. Billy – in death somehow putting him right.

Time passed. Those paying homage left and were replaced by others and others still. Ben stayed.

A woman crept close to him. He did not see her. Did not twitch a muscle or blink an eye. It was as if he had turned to stone. Every bit a statue like those being erected, in ever increasing intervals in this sad and blessed region, in memory of the 'glorious dead'.

She watched. She waited. She gained nothing from him, except the occasional sight of his lips moving in silent speech or prayer. It was true what she had heard about him. He was young and immensely good-looking, war-wounded in one eye, and so full of melancholy one instinctively wanted to reach out and comfort him. Mothers were said to long to take him home to replace beloved lost sons.

She must not disturb him. It was time to leave him to whatever it was that plagued him so much.

The sudden shift of her going caught his eye. Ben looked up. Stared at the neat, sparely shaped female in a plain black suit and a small hat; a little black tasselled bag was hanging from a draw-string over her gloved wrist. He grimaced to ease his stiff facial muscles.

'Oh, dear, I'm so sorry. I never meant to intrude. Please forgive me.'

He was further surprised at the mild American accent. 'No, I . . .' He consulted the skies. The sun had gravitated a long way west. 'I've been here nearly all day. I'm . . .'

To cover his confusion, she shot out her hand, making her unpretentious little bag sway, and for a moment he was mesmerized by it. 'Brooke Wilder. From Wyoming, United States. Pleased to meet you. Although my pa died in the Argonne forest, in France, I've come here to look for the grave of a cousin of my mother's. She originated from England, and he was a private in a West Yorkshire regiment. Sorry, I don't know what else to say.'

'Ben Harvey, from Cornwall, England.' He returned her firm handshake.

'I'll leave you now.'

Discreetly, he shook out the rigidity in his limbs. 'No, don't. I mean, I can't stay here for ever and you're not disturbing me. Have you just arrived or are you leaving?' According to the dried tears on her cheeks, she had already made her pilgrimage. She appeared cool and unruffled despite the atmosphere having turned humid and airless, but was prettily flushed. She was about twenty years old, with bobbed, light-brown hair shot through with gold flecks and had a smile that was unobtrusive and warm and somehow uplifting.

She read the name on the grave he was attending, and the inscription. '"After Conflict Rest." That's well said. They all deserve their rest. Was he a relative, may I ask?'

'A friend. I had three close friends as a boy and I've lost them all.'

'I'm sorry. Are the other two buried here?'

This made him smile. 'No. They're alive and back in England. Actually, they're both women, one is the sister of Billy lying here.' His prolonged inactivity had made his head throb. He needed oxygen to course through his body and clear his befuddled mind. 'I walked here, Miss Wilder. May I escort you to your motor car or whatever?'

'I've hired a touring car. I take it you're staying at Ypres? If you want to spare your feet I'd be glad of the company.' She had an endearing way of leaning forward and giving self-deprecating little laughs. 'Hope you don't think I'm being forward.'

Ben's heart leapt with triumph, for all at once he no longer felt the crushing need for solitude, and this unassuming young woman was just perfect to begin the process of rejoining life and order. 'Not at all. I'd appreciate that, Miss Wilder.'

Fifteen

Emilia and Dolly were coming out of a ladies' fashion shop in Truro, each lightly laden with a carrier bag.

'You should've treated yourself to something more than just a nightdress, maid,' Dolly said. 'Like one of those summer sweaters. They're all the fashion now. I read about it in the *Woman's Weekly*. Alec said you should pamper yourself today. You're lucky to have a man who don't mind spending money.'

Emilia pretended to look in the shop windows, hoping to put an end to the nagging that had been coming her way all morning. 'I didn't see anything I liked, Mum. Anyway, you've only bought yourself some new knickers.'

'Emilia, don't you dare mention such a thing in the street! Darn, you can be deliberately difficult sometimes. What I meant was you're a young woman, you should want to look nice.'

'I do want to, Mum.' To compensate for shocking her mother Emilia linked arms with her. 'You needn't worry about me, you know.'

'Can't help that, can I? To worry is the lot of a—' Dolly looked apologetic and gazed down at the wide paving stones.

'You can say it, Mum. To worry is the lot of a mother. We've both lost a child, it gives us an even closer bond.' They were heading down Kenwyn Street towards Victoria Place, known locally as Victoria Square. People stopped, it seemed, every few steps to greet Emilia, to say how pleased they were to see her out and about again after her 'great sorrow'. Other times they were hailed from slow-moving motorized or horse-drawn vehicles.

'You certainly know a lot of people now. It comes from being the wife of a country squire,' Dolly remarked proudly. She homed in on a restaurant tucked away in the corner of the square. 'Now we're here, shall we pop into Henderson's for a cup of tea? After that we'll go on to the West End Stores where I'll make sure you treat yourself.'

'Whatever you say, Mum,' Emilia replied, trying to work up an appetite to please her mother. In the past, she had always enjoyed being in Truro, taking a break from the farm and her busy life, but she could hardly retain interest today.

'I'll see what's on the menu to tempt you to eat, don't like seeing you this thin. Then I'll raid their bakery department and take something home to put a bit of meat on Alec. He's a little too gaunt these days.' The stern approach left Dolly in favour of a little satisfied smile. 'The boys were some excited about him taking them out today. Cricket on the beach, what better for all of them?'

'He's up to something.'

'Who is?'

'Alec. I know when he's scheming.'

'Well, it can't be anything too sneaky with the children in tow.' Dolly hooted in laughter but quickly grew serious. 'Everything's all right though, isn't it, dear? There's been a bit of an atmosphere since Alec had those words with Tristan.'

'Of course, everything's all right, Mum.' Emilia kept secret her frustration with Alec for refusing to telephone Tristan and apologize over his unmerited outburst. 'Come on, let's slip inside and get a table near the window.'

They freed their arms to be able to pass through the low door of the small classy restaurant, its windows curtained in brilliant white lace. A male voice called out Emilia's name.

She went to the edge of the pavement where a trap and ponies were being brought to a halt. 'Perry! I didn't know you'd be in town today. Hello, Selina.'

After the usual polite exchanges, Perry said, 'I've just attended a meeting, Emilia, for one of my charities. You're welcome to bring Will and Tom to the house for tea with Libby this afternoon.'

'Thank you. I'll do that if Alec brings them back in time from the beach.'

'Where's he taken them?' Selina asked, puzzling Emilia and Dolly, for she didn't usually keep on with this sort of commonplace conversation.

'He didn't say,' Emilia frowned. 'Perranporth, I suppose.'

'Any news yet from Ben?' Perry enquired.

'Oh, I saw Eliza Shore in the village yesterday,' Emilia replied eagerly. She always enjoyed talking to Perry and spun out her tale. 'All I got out of her at first concerning Ben was that he'd written to say he was now somewhere in England. Somewhere in England, I said. Sounds like an introductory sentence to some creepy movie. Where about in England is he? Then I received ten minutes of rapture from Eliza about Rudolph Valentino. Who'd have thought she'd be capable of idol worship? Never seemed the least bit interested in men before.'

Perry smiled down on her. 'So she gave you no clue as to where Ben is?'

'Eventually. West Yorkshire. Strange, I thought. Why there? I could imagine Ben living it up in London.'

Dolly cut in to ask Perry in her blunt manner, 'When are you sending your little girl to boarding school, Mr Bosweld?'

'Yes, when will it be, Perry?' Emilia took the conversation back. 'I shall miss Libby very much.'

'I beg your pardon, Emilia?' Perry's eyebrows shot up high on his handsome face. 'Whatever gave you the idea that I'm sending Libby away?'

'Well, Selina mentioned it during our first meeting.' Emilia looked from the amazed brother to his sister, who with guarded eyes, promptly said, 'You are mistaken, Emilia.'

'I am not. It's what you said.' Emilia was not going to allow Selina to further embarrass her by allowing her to get away with a lie.

'Then it must have been some silly notion of mine,' Selina replied, with a fleeting smile. 'Well, we really mustn't keep you. Come along, Perry, I need to get back home. I'm on duty later.'

Perry tipped his hat and ordered the ponies to walk on, and Emilia stared after the trap. He had given her one last deep smile but his annoyance with Selina was obvious.

'She's a bad'un, that one,' Dolly snorted, rearranging her home-knitted cardigan and shuffled her shoulders as if shaking off something irreverent. 'Don't ask me how I know, I just do.'

Emilia confided much in her mother but had thought it wise not to mention that Selina Bosweld was Jim's seducer. Alec had described Jim's behaviour as of one being in the grip of an addiction, and while Emilia was grateful for Selina's sympathetic care on the day she had allowed herself to get sunburned, she grimly considered that the nursing sister had corrupted Jim. When Selina finished her association with him, she hoped Selina did so with gentleness. 'She can be very kind, Mum. She must be a wonderful nurse.'

'I'll have to take your word for that, maid. The brother's easy to rub along with though, isn't he?'

Emilia couldn't help smiling with pleasure. 'Perry's a thoroughly decent man, everyone likes him.'

'Pity his sister isn't more like him. Well, come on then, maid, let's eat before you fade away.'

When the Boswelds had left the town behind and were making for home through the back lanes rather than following the longer route by the main roads, Perry demanded, 'What's this all about a boarding school for Libby? You know I'd never dream of sending her away. I want her with me while she's growing up.'

'And I want what's best for her. A good schooling, then university.'

'I'll send her to a girls' day school when she's about twelve. She can go on to university from there, but only if it's what she wants. I don't understand why you made a decision about Libby without consulting me first. It's what we agreed we'd always do.'

'There's no need to be so possessive. Don't forget she's my daughter.'

'I won't, but our arrangement made me her father, don't you forget that.'

'Few things stir your passion, Perry, apart from Libby.'

Keeping his face straight, he turned the team out of Church Lane and they were soon starting up the long hill that led towards Devil's Arch. 'Is that a snipe of some kind?'

'Yes. No. Let's forget the whole silly argument.' Selina leaned back with her arms along the back of the red padded seat. 'Sorry, but I can't help being curious. Why aren't you looking for a bed partner? As far as I'm aware you haven't done it for ages. What's wrong with you? It isn't normal to go without sex for so long. Or are you getting it from someone and not letting it be known? Let me see. The only woman you're alone with for any length of time is—'

'Shut up, Selina!'

'Ah, so that's it, is it? Emilia. You've got a thing for the little earth mother? I can understand that. She's fascinating, and I'm sure when roused she's full of passion underneath her apparent respectability. So, are you bedding her?'

'Of course not!'

Selina looked up in under his flamboyant hat. His dark skin was on fire. 'Ah, passion at last! You'd like to, eh, Perry?' She looked ahead when she said, 'I think a lot of people would. I could help you out by seducing Alec.'

'Don't start. I don't want to have to leave another home because too many wives were getting suspicious that you're giving their men sexual favours. Keep to Jim and the consultant you're screwing at the hospital.'

'I've had enough of Jim.'

'Then for goodness sake tell him, and gently, the poor boy's besotted with you. And don't start on anyone else in the village, including Ben Harvey when he gets back.'

'Don't tell me what to do!' Selina poked him hard in the ribs.

Perry yelped. As a nurse, Selina had the softest of capable hands, but she also knew how to hurt and spin out the pain. 'Look, please don't make things difficult, Selina. Libby's getting older now and that means you have to behave more responsibly. Your affairs could lead to her being shunned and I won't have that for her. The war stripped me of everything, I had nothing left to live for until you got in touch with me about your terrible fix and we agreed that your baby would be thought of as mine and Ada's. We've had to move a long way to ensure there would be no one who could compare dates. You had better not dare do anything that might spoil Libby's security and happiness.'

'That sounded like a threat, Perry.'

'I suppose it was. Damn it, Selina, she deserves only the best out of life. You've no idea who her real father was out of half a regiment of American soldiers! Your free and easy lifestyle is risking a scandal. Let me warn you again, I love Libby like she's my own daughter and if I'm forced to I'll do anything, absolutely anything, to protect her.'

Sixteen

Jonny was up in the storage attics of Roskerne. Usually he came up here to indulge in a lonely party of self-pity, to plan his next wayward prank and to snatch a forbidden smoke. After the burning-couch incident he had been sent up to tidy the entire confines, which were dusty and dark despite a skylight and a lit ship's lantern, hanging safely from a hook on a massive beam. Today he had been asked by his father, so pleasantly it had given no room for cheek or protest, to come up for a different reason.

Supposedly, because of his recent punishment, it was considered that he knew best where 'things of a particular interest' could be found, and he had been given the task of seeking them out and setting them aside. It had been raining hard since dawn, and although he would rather be up here than hanging aimlessly about the house, and although every now and again, when filtering through the amazing amount and manner of past Stockley belongings, he felt a spark of curiosity in his father's intention of opening an antique and curio shop, he was tossing things about, half-hoping something would break.

He had cleared off the chipped black marble top of a creaking washstand, and despite himself had a growing collection on it. A bronze cigar cutter shaped in the form of a bulldog, Vesta holders, miniature watercolours, boxwood models of boats, foreign shells and fossils, a set of animal-shaped jelly moulds and a Sheffield plate decanter stand. He was adding a ship's brass companionway lamp to the hoard when he heard steps on the stairs.

He scowled as Vera Rose's beribboned fair head appeared.

'Don't tell me you're back from ballet already? What do you want?'

'I thought you might like to know it's stopped raining at last.'

'So?'

Ignoring his rudeness, she came through the doorway, still in her frilly, stiff-netted, pale pink dress, and started to sift through the things in an open sea chest. 'I think it's a great idea of Uncle Tris's. You should be proud.'

'Why should I be proud? It's boring.'

'But you're going to have your name put on the shop front, Harvey and Son. People don't do that sort of thing for girls.'

'Course they don't. Girls only get married. Put that barometer down. I'm supposed to be doing this. I don't want your company.' Jonny strode towards her and slammed down the heavy carved lid.

She leapt back in fright. 'Be careful! You nearly jammed my fingers. These are my family's things, you've got no right to exclude me. And don't be so horrid.'

Jonny glared at her and chose the most offensive expletive he knew before ending, 'So bugger off.'

'You're absolutely beastly, Jonny Harvey,' she gasped in disgust. 'I hate you! I wish you'd never come here to live.'

'Not as much as I do,' he snarled. 'I can't wait to get away to university. And when I join the RAF, I'll never come back.'

'Good. I hope you never do!'

'And anyway, Aunt Winnie's given my father permission to take what he likes. He should have bought a house in Truro and set up a shop there. He would have done if they hadn't got married because your mother was so hard up and he was so set on getting sex all the time.'

'What are you talking about?'

'You wouldn't understand, you're just a stupid girl. I know all about what men and women do in the bedroom, after spending so many years on a farm. Haven't you heard them? They're at it like bleddy rabbits.'

Vera Rose clenched her fists. Her face seemed to be filling up with steam and she looked about to explode. 'I wish you'd disappear for ever. I hope you fall on the way back down and break your rotten neck. I hope you drown in the sea. I'll never forgive you for saying those terrible things about my mother.' Then, letting out a high-pitched scream, she began to sob with an arm in front of her face.

Jonny shushed her. If his father heard her and asked why she was so upset, he'd be in trouble again. He was also blushing with shame. Vera Rose must be distraught; it took a lot to make her cry. 'Look, Vee, I'm sorry. Be careful, you can't see where you're going like that.'

Vera Rose walked into a box and wailed at the excruciating pain in her shin. Afraid she would scream again and cry even louder, Jonny dashed to her and put an arm over her shoulders. 'Quick, sit on the couch. Be brave, it won't hurt for long. I'm sorry for upsetting you. It's just that I miss the farm and Uncle Alec so much. I'll miss being there for the haymaking. They'll be starting tomorrow. I promise I won't take it out on you again.' He tried to curl his little finger around her little finger. 'Friends again? Dad stopped my pocket money but I've still got thruppence. I'll buy you a big ice cream.'

Vera Rose sat down but she shoved Jonny away violently and he ended up on the planked floor. She sniffed a last tear and glared down on him. He was wearing a pleading expression. 'Oh, you! You're so full of gab, Jonny Harvey. I will have your thruppence but I'll save it. I'll get so much money together you'll never be able to accuse me and Mummy of sponging off you and Uncle Tris again.'

'I didn't mean sponging, Vee.'

'Yes, you did. You're horrible to everyone. I don't know why Uncle Alec likes you so much. Anyway, I bet he's forgotten you by now. He's got two sons of his own.'

'Oh, you don't know him like I do.' Jonny got up and rubbed at his hurting backside before returning to the chest. 'I'd better get on. Show Dad I'm willing. Perhaps he'll let me go down to the beach later. He might if you ask him.'

'Are you hoping if you show enough interest in his business

that he'll let you stay at the farm? I know you don't want to miss the sports day. You usually win all the events.'

'Do you think this fishing reel will do? It might be of benefit if I did try working with Dad. If I can get him to change his mind, you'd be able to stay at the farm too.'

'I could go there anytime I want. Aunty Em telephoned me to say so, but I replied that I'd rather stay home and keep you company.'

'Really?' Jonny gave his cousin a disarming smile, a smile that spoke of his charm with females to come. 'That was jolly sporting of you, Vee. I forget you're nearly as loyal and as much fun as a boy.'

'Well, don't ever forget it again or I might forget about loyalty and cause you the most trouble you've ever had in your life!'

There was a loud persistent honking of a car horn. Jonny flew down the attic steps and ran to the nearest window. Seconds later he was shouting up to Vera Rose. 'It's Uncle Alec! He's here! I told you he wouldn't forget me.'

Jonny tore out of the house before Alec had let Will and Tom out from the back seat. 'This is a brilliant surprise, Uncle Alec. Hello, boys.'

Tristan joined the throng in time to see his son and his brother exchange an affectionate hug. He and Jonny had not enjoyed this sort of closeness since the boy was little.

'Hello, Tris. I'm glad the rain's stopped. It was dry until we hit the coast road,' Alec said. He was calm and breezy.

Tristan eyed him warily.

Winifred came outside wearing her charming old-fashioned hat and joined Vera Rose at the foot of the steps. The boys were chatting excitedly about the beach and cricket. Vera Rose felt left out.

Alec sauntered up to Winifred and kissed both her cheeks with a resounding smack. He was all smiles. 'I must say you're positively blooming today. I've never seen you looking so much in the pink before.'

'Save your compliments, Alec Harvey,' she replied with unaccustomed fierceness. 'You owe Tris—'

'An apology,' he finished for her gaily, turning to his brother. 'I behaved abysmally towards you, Tris. I'm very sorry. I couldn't let another day go by without making amends which I'm certain I can do because you don't bear grudges, like I do.'

Tristan stared at the hand Alec directed at his chest as if he'd never been offered such a gesture of reconciliation before. The apology was welcome, but he wasn't fooled by the reason behind it. Alec was here to renegotiate the question of Jonny's summer break at the farm. When Alec took the handshake a stage further and wrapped Tristan in a brotherly hug, Tristan whispered down his ear, 'You can be a right bastard at times.'

'I know. Polly Hetherton has pointed this out to me, but of course she used different language. I really am sorry though, Tris. How about a game of cricket on the beach? The sand is wet and firm and we've brought a huge picnic, plenty for everyone. Then you can think it over about Jonny. I'll abide by your decision.' Alec smiled at Tristan until he too broke into a smile.

'I was busy doing something else, but go on then, you ratbag. Afterwards I'll tell you about the business I'm going to set up.'

Jonny was already organizing his team, defying the grumbles of the other boys by choosing Vera Rose, and putting her in a state of being in heaven, to bat first.

Winifred was listening through the buzz of voices. Another motor car had started down the drive. 'Who's this?'

As the others became aware of its approach they gradually fell silent and all watched.

'It's Uncle Ben!' Will exclaimed.

'And a strange lady,' Tom added, his little brown head bobbing as he went on tiptoe to gain a better view.

Tristan shot Alec a warning look. Alec lightly shrugged his shoulders.

It seemed Ben had bought a new car, this one was a nippy Austin Tourer, quite unlike his other fast model. He turned off the engine and got out, but Jonny beat him round to the passenger side and opened the door for his companion.

'Welcome back, Ben.' Tristan hastened forward to greet him. 'This is the second welcome surprise arrival here today.'

Ben waited until the stranger with him had taken his arm. 'It's good to be back, Tris.' Smiling, quietly confident, he included Alec, if he cared to listen, in what he next said, 'Everyone, I'm proud to introduce Brooke Wilder Harvey, my wife.'

There was a moment of stunned silence, broken by Winifred, who, thrilled not only at the announcement but the fact Ben had chosen someone of his own age to marry, dashed off the step to the couple. 'Oh, Ben, this is marvellous news. Congratulations! And you look so well, I'm glad to say. Welcome to the family, Brooke. My, you're pretty. I'm Winnie, Ben's cousin.'

The two women joined in an easy embrace. 'I'm pleased to meet you, Winnie. Ben's told me all about his family. You're married to Tristan, his brother.'

'Good heavens, you're an American. How exciting.' Winnie looked from her neat, glowing new sister-in-law to Ben. 'Did you go to New York?'

'Actually, Brooke and I met at Passchendaele. I went there to pay my respects to Billy Rowse. It's a long story which I'll tell you about later.' Ben glanced at Alec, who was expressionless, and homed in on Tristan, his mood dropping into sorrow. 'I've visited Henry's grave too and I've brought back photographs.'

Brooke pre-empted any more introductions by picking out the rest of the family members from the descriptions Ben had given her. Warm greetings were passed until she faced the eldest of her brothers-in-law. 'You must be Alec. Hello.'

As she approached, Alec had been asking himself how he felt about Ben's presence. Until Polly's rebuke he had hoped Ben would sell up through a land agent and never come back to Hennaford. Since then he had kept his feelings about him on hold. He was glad he was safe and well, and married to someone who looked suitable for him. Now he studied

Brooke Wilder Harvey in the same way she was studying him. Carefully. Deeply.

Ben came forward, stiffly alert, and protective over his bride. Both were expecting at least a cool reception from Alec. Another silent moment passed.

Then, recalling Emilia's desire for old wounds to be healed, Alec reached out to Brooke and bent his head and kissed her cheek. He was aware of a great many cautious gasps and murmurs. 'I'm glad to see my young brother has finally settled down. You're very welcome to the Harvey clan, Brooke.' To Ben, he said, 'We've *all* been worried about you, Ben.'

Ben was bewildered and did not hide it. 'I don't understand this but for Brooke's sake I'll accept the sentiment. I hope you meant it. You've got a horrible way, Alec, of making one feel out in the cold.'

'Well, it looks like new beginnings all round,' Tristan said. He glanced hopefully at Jonny, hoping today's event would bring him and his son closer. 'This means we've got two more for cricket.'

Brooke elected not to play and strolled with Winifred down to the beach after the men and children. 'It's best to let Ben and Alec underpin their reconciliation, and it's good to talk with another woman in my new family. First though, I'd like you to tell me if you think Alec was really sincere with Ben. Ben says he's complex, even a little disturbed.'

'Perhaps Alec wasn't being entirely sincere, but mostly his heart's in the right place. It's up to both of them to build on the events of today. As for Ben's observations, it has to be said that Tris and I have similar worries. Alec feels things so acutely and he does have a tendency to see them in a different light to most. But Emilia's level-headed, she keeps Alec firmly in the real world.'

The women settled themselves in the deckchairs that Ben and Jonny had carried down the long winding cliff path for them. Winifred sat sedately, hugging her middle, occasionally caressing it. She held up a parasol to ensure the sun did not hit her face and hands. Brooke stretched out and had already taken off her shoes and stockings. They were the difference between a satisfied mother cat and a confident growing kitten with still a hint of playfulness.

'I know about the women formerly in Ben's life. He's told Mrs Hetherton about us over the telephone. She wished us well, so there won't be a problem with us socializing with her in the future. We're going to call on her soon so Ben can see her little girl. I know about Louisa's tragic origins. The woman I'm really looking forward to meeting is the one whom Ben calls Em.' Brooke laughed, and Winifred was interested in what was amusing her. 'Ben told me how embarrassed he was over Emilia and Honor Rothwell preferring other men to him, even though he'd fallen out bitterly with Emilia in their case. When he proposed to me and I accepted immediately he went straight out and bought a special licence. It was love at first sight for me, there was no chance I'd have changed my mind. We still managed a little family affair, with my distant cousins way up in Yorkshire. The land up there's like it is here, lush and green and full of hills and valleys, absolutely beautiful. There's more of it, of course, and the moors seem to go on for ever. Where I come from it's hotter and drier and the spaces are vast. It's cattle country, and you could put the largest farm over here in a tiny pocket of a single ranch. It was lonelier and the folks were tougher. Ben says his farm and the village of Hennaford are in the thick of the countryside. It will be great though, having the good old Atlantic within easy reach.'

'Tell me all about your whirlwind romance,' Winnie said dreamily. 'I'm quite starved of feminine gossip most of the time.'

Brooke related the poignancy of her first meeting with Ben. 'My mom died a few months ago and I sold the family business, a mercantile in a little backwater town to fund my trip to Europe. It was Ben's suggestion he help me trace my mom's family. Can't tell you how happy that made me, I couldn't have endured being parted from him.

My travels took me to Ben and there was no going back. Life's like that, I guess. Full of deciding moments. Like when Ben's eye was partially blinded. If not for that, he probably would've married Emilia and I wouldn't be here now, and Alec would've still been at his loneliest.'

There was an exuberant shout of howzat from Alec as the wickets fell against the opposing team. Brooke gazed his way. 'He's usually quieter, so I understand. Somehow, I can't get him and what I know about Emilia settled in my mind as a suited couple.'

'They're different in a lot of ways, I grant you, yet they share a deep love and have a strong marriage. Alec's here in this mood today because he's contriving to take Jonny home with him.' She gave Brooke a potted history of the boy's disruptive behaviour since her own marriage. 'It's put Tris in an impossible situation, and just when Jonny was reluctantly showing an interest in his new venture.'

'What Jonny needs is to see a side of his father he can also hero worship.'

'Yes, I agree. I'd be lying though if I didn't admit I'd welcome a break from Jonny. I'm not used to having a noisy, demanding boy about the place. And I'd appreciate some time alone with Tris.'

Brooke's bright eyes were on Winifred's tender caresses. 'Just you, Tris and your baby?'

Not used to open discussion about this delicate matter, Winifred blushed, then her joy shone through. 'Oh, I've given it away, have I? Please don't mention it to anyone else. I want to spare Alec and Emilia's feelings, and well, I don't think Jonny would take too kindly to it yet.'

'I'll keep silent about it. I think I might be starting a baby too. Have to wait a few more days to be sure. Hope so, Ben's longing for a son.'

Winifred squeezed Brooke's hand. 'Congratulations, I hope you are expecting. I can't help feeling excited about my baby.'

At the same moment that Ben met Brooke's eyes and blew her a kiss, Tristan waved to Winifred.

Winifred sighed in bliss, 'Now all we need is for Alec and Emilia to be happy again.'

Emilia was searching about in the hay house. Spying a new formation, not unlike a fort, in some of the bales, she climbed over them. 'Well, Jonathan Harvey, you're only back a few hours and I'm forced to look for things that should be inside the house.

'What on earth do you want this for?' She bent down to retrieve one of her best tablecloths and shrieked when she was grabbed from behind. When she recognized the size and gentleness of the hands, her shock vanished and she grinned. 'Alec, what are you doing?'

'The house is full. This is the only place where we can be alone.'

He turned her round and she launched herself at him and clung with both arms around his neck.

'That's your fault. Look what your nephew's brought out here. Blankets, cutlery, mugs, pen, paper and ink from the den. Everything except the best silver.'

He pulled her body in tighter against his. 'I didn't follow you out here to talk.'

The desire he had enflamed in her at their contact flared into the unstoppable. She kissed him with a passion that equalled his, pressing her breasts into his chest. Alec took her down on to a blanket spread across the bales. She yanked his shirt out of his trousers. He pushed up her skirt.

They were too keen, too impatient to spend time with preliminaries and Alec got himself ready.

Emilia moved herself in under him a fraction. 'You have brought something with you?'

'What? Oh damn.' His hot breath fanned over her face and his mouth demanded hers again as he realigned her back into position.

She pushed on him. 'Then we can't go this far.'

'We can't stop now, darling.'

'We have to.'

'Please, angel.'

'Don't be selfish, Alec.'

'Nothing's likely to happen.'

'I don't want to risk it. We'll finish this later.'

'You're joking? Emilia please.'

'Get off me, Alec. Don't be so thoughtless. Damn you, Alec, move!'

'Ouch! Bloody hell, there was no need for that.' He rolled off her, panting, gasping.

'Serves you right.' Putting her clothes back in order, Emilia got to her feet, shaking off tell-tale bits of straw. 'You had no right to insist, Alec. You should have stopped.'

'I was going to!' He let out a blasphemy. 'Since when did I ever force you?'

Emilia gazed down on him and kicked the bales he was sprawled out on. 'You shouldn't even have tried to persuade me. You agreed there'd be no more babies yet. I thought you understood how I felt. I carried Jenna for nearly nine months in my body. I don't want another baby inside me yet, to have to feel it growing there, to have to give birth and feed it and wonder if it will survive, to, to . . . Oh, damn you, Alec. I'm going outside. You can bring in all these things the boys and Vera Rose have brought out, and don't forget you promised Tris that you'd keep Jonny in line. Jonny has to learn more obedience. No more doing things your own way.'

Alec was up and on his feet. Emilia was about to climb out of the cleverly made camp, now spoiled by their actions, but he restrained her with a firm hand. 'I'm sorry about trying to make love to you without precautions. God knows, I'm sorry for upsetting you over our little girl. I know my tendency to slip away into my own thoughts sometimes actually turns me into a thoughtless swine, but what does that last remark mean, Emilia? Are you accusing me of trying to take Tris's son away from him?'

'Of course not.' She twisted until she was free of him. 'But you've just behaved in the most unfeeling way towards Tris. He and Jonny should have been allowed the whole of this summer to work out how they feel about each other as father and son. Your selfishness has only succeeded in keeping them emotionally apart. Jonny has little enough respect for Tris and your blatant interference for your own ends has reinforced this. How would you feel if Will or Tom preferred Tris to you? Sometimes, Alec, you are the most sensitive man in the world, other times you're exactly the opposite. To further your cause at Roskerne today is the only reason why you've invited Ben and his bride to dine here later in the week, isn't it? You made it impossible for Tris to say no to your scheme. Have you thought for a moment how he must be feeling now?'

Alec swept a hand through his hair, dislodging chaff, which settled on his broad heaving shoulders. 'No, I didn't think about Tris, but I will from now on. I'll point out to Jonny how he should behave as a son. He'll understand and I'm confident he'll behave better in the future. I'll telephone Tris and set his mind at rest. As for Ben, you're wrong about my motives there. When he suddenly turned up I was pleased to see him, honestly. Emilia, why couldn't you simply say all this to me? Why the bitterness and spite?'

'Bitterness and spite? Charming! Why couldn't you tell me you thought differently about Ben? It's about time you opened up. About time you stopped living half in a mental fog.'

'I heard Ben call you a bitch once. You certainly can be when the mood takes you. Do you want me to cancel the dinner?'

'No. Of course not. I'll invite Perry and Selina too. It's time we entertained again.'

She made to go but a dreadful feeling assailed her, as if ice-cold rain was falling in her soul. She had never quarrelled with Alec like this before. Not having his usual comfort and unconditional love made her feel empty inside. She fell down a bale of hay and let a rush of tears cascade down her face.

Alec sat beside her and held her in his arms. He cried with her. They knew who they were crying for, what this was all really about. There they stayed. Close and silent, until he cleared his throat and whispered, ‘Are you as afraid as I am?’

‘That it’ll never get better? I suppose we’ll just have to wait.’

‘There’s nothing else we can do.’

Seventeen

Jonny was having the best of times. When he wasn't leading his gang on some riveting adventure he was haymaking alongside his uncle, or playing chess or stripping down the motor car engine with him; the workings of an engine fascinated them both. Always they joked and larked about.

This morning they had got up long before daylight to attend the difficult birth of a female kid. Uncle Alec had saved both its and the nanny goat's lives – to Jonny's mind – and he had been allowed to choose the kid's name: Minnie, because it looked silly and cantankerous like Mr Miniver, the geography master at his new school. Then they had shared a secret breakfast of thickly sliced toast spread with 'thunder and lightning' – golden syrup and clotted cream – and had cut hugely into a pork pie and destroyed a perfectly set strawberry blancmange, and Aunty Em had scolded Uncle Alec over them leaving the kitchen in a mess and for eating food earmarked for later in the day. Uncle Alec had crept up behind her while she had set to with a dishcloth and he'd grabbed her and kissed her and she had smiled and stayed in his arms. While it embarrassed Jonny to see affection pass between his father and stepmother, he liked Uncle Alec and Aunty Em to show it. It made him feel good and made him feel safe, as if he was 'back in the old days' when he had been so happy living here.

Now he had finished his allotted jobs in the yard, feeding the pigs and replenishing the food stocks where necessary, he was shortly to join his uncle and the workforce in the fields, to help 'pook' the hay into small mounds roughly four feet high as protection against rain. But wanting, as he occasionally did, to be alone, he slipped away on his Aunty Em's bicycle.

Whizzing down the lanes, he leaned the bicycle against a field gate, climbed up on top the hedge and took his slingshot out of the waistband of his shorts. He had already filled his pockets with hard round stones and he aimed them with keen accuracy at white dead-nettle heads in the hedge across from him. In this way he soothed the rumblings in his soul, easing some of the frustration at not being able to live at the farm permanently.

He wondered for a moment if his father was moving goods into the shop in Bank Street at Newquay. His father had said he'd take him all over the country to look for suitable stock. That promise at least appealed to him: there had been no opportunities for him to travel far yet.

His pockets empty, he jumped down off the hedge, gathered up more stones, then scrambled up through the tough grasses, long stalks of lacy cow parsley, and pink and red campion of the opposite hedge to shoot the stones back across the lane. He had emptied one pocket when he was forced to stop as someone was approaching. It was Selina Bosweld on her bicycle, an upright, almost daring figure, like a heroine in an adventure comic in cape and nursing sister's uniform. He hoped she would ride straight past.

'I say, brilliant shots.' She halted, one foot resting on the dusty lane. 'You should suggest a contest of the sort at the sports day.'

There was something about this woman that made Jonny feel strangely disturbed. He was too young to recognize the first beguiling stirrings of interest in the opposite sex. 'Shan't, grown-ups are stuffy when it comes to this.' He held up the sturdy Y-shaped piece of hazel tied with an elastic trigger.

'I suppose they are and with good reason at times. You will be careful with it? You could take out an eye or cause a serious head injury with a wayward shot.'

Jonny crinkled his strong dark face at her. 'Of course, I'm careful. Jim taught me how to use a slingshot ages ago, when I first went to live with my Uncle Alec. I lived at Ford House before that. I suppose you know my mother died there.' It had been a long time since Jonny had felt the grief of losing his mother and now he was embarrassed by the wobble in his voice.

Selina leaned her bicycle next to his. 'Do you want to talk about her?'

Suddenly he did. This woman was straightforward and unlikely to feed him a load of superstitious twaddle; on this score he differed from his Uncle Alec. In one mighty leap he was down beside her. She put a hand on his shoulder and ushered him to the field gate, where they looked down over the rolling field to the one beyond it and saw the small shapes of Alec, Edwin, Jim, the other farm workers and some casual labourers – men, women and children, including Will and Tom, about to start work.

Jonny had not realized how the time had run on and now he only wanted to join the haymakers. He'd hate for Uncle Alec to feel he was lazy or disloyal after the clever manipulation of his father. And he did not want to be seen talking to a female, especially one who was considered a 'smasher' in the village. With his ample height and adult ways he was often considered older than his age and he might end up as victim to the sort of teasing that would make him squirm. And he knew other things about Selina Bosweld. Jim wouldn't like any such teasing. He could be mean these days and there were times when, to his shame and consternation, Jonny felt a little afraid of him. He moved away to where he was hidden from sight of the haymakers behind an overhang of foliage and brambles.

Selina joined him, smiling kindly. 'Go ahead, Jonny. What's on your mind? Don't be shy.'

He suddenly didn't want to confide in someone who was little more than a stranger, but he had committed himself and there was nothing for it but to go ahead. He prayed Selina Bosweld wouldn't keep him talking for long. 'Well, people say my mother haunts the house. Many times I've looked up at the windows to see if she's there. She never is. Have you seen her? Felt her presence?'

Selina put her arm round him. He felt uncomfortable, then he remembered how kind she had been to Wilfie Chellow, how her compassion had changed the villagers' impatient attitude and fear of him. She had given Wilfie back his dignity and the poor chap rarely 'went off his head' anymore. First and foremost she was a caring nurse. 'I can't say I have, Jonny. I think your mother's resting in peace. Don't take any notice of silly rumours.'

'I won't, Miss Bosweld. Thanks.' He wanted to repay her for her kindness and thought he should give her a warning. Any day now she would be caught out doing the thing he had accidentally witnessed in the woods and everyone would hold a different view of her then.

'Are— I mean,' he hoped his face wasn't burning too brightly. 'Will you, um, be seeing Jim later today?'

'There's no special reason why I should.'

He wanted to protect her and dared to look into her face. She gazed back from her dark violet eyes. They were nice and peaceful but if she were found out they would fill up with tears. 'There's something—'

She let go of him. 'Well, I must get off home. I've been on duty all night and I'm tired. Goodbye, Jonny.'

She was going. He sighed in relief. His warning was too delicate to voice and why get himself involved with something that was none of his business anyway? But she was a kind lady. When she reached her bicycle, he found courage and blurted out, 'I know!'

She strode back to him. 'What do you know, Jonny?'

Her face had turned hard. The delay had angered her. Jonny's nerve went. As she came closer and closer to him, he retreated until he could go no further, his back coming into contact with the brambles. He wished himself anywhere but here. He was out of his depth and sinking fast.

'Answer my question, Jonathan Harvey.' She was looming over him.

'Well, I know . . . about you and Jim. What you do . . . together.'

'We don't do anything, Jonny.'

'But I've seen you. I only want to warn you—'

'Threaten me, you mean?'

'No! Look, you've got this all wrong. I won't say anything.'

She pushed on him until the thorns were scratching his back through his shirt. 'You'd better not, boy. You'd cause all sorts of trouble for me and it would upset my brother and Libby. Is that what you want?'

Jonny shook his head. He was afraid of her now. 'No, I swear. I only—'

'If you ever say anything, then I'll . . .' She put her lips close to his ear. Jonny paled and trembled at her harsh whisper. 'Remember boy, I'm a nurse. I know exactly how to do it.'

When she had gone Jonny raced across the lane and tossed himself over the other side of the hedge. Out of sight, for the first time in years he cried like a young frightened child. Never had he felt so wretchedly alone. He couldn't even go to Uncle Alec about this.

Emilia was on her way down the lane to issue the dinner invitation to Perry and Selina and she was carrying the Boswelds' weekly supply of eggs and dairy produce. She also had some of Tilda's scones in the basket, knowing Perry liked them.

Something whooshed past her and she missed her footing and nearly fell into the ditch. 'Can't stop!' Selina bawled over her shoulder from her bicycle. 'Need my sleep. If you're going to my house, don't disturb me. I'll see you another time.'

'Careless cow,' Emilia mumbled, righting herself. She watched as Selina splashed through the ford, obviously unconcerned about wetting her shoes and soaking the hem of her nurse's dress. 'Well, you won't stop me from seeing your far more pleasant brother today.'

Perry was at the breakfast table in his dressing gown, reading the newspaper, and looked up in alarm as Selina blazed into the house. 'Where's Libby?'

'She's out for a walk with Vera Rose and Casper. What's wrong?'

'Nothing! You get off your lazy backside, get dressed, fit your artificial leg on and try to walk properly, damn you! There's nothing stopping you except something in your mind. You know that. Whatever it is, come to terms with it. Sometimes I hate you!'

She stamped up to her bedroom, slamming the door so violently Perry thought the ceiling would come down on top of him. He sighed deeply in vexation. She would be in a foul mood when she resurfaced and it would escalate into an even worse one if he didn't get on and obey her orders. He knew he would have made better progress with the prosthetic if he received the right sort of encouragement. Selina was excellent at physiotherapy but her ministrations were relentless and tiring. She bullied him throughout each session. Sometimes, he felt he hated her too.

Getting to his bedroom on his crutches, he sat up on a high-seated chair and strapped on the wooden limb. Gripping the arms of the chair, he hefted himself up, bearing his weight on his good leg.

Now to take that first vital step forward away from the safety of the chair without Selina being there to cajole or support him.

A rush of blood sounded in his ears and he felt sick. As if he was on a precipice and about to plunge down a bottomless pit. He closed his eyes. *Fight it! Don't give in. Just one tiny step. It'll hurt like hell, but no matter. It will be good to walk again, for Libby's sake and your own.*

'You can do it, Perry. Look at me.'

Instinctively he smiled. It was Emilia's wonderful voice, with its lovely evocative intonation. Soft and encouraging, just for him. He opened his eyes and saw her in the room. She was holding out her hands to him. And she was smiling. He concentrated on that hopeful, beautiful smile. He didn't feel the step he took. The next one. Or the next. He didn't know if his movements were strong or shaking or if the prosthetic was rubbing his stump. All he was aware of was that he was getting closer to her. Closer. Wonderfully closer. He knew then he was in love with her. Hopelessly, deeply, gorgeously in love with her.

'Keep coming. That's right. You've nearly reached me. Oh, Perry, you're doing it!'

He kept moving towards her smile, her lovely face, her waiting hands.

'Perry, reach for my hands. Keep coming. Take hold of my hands. I won't let you fall.'

'I know you won't, Emilia.' His outstretched arms felt heavy but he was able to obey her. When her hands were taking hold of his he felt as if his whole body was floating on air.

Emilia backed away and pulled on his hands, taking him with her. She was laughing now. 'I'll take you to the bed. I think you'll need to sit down at any moment. You mustn't overdo it.'

Suddenly he was falling but he was not alarmed. He was taking her with him down on to the bed. And he was clinging to her. Laughing with her. Holding her. He didn't ever want to let her go.

It was the first time in months that Emilia had felt happy, and it was due to the triumph she had witnessed and been a part of. She stayed where she was, lying on her side next to Perry, hugging him. 'I feel I've just seen a miracle.'

'You have. Thank you, Emilia.' He was bubbling over with joy. He looked into her eyes. 'Thank you so much. You're wonderful. You're just what I needed to break through the barrier that was holding me back. I feel as if my life's started all over again.'

Alec and Ben had been the only two men she had been this close to. She knew it was wrong to stay like this, but she couldn't stop herself revelling in the feel of his strong arms, and gazing into his handsome face. When he touched her face, when he kissed her cheek, when he softly slid his warm lips to press over hers, she told herself it was the affectionate kiss of a friend.

She sat up but did not move away from him. 'You'll need

someone to make you a well-deserved cup of tea after this. I saw Mirelle walking off towards the village with a basket. She was looking at a shopping list. Can she read English?'

'A word or two. She'll give the list to Mrs Eathorne. It's so good to see you, Emilia. I thought you'd be toiling in the fields.'

'I've slipped away from the kitchen, I'm helping with the food today.'

'Pity you're not at a loose end.'

'If I'm not back in time then Tilda, Sara and my mother can manage without me. I was going to take the crib and beer on the cart to the fields but Sara seemed desperate to swap places with me. I'm hoping it's because Wally Eathorne from Druzel Farm will be there; neighbours always get together to help each other out with the haymaking. Wally is trying so hard to get Sara to notice him but Jim stamps on anyone who tries to get close to her. Poor Sara, she's so worried about Jim. You know it's Selina he's seeing?'

Perry nodded. 'So it's still going on? Selina said she was going to finish it. Don't worry about it, Emilia. I'm sure it will fizzle out in time.'

She was about to say, 'That's what Alec says,' but it didn't seem right to mention him while she was sitting so close to another man, on his bed.

She felt Perry's hand on her waist. 'I'm so very fond of you, Emilia. Have you guessed?'

'Yes. I value your friendship highly, Perry.' She knew she should go, run away, but instead she settled on something marginally safer. Ada. A photograph of his wife was on the dressing table, a portrait of a small, young woman with an uncertain smile. 'Do you still miss her?'

'Not really. Ada was a silly sort of little thing, but she was a dear and was devoted to me and I thought we'd make a go of it. I married her in a moment of madness at the outbreak of the war. I didn't expect her to die at home in bed while I was out there in the slaughter fields. I should have been a lot sadder at losing her if she'd been anything like you, Emilia.'

His hand was caressing her waist and Emilia laid a grip over his sensitive fingers. 'You mustn't say things like that to me.'

'Sorry, but it's the truth.' He felt Emilia making to get up, so he said, 'And another truth is that Ada wasn't Libby's mother, but please don't think me the sort who indulges in casual affairs. There's more too that you don't know.'

'Don't tell me.' The fight inside her to leave him yet wanting so much to stay was won by her resting her head against his chest. 'I'd never think badly of you, Perry.'

He entwined his fingers in her hair, lifted it and kissed it. 'Darling Emilia, Em . . .'

'In a minute or two I'll help you to walk again. It's as important to me as it is to you that you continue making progress. Then I'll make the tea.'

'For both of us?'

No, then I will go.

She said, 'Yes, for both of us.'

Eighteen

Emilia reached the stone footbridge at the side of the ford, telling herself that only a respectable short time had passed since she had first gone over it. She had stayed in Perry's embrace for the two minutes she had stipulated, telling him that the tea would be drunk in the parlour. This had been done with him in his wheeled chair and she at a sound distance across the room. They had chatted about the children, the garden and the weather. Good, honest subjects.

She could justify her actions how she liked, but when she was climbing the short steep hill up to the farm her heart was thudding, her face was aflame and she had a tight, hurting grip on her fists. Perry had wheeled himself to the front door to say goodbye and she had allowed him to take her hand and leave a lingering kiss there. Then she had stooped and kissed him on the lips and there had been nothing respectable or honest about the manner in which she had done it. Her body had wanted him then in the same way it had wanted him when they had cuddled together on his bed. Now her mind was filling up with shame, but not all the way to the top because she didn't regret one moment of what had happened. Perry was handsome and sensuous, and he was fun and open in a way that Alec was not. The danger was exhilarating for she knew her attraction to Perry was not just a means of sheltering from her grief over Jenna.

When she had helped him to rise off the bed and walk to his wheeled chair in the parlour, Perry had said he would find it easy to start out on his own from now on, that he would only have to picture her encouraging him, holding out her arms to him. He had also said his room would never be as lonely for him again. She would not, must not, venture to his house alone for some time, but she was already looking forward to seeing him again for the dinner party at the weekend.

Something filtered into her mind. Someone was calling to her. Perry? Had he managed to follow her this far so quickly? She turned and found herself staring at two people only a step or two behind her. It was Ben and a young woman who could be none other than his bride.

'Have you developed cloth ears?' Ben grinned at her. 'I've been shouting to you for ages. I thought I'd bring Brooke over to meet you rather than leave it until the dinner. Brooke, this is Emilia.'

'Hello, Emilia. I've been eager to get to know you,' Brooke said, leaning forward in her sociable unaffected way.

Emilia felt so strangely happy that she hugged Ben and then Brooke, whom she at once took a liking to. 'It's good to see you again, Ben, and to meet you, Brooke. This calls for a little celebration.'

'I won't argue with that,' Ben laughed, and Emilia was glad to see him happy. 'I must say you're looking good. I was half-dreading to find you pale and downcast.'

'I've got a lot of good people around me.' Emilia walked on between him and Brooke. 'Come on, let's sit on the goat house steps and catch up on all our news like we did in the old days. I'm eager to see the photos you've brought back of Billy's grave. So are my parents. We're all grateful to you for that, Ben.'

'Jonny must be thrilled to be back at the farm,' Ben said.

'He is. It really is something like the old days. I think I'm at my best when Ford Farm's bursting with people.'

'I liked Emilia a lot,' Brooke said, when she and Ben were making their way, arm in arm, back to Tremore, this time taking the route across the field behind the farm so he could show her the woods where he had once played.

Ben kissed the side of her head. 'Well, she's down to earth, like you. Now Em seems to be getting over the baby's loss

I think we'll be able to break our good news soon. So will Tris and Winnie.'

'I think I might have some interesting things for Tris's shop when my things arrive from Wyoming. Some originated from England, you know, from the early settlers.'

'Oh, but you must keep them, darling. They'll be part of your family history. You are good to think of others. It's one of the things I love about you, you're so completely unselfish.'

'Thank you, kind sir.'

They entered the woods, wandered under the awning of trees. Ben showed her his old camp – now Jonny's – then he took her to a secluded copse, where the foliage was dense and created good cover. 'Are we going to watch some animal in its natural habitat?' Brooke parted the leaves and peered through the space she had made. 'Tell me about all your fascinating British creatures, Ben.'

Using his strong hands gently, Ben dragged her down on to the springy undergrowth of the forest floor. 'Badger watching or anything like it isn't the reason why I've brought you here.'

Brooke succumbed eagerly to his kisses. She found Ben a captivating mixture of reserve and passion. They had been inseparable since the day they had met, yet despite her willingness to share a bed with him he had insisted they wait until their wedding night before making love. It had been important to him that he did everything right, that their union from the platonic into intimacy was perfect.

'I adore you, Ben Harvey,' she whispered.

'You're everything I've ever wanted,' he said with emotion, making her totally his again.

Much later in the day, after Alec had finally called a halt to the haymaking because of failing light, Jim was in the woods, near the outskirts, where he could just make out the figure of Selina approaching him. He had met her here so many times he was able to walk back home in the dark without stumbling.

He grabbed her roughly, the way she liked him to. Selina shoved him away. 'Not now, Jim. In fact never again. I've come to end it between us. It's time for us to stop.'

He came after her as before, his big hands calloused from his graft. He had not washed and smelled of sweat, but not offensively; a tantalizing draw, he knew, to Selina. 'You've said that before, yet you keep coming back for more. You need me, Selina. Don't play games.'

She stroked his brawny shoulder, then yanked on his fair hair until he was forced to lean his head over to the side. 'It has to end this time. We've been seen. I can't risk there being a scandal.'

'Who's seen us?' he swore.

'That boy, Jonny. We've been lucky to have gotten away with it this long. I'm sure Emilia guessed about us a while ago, but as I was certain she wouldn't say anything I let it continue with us for a while longer, but enough is enough. We've had a good time, now we must move on to other things.'

'But I don't want to.' Jim snatched her hand from his hair and gripped her wrist. 'We could make it official. Tell everybody we're courting. In love.'

Selina laughed and laughed. 'Don't be foolish. I'll never fall in love. I enjoy my freedom too much for that outdated notion. Now let go of me, Jim.'

Jim was shaking his head. 'Don't do this to me, Selina. I couldn't bear it.'

'Well, it couldn't last for ever, foolish boy. I've kept on with you longer than anyone else before. It's time for you to go after Elena Rawley again or someone else. You've got all the experience you'll need. You should have the confidence to get whatever you want off any woman you like.'

'But I want you. I love you.'

'No, you don't. Now let go of me before I make you. You're very strong but I'm perfectly capable of getting you off me. I hate scenes, Jim. Be a good fellow and say goodbye.'

'You heartless bitch!'

Selina smiled sardonically. 'See, I told you that you didn't love me. No man could say something like that to a woman if he loved her. Look, I'm not rejecting you because of you, yourself, Jim. You're a nice boy. You're a good lover, you can be proud of your prowess when it comes to that. Not every man can say he satisfies a woman every time. If it makes you feel any better I won't do it with anyone else in the woods, it will remain our special place. We'll always have special memories, won't we?'

Jim was almost in tears. 'I s'pose.' He let go of her wrist and crumpled forward, placing his head on her breast.

Selina kept it there and stroked his hair then she lifted his face, kissed his mouth and pushed him away. 'I'll see you around the village or at the farm, Jim. Now be a good chap and run along home.'

Weeping quietly, he followed her at a distance where she couldn't see him. She did not go inside Ford House but sat on the front garden wall, smoking. He knew it would be impossible to get her to change her mind.

'Whore,' he muttered under his breath. A woman had to be a whore to have seduced him the way she did and do the things she had taught him to do. Was she going after Ben Harvey now he was back, even though he had brought a wife home with him?

When Selina had finished the cigarette she remained where she was. Jim was keyed up, preparing a speech for when she went inside. He would go in after her, force his way in if he had to and give her a piece of his mind and call her the names she deserved in front of her brother, and tell her he was glad it was over between them and he wouldn't ever miss her. Keeping watch, he moved up to a better vantage point.

Selina moved off down the lane. He heard a motor car. It halted, the engine rumbling slowly. He had a good view of it. Selina got into the motor car, beside an older man in a dark suit and trilby hat. It was no surprise to Jim when she reached across and kissed the man in an open-mouthed way. Selina was hungry for sex. She always was. He should have known she would have someone else already lined up to take his place. Then with a plummeting heart and a dreadful fury it occurred to him that she probably had been seeing this other man all along. He had only been her 'bit of rough'.

He was determined now to spread it all round the village what sort of woman Selina Bosweld was, to let everyone know there was another side to the caring nurse they thought she was. But it would involve himself and not help his case if he did decide to make a fresh play for Elena Rawley, and it would embarrass Sara. He must think of something else, a better revenge, and thanks to his calculating mind, developed as both a defence and an assault tactic in his vulnerable early years, he knew exactly what he would do.

Before the motor car pulled away, he noted its number. 'Right, matey, I'll find out who you are. Something dodgy's going on here if you couldn't go up to the front door and call for her. As for you, Selina Bosweld, I'll bide my time, then I'll get even with you for what you've done to me.'

Nineteen

Arriving at the doorstep of the schoolmaster's house, Perry removed his hat, straightened his lightweight jacket, and ironed out the discomfort in his face from wearing his artificial leg. He had learned from Libby, who was absorbing the affairs of the village, that a meeting had been called here this morning of the social committee to plan for the coming sports day. He was about to ask if he could join in.

He had a whole tropical forest of huge restless butterflies in his stomach. Not because he was unsure of receiving a welcome but because Emilia was attending today – her first outing of this kind since her bereavement. He couldn't wait until the dinner at Ford Farm to see her again.

Mrs Frayne, the schoolmaster's wife, motherly and bountiful, comfortingly plump and smiley, opened the door to him. 'Of course, you're welcome to join us, Mr Bosweld. Oh, I forgot, you like to be called Perry, don't you? Come along in, Perry. How splendid to see you up and about, I've only seen you in your wheeled chair before. Do you, um, need any help getting over the doorstep? Oh, you don't, how resourceful of you. How did you get here, if I may ask?'

'On pony. I tethered it to the field gate, took a look at where the sports day will be held. It's perfect for the occasion, such a long, flat, straight field is a rarity in this area.' Perry had also noticed the school was the usual small, two or three classroom affair, with separate concrete playgrounds for the boys and the girls, divided by a four-foot forbidding wall, topped with something that looked like thick dried tar. The little wrought-iron gate was rusty and he thought to offer to commission the blacksmith to produce a new one, something more solid and picturesque. Offer anonymously, he didn't want to be seen as a pushy intruder.

'Yes, Mr Harvey always does his haymaking there first. He allows the school free rein once his crop is in, we hold rounders there as well, and nature studies on other parts of his land.'

He was soon inside the pleasantly furnished, dark but not gloomy front room, facing all those who had been expected to come, and the one other newcomer, Brooke Wilder Harvey, who had arrived with Tremore farm worker Eliza Shore. He had met Ruby Brokenshaw on the two occasions he had taken an evening drink in the Ploughshare. Next to her was her longest and most regular customer, a small wizened toothless individual in a grubby cap, known as old Mr Quick. Perry was to learn that old Mr Quick had come only for the company and a cup of tea and a slice of cake.

Elena Rawley was there, mousy and friendly, seeming in support of his involvement on this occasion, and Mrs Eathorne, the chatty shopkeeper, and Mrs Chellow. Brain-damaged Wilfie, so Perry was told, was amusing himself in the Frayne children's playroom – the source of harmless intermittent chinking noises and the occasional watery inane chuckle. The most dignified of those in the gathering, whom Perry had not met before, was Mrs Oscar Dowling, the rector's wife, slender and wearing pre-war fashions with pride, as if she wanted to convey that thriftiness was a virtue. Perry had heard somewhere that she was called Daphne, but she was nothing like the slightly dizzy, amiable Daphnes he had been acquainted with before. She offered him a formal, 'How do you do,' then turned her stiffly hatted head away quickly, and Perry thought perhaps she did not approve of him because of his non-attendance at church, or perhaps it was the terracotta hue of his jacket. He had taken up his unconventional style of dress while reading for his science degree at Oxford, where, thankfully, individuality was not frowned upon.

He baulked at being shunned for any reason, but he had no

care about it today when his eyes fell on Emilia, seated in a dark corner, lovely in neat black and a small hat. She gave him a beatific friendly smile. No, it was more than friendly. The light and energy shining back from her showed she was just as delighted to see him. He wasn't sure if he believed in the Divine – Elena Rawley's father would never succeed in securing his presence in the Wesleyan chapel either, but he thanked the gods, anything and everything that she obviously did not regret their intimate moments of two days ago.

Miserably, there wasn't a free spot close to her where he could fully enjoy the sight and sound of her, where he could smell her sweetness and perhaps even touch her, and he accepted a high, hard-backed seat near the door, which Mrs Frayne in her worries for his comfort, hoped was suitable for him. She had sent her daily help for another cup and saucer and plate, and he was left juggling the ridiculous dainty crockery and the last slice of a crumbly ginger cake as best he could.

The desk top of a walnut bureau had been pulled down and from there, with writing paper and fountain pen poised, Mrs Dowling popped on a pair of gold-rimmed pince-nez and called the meeting to order. While allowing his eyes to wander often to Emilia, Perry learned, with satisfaction, that regular village events were swiftly and efficiently organized.

Mrs Dowling had written out a quantity of lists beforehand. 'Before I start I'd like to say how pleased I am, as I'm sure all of us here are, to have Mrs Harvey back with us after her sad loss.' Allowing a few seconds of murmured agreement, she droned on in well-bred tones, 'And I extend a welcome to Mrs Wilder Harvey and –' slight pause – 'Mr Bosweld. I'm sure both of you will pick up what happens as we go along. Thank you all for attending. Are we happy to go ahead with roughly the same plans as last year?'

Perry thought Daphne Dowling the sort to ruthlessly conspire to have things her own way, but she took a moment to pass round an enquiring look to each individual. Except for him. He was content to gaze at Emilia under the cover of sipping the stewed tea.

No one had any comment and Daphne Dowling went on. 'Well then, thanks again to Mr Alec Harvey's generosity we shall use Higher Cross field. He will also supply the sheaves for pitching, the greasy pole for the pillow fighting, etcetera. The preparations of erecting the marquee, etcetera, will begin as usual in the early morning. Mr and Mrs Frayne will be in charge of the races, children's and adults'. Mrs Harvey and I will award the monetary prizes, the trophies, etcetera. Mrs Eathorne will run a stall of sweets and lemonade, etcetera. Mrs Brokenshaw, the beer tent and pasties. Miss Rawley and Mrs Chellow will be in charge of raising the funds for the children's saffron bun treat and distributing them, with lemonade on the day. Mr Benjamin Harvey will supply the piglet to be bowled for. Miss Shore, I can take it you will be in charge of the creature again?' Mrs Dowling looked down over her pince-nez at Eliza. Perry could almost feel her disapproval of the farm worker's presence. Eliza Shore was turned out in trousers, gaiters, a man's shirt and hobnail boots, her habitual garb, her chin-length cropped hair was greasy and the whiff of the farmyard was coming off her.

'Wouldn't have come else, would I?' Eliza Shore grinned, exposing her big teeth. Squashed on the clumpy two-seater settee between Ruby Brokenshaw and her new mistress, she elbowed Brooke in the ribs. 'The bugger got away last year. Chased it halfway round the village, I did, 'fore I got it back. Hector Crewes, the postman, won it. Only just beat you, didn't he, Mr Quick?' Her voice boomed across the room for old Mr Quick's sake; he was nearly totally deaf. 'You got a steady hand for a bowling ball, haven't you?'

Old Mr Quick did not comprehend what she was saying. He nodded cheerfully and went on sucking up his tea.

'We didn't need to hear about last year's misfortune in those terms, Miss Shore,' Mrs Dowling remonstrated. 'There will be tug of war between the usual teams captained by Mr Alec and Mr Benjamin Harvey.' Perry had heard that some of the villagers thought this would not be so interesting now there was no contention between the two brothers. He pictured

Alec and Ben urging on their teams with gritted teeth, just the same. 'I'm sure the usual villagers with a musical talent can be called on to provide a band again. Miss Rawley has already volunteered to do the rounds and confirm this while she's collecting for the tea treat. Now, does anyone have any new ideas to propose?'

All eyes travelled to Brooke and Perry. Brooke was about to speak, glanced at Perry and hesitated. 'You go ahead, Mrs Wilder Harvey,' he said gallantly.

'Thank you, Mr Bosweld. Ben and I would like to suggest a large wooden platform be laid down for dancing later in the evening.'

Her accent sounded new and adventurous in the old-fashioned atmosphere. Prior to Perry's arrival, Emilia had been chatting to her, drawing closer to her in friendship, and Emilia thought now how fresh and pretty she was in a shimmering asymmetrical cardigan. Fresh and pretty, because she was in love. Perry being here made Emilia feel fresh and alive after so many weeks of grieving.

'Splendid idea. Everyone agree?' Mrs Dowling looked for a show of hands. Received them in an unanimous vote except for old Mr Quick's, but his views didn't count anyway. Wrote at the bottom of one of her lists. 'And I can leave it with you and your husband to provide the timber and build this platform, Mrs Wilder Harvey?'

'We'd be delighted to,' Brooke said, glancing at Emilia, who smiled back in encouragement.

The smiling interchange made Brooke think she wouldn't have to leave it much longer before she could tell her sister-in-law she was pregnant. Emilia seemed so calm and rested, and a little sparkly.

There was a vacuum of silence and Perry plunged in with the idea he had come up with. 'How about archery?'

'I beg your pardon?' Mrs Dowling glared at him as if he had suggested something outrageous.

'It's an ancient noble sport, Mrs Dowling,' Perry replied, wanting to call her Daphne in true Selina-style mischief, refusing to allow her disapproval of his presence to unsettle him. If she was a religious bigot, or if she considered him an outsider because he wasn't married to a local, as was Brooke, or if she felt he had not finished his apprenticeship as a newcomer and had not proved his worthiness yet as a villager, it was too bad.

'I think archery will make a welcome addition, Perry,' Emilia said, smiling at him, loathing Mrs Dowling for her coldness towards him. Mrs Dowling was a snob and a stickler for convention. She had made it known that she disapproved of Selina working. But she was fair-minded and Emilia couldn't fathom what she had against Perry, who was liked and respected by the rest of Hennaford.

Perry answered the woman he had fallen hopelessly in love with. 'Thank you, Emilia.'

'I also think it's an excellent idea,' Elena enthused. 'But best kept strictly to the adults, of course. We don't want any young Robin Hoods being hurt.'

'Who around here can use a bow?' Mrs Dowling's tone was argumentative, sour.

'I'm sure I can master it,' Eliza Shore bawled out. 'And so could Cyril Trewin and Mr Ben, eh, Mrs Ben?' Eliza was devoted to her new mistress.

'Absolutely, Eliza, and I'd like to try too,' Brooke replied, frowning at the rector's wife.

'Just about any adult I know could try,' Emilia said. 'A prize for the three closest shots to the bulls eye, was it something like that you had in mind, Perry?'

'Something like that, Emilia,' he replied. Their empathy was so strong that for them it felt as if they were the only two people in the room.

'Show of hands!' Mrs Dowling suddenly boomed.

Old Mr Quick heard that and was alarmed. He clattered his teacup down on the saucer and shot his shaky ancient hand up with all the others.

'Very well, I'll add an archery contest to the posters. You will be responsible for everyone's safety, Mr Bosweld. Anything else from anyone?'

There wasn't. A short time later Perry invited Emilia to

walk with him down the short track on the other side of the schoolhouse wall to his pony.

Brooke went with them. 'I wonder why that old battleaxe didn't like you, Perry. Sorry, but it was obvious. If it wasn't for the good cause, you would have been justified in leaving early.'

'She doesn't bother me, Brooke. Emilia, are you walking home?'

Emilia knew he was hoping they could spend time alone down the quiet lanes. She tried not to show her own disappointment. 'Brooke's invited me over to Tremore for lunch.'

Crushed, Perry nodded forlornly.

'Where's your little girl, Perry?' Brooke asked.

'She's at home with the maid. She's got no one to play with today, the other children are caught up with the haymaking.'

'Why not ride home and fetch her and join the rest of us? Ben mentioned that you'd been to the house for dinner, but you haven't seen the farm, have you? Come and look around with us. Bring Libby's puppy too, if you like.'

His handsome face was a picture of happiness. 'Thank you, I'll do that. You make it sound cosy.'

'Well, it's important we all get along, isn't it, Em?'

'I couldn't agree more, Brooke,' Emilia agreed. She was looking at Perry.

Elena Rawley had spent a blissful day cycling from cottage to house, from field to farmhouse, to and from local businesses; the blacksmith, the flower and vegetable nursery, the animal feed shop, etcetera, as Mrs Dowling would have said, until the full complement of local musicians were duly engaged for the sports day. She had also collected the sum of one pound, three shillings, already more than enough for each child's tea-plate-sized saffron bun. It was getting near teatime, and although her father had been invited to lunch with other ministers on the circuit, in Truro, he would be home by now and expecting her to soon be putting his next meal on the table.

She was happy despite being sorely hot and perspiring,

happy though her skin was raw and itchy due to the sultry heat of the sun and the number of hills she had ridden up, and her throat being desert-dry. Nothing satisfied her more than a well drawn-up spot of organization, and serving others. It was what she was born for. Serving God and the community. A person didn't have to belong to her father's flock to benefit from her good works. And she intended her works to be of the genuine, not the interfering or self-generated-to-earn-praise kind. It was all she wanted to do. Not for her, a husband and marriage when she wouldn't have so much self to give freely. She was a sort of nun, God's handmaiden without the habit and cloisters.

The sports day was always a delightful occasion, when the children ran races for fun as well as the hope of winning a little silver to spend, when the women proudly displayed a newly decorated hat, and the men – and Eliza Shore – competed by flexing their muscles to pitch a sheaf of straw on a long two-pronged fork the highest height over a graduated climbing horizontal pole. Sometimes the squire won this prestigious event, sometimes Eliza. Mr Ben Harvey always got into the last four or five. But last year Jim Killigrew succeeded in outclassing everyone.

Jim Killigrew. Now there was a sad young man, she mused. Then she dismissed the salacious rumours about him of winning and losing some woman-friend, said to be the cause of his recent depression, and she recalled how one year he had asked, via Ruby Brokenshaw, if Cornish wrestling could be added to the sports day activities. Mrs Dowling had remarked it was worth pursuing but there hadn't proved to be enough local men with the necessary expertise. Jim had not mentioned it again, but Elena knew he was still bitter over what he saw as a personal rejection.

Elena had climbed the hill past Ford House – where Perry Bosweld had been arriving home with his daughter and her puppy; they were as happy as she was, going by the boisterous way they had waved to her – and she was now heading towards the main road, which she would cross over and then after riding on a few hundred yards away from the heart of the village, she would turn down Henna Lane, go on for half a dozen twists and turns to finally reach the Manse. A journey of ten minutes, but once she was in Henna Lane her legs were aching unbearably, their pumping action suddenly wavering and before she knew it she was falling sideways into a ditch.

Screaming in fright, she landed awkwardly amid long grass, brambles, stinging nettles and wild garlic, picking up a multitude of bumps, bruises, scratches and stings. There was the pungent onion smell of the crushed foliage.

'Ohhh.' She put a hand up to her tangled hair. Felt blood there. And felt the terrible pain where her legs were at odds either side of the back wheel. 'Ow! Ouch!' Always hating the sight of blood, she shut her eyes, afraid to look at her wounds. 'Oh, God help me. Help! Help!'

The answer to her prayer was almost immediate. 'Keep still,' came a voice from somewhere high above. But it wasn't a heavenly voice, her guardian angel's voice. The tone was gruff and impatient. 'Your ankle's badly twisted and you've got deep cuts.'

'Jim? Is that you, Jim Killigrew?' Her voice sounded weak and pathetic and she even wasn't sure if it really was hers.

'Don't move, Miss Rawley,' Jim said, terse and unsympathetic from where he stared down at her from the highway. He had hurried towards her from the opposite direction after witnessing her plummeting into the ditch. He had no business to be here, idling away his boss's time and he would be in for another roasting for absconding from the fields, but he didn't care. He didn't care all that much about this young lady's distress. He tossed away the cigarette clamped between his teeth. 'I'm going to move the bike out of the way. It'll hurt like hell but you'll just have to put up with it.'

'You will take me home?' she cried, trying to fend off the hands he put on the back wheel, fearful of the promised pain.

'Where else would I take you? Do you want my help or not?'

'Perhaps you ought to take me to Ford House. Mr

Bosweld's a former surgeon and perhaps Miss Bosweld is at home. I don't think I want Dr Holloway sent for, no one trusts him now.'

'I wouldn't take you to Ford House if you was dying!'

The expletive he added to this so shocked Elena she stared up at the furious face framed by his mop of fair scruffy hair bending over her and she wasn't ready for the bicycle to be shifted. The excruciating pain made her faint.

When she came to she found herself looking up at the ceiling of her own bedroom. 'How did I get here?'

'Killigrew's just laid you down on your bed, my dear. Be brave.' It was her father and he was holding her hand.

'Want me to fetch Dr Holloway?' Jim growled at the Reverend John Rawley.

'If you please, young man. I'm grateful to you for bringing my daughter home but I would appreciate it if you would dispense with your aggressive manner.'

Jim had his hands stuffed in his pockets. 'Oh would you? Forgive my disgusting manners, but I didn't think you'd want anything from me, even help. Never had time for me before, never thought me good enough to lick your blasted shoes. Or hers.'

'Well, yes.' The minister, baggy clothed and baggy featured and almost hairless, blanched then reddened in equal amounts of annoyance and shame. He rallied quickly. He was at times a direct speaker and occasionally, when brought to passion, had been known to issue a mild swear word. 'Now look here, Killigrew, I can't leave Miss Elena and there's no one else here who I can send to fetch the doctor. I'd be most grateful if you would go for me.'

What Jim really wanted to say next was, 'Go to hell!' The anger and frustration inside him overwhelmed any finer feelings. Then Elena said in a frail, frightened voice, 'Thanks for your help, Jim. I could still be lying out there if it wasn't for you.'

He saw her then not as a condescending young madam but a woman, a woman with shapely long legs exposed by her ripped skirt, and made all the more sensual by the blood on them. He was assailed in the loins by the sort of lust that Selina Bosweld had bred in him, the lust that had no outlet now unless he went looking for one. Its intensity, the shame of feeling like this here in a sedate virginal bedroom, the humiliation Selina Bosweld had subjected him to when throwing him over, and the anger he felt about all the trouble he had got into at the farm made him hurl himself towards the bedroom door. 'I'll call at the bleddy doctor's for you. I'm not heartless.

'I'm not!' Outside he was running, running back down Henna Lane with a primal rage growing inside him and crying scalding hot bitter tears. 'I'm not! I'm not . . . anything! But just you wait, Selina Bosweld, I'll be somebody soon when I bring you down!'

Twenty

'What music have you got, Alec?' Polly said, at the mahogany-cased gramophone.

'All sorts, my dear.' He came to her, debonair in his dinner suit, tanned, rugged. 'Jazz. Ragtime. Opera. There's an outstanding recording by the American blues singer Bessie Smith, although we haven't played it since we bought it last Christmas.'

'I don't fancy that. Let's take a look.' For Polly there was already too much American presence in the room. Wishing Ben well in his marriage over the telephone was one thing, but it had been different altogether when actually faced, on the visit to see Louisa, with the homely but sparkling pretty young thing that had taken her place in Ben's life. It was hard to be polite to Brooke now, particularly with Emilia, the rather gleeful little bitch, watching to see if she would be ungracious. And it somehow seemed a slap in her face that Ben was on good terms again with Emilia.

Life wasn't fair, so Polly thought, and even more so when Alec reached round her to the shelf on which the music recordings were stacked. The sheer silvery stuff of her dress was slashed nearly to the waist and feeling the tantalizing contact of his sleeve on her skin and his warm breath on her neck brought to her mind his attractions, and she wanted to lean against him. Alec had left his haymaking to issue a personal invitation to her to attend here tonight, but unfortunately she could read nothing into it. Alec was the faithful sort, damn it! How lonely life was.

Alec withdrew a handful of shellac discs. Although not inclined to eye women, for a brief moment, because his love life had lost some of its sparkle and spontaneity now Emilia was insisting on contraception, he treated himself to the alluring sight of Polly's bottom moulded within the clinging material. 'What would you like, Polly? Caruso? Dame Nellie Melba? Something faster? How about Creole jazz, we've got a couple by Joseph "King" Oliver.'

Male company. A lover. A husband. 'Anything you'd like, Alec, is fine with me.'

Emilia was down the other end of the room, near the door. With her parents opting to spend the evening in the small parlour, their own little domain, apart from Alec and Polly, and Selina who was finishing her coffee alone on the sofa, she had an eager audience of the other dinner guests, including Reggie Rule, who had made up the numbers at the table. 'Isn't it wonderful that Perry can now walk with just the aid of a stick? I couldn't believe my eyes when I saw him coming towards me on two legs, so to speak.'

Her eyes were glittering and fastened on Perry, who was close beside her. He had one arm propped on the bureau to underpin his balance, his walking stick near at hand. His confidence, his happiness was infectious, and when he made some silly remark the group laughed, although not with gusto. No one had forgotten the household was still in mourning.

Selina viewed the larger clique with unquiet eyes and started on the champagne – Perry had brought a magnum along to celebrate his achievement. Would anyone else notice the other reason for his happiness? She had a secret reason to hope he would quickly work this new happiness out of his system, but an affair appeared to be in the offing. Emilia was equally attracted to Perry – it was what was making her so dazzling tonight.

Selina wanted to move on again, to a more exciting area, London perhaps, with all its challenges, opportunities and thrills. And where, as her one and only lover at the moment had suggested, she could train as a doctor. It was something that had passed often through her own mind and was now her burning ambition. She could go now, of course, set out on her own. Her consultant lover was a generous sort and had offered to fund her studies, but she could never leave Libby behind. Her daughter was the only person she had ever loved.

She had ignored Ben and his bride since their introduction, not sharing Hennaford's decree that Brooke's transatlantic origins were exciting. All this stupid talk about cowboys and Indians. Boring! To pass away the time she flicked over the remaining guests. Tristan Harvey and his comely wife; a couple ingrained in the institution of marriage. *Nice* and lacklustre. Tristan Harvey and Perry were to form a link in their charitable activities for ex-servicemen, well, bully for them, but they'd bored her half to death about it over dinner. She wished Reggie – the poodle – had not been invited. It seemed he had chosen her as a likely wife for himself and dogged her movements, given the chance. Only her abrasive stares were keeping him presently at bay.

There were only two people here, or anywhere else locally, she would enjoy seducing. Alec was one of them. How sexy he was. Emilia, comfortably married for a few years had forgotten how alluring he was. She had not noticed the doe eyes Hetherton had turned on to him. If he so desired, Alec could easily win her over, and the divine young creature that was Sara Killigrew. Selina smiled to herself. Earlier this evening Jim had tried to harangue her with insults, with threats. She had told him if he made trouble for her then she would make trouble for his sister. Jim had had no notion what she was talking about but it had sent him skulking off.

Alec was a worthy prize, and winning him over was something to do while she stayed hereabouts. He would be one of her greatest challenges, yet the other person in her sights would be her ultimate conquest. That person, who was never likely to capitulate, made her dizzy with desire, shaky in the limbs, break out in a nervous sweat, sensations she had experienced only at the beginning of her long and varied journey into sensuality.

She lit a cigarette. 'Does anyone know any of the new dances?' Her voice cut through the pleasantries. 'Brooke? There's a new marathon dance craze in America, isn't there?'

'Oh, that's not happening anywhere near where I come from,' Brooke replied.

'Do you know any, Selina?' Polly asked. She thought to suggest a tango to Alec, far more provocative than kicking up one's feet and flapping one's hands about.

'One or two, but I can't be bothered to dance tonight.'

'Have you been run off your feet all day in the hospital?'

Selina dismissed Polly's enquiry, made only, she was certain, to infer to the company that she had to work for a living. She zoomed in on Emilia. 'You can take all the credit for Perry's triumph, you know. He'd never have walked off without you. You arrived at the house at just the right moment. He always looks forward to your regular visits. I believe you've been good for each other. And tonight, Emilia, you are the most beautiful woman in the room. Isn't she, everyone?'

'Yes, she is,' Polly answered at once, truthfully, trying to conceal her jealousy. She had hoped Emilia would grow fatter and plainer with each succeeding pregnancy. And now Alec had deserted her and was staring at his wife as if he had never seen her before. Polly, who had thought of Selina Bosweld as witty and charming at Ben's dinner party, now saw her as more common than Emilia, someone who should never be invited to a refined table, and she was sure she was trying to cause trouble with her carefully chosen remarks, but she was not above shooting a barb herself to unsettle a rival. 'I do like your silver locket, Emilia. Alec gave a smaller version of it to Louisa a while ago. He does spoil her.'

'She's worth every bit of it.' Apart from preferring Elena Rawley as Reggie's opposite number tonight, Emilia had given Polly no thought, nor did she now. She was too involved in keeping her emotions under control at Selina's shamefully accurate observation about her and Perry being good for each other. Did Selina suspect? She and Perry must be careful. No, what was she thinking of? There was no 'she and Perry' needing to 'be careful'. She must put an end to the inappropriate closeness she had allowed to spring up alarmingly fast between them. She should move away from him and keep a distance. But she didn't. It wasn't as if they were going to do anything while in a roomful of people, Alec included. 'I haven't seen Louisa for a while now. You must bring her over to the farm for a picnic with the other children, Polly.'

Polly said she would think about it. Emilia noticed how Tristan had glanced down at mention of his dead wife's child.

'You look stunning, darling. Gorgeous. You always do.' Alec's voice was low and husky, he was unaware there had been any other subject but Emilia's appearance. He could not remember if he had complimented her tonight. She was a pagan creature, enthralling and divine in a sleek beaded dress, complemented by some of the jewels he had given her.

'Simply captivating,' Perry whispered to Emilia alone, and he gently grazed a trail up her arm with a stealthy forefinger.

When Emilia smiled and said, 'Thank you, darling,' she wasn't sure to whom she was replying.

Forgetting Louisa Hetherton-Andrews, Tristan had reason to be enjoying the evening. 'I must say, Em, that you and Alec are doing wonders with Jonny. He's much quieter and more polite. Wanted to know all about the shop, didn't he, Winnie? You must all come over and see it when it's up and running. Everyone's invited.' He cast his soft grey eyes over the whole gathering.

'I'd like to do that,' Perry said blatantly to Emilia. 'We could take Libby and the boys.'

Ben had been grasping Brooke increasingly tighter round the waist. There was a strange, almost foreboding atmosphere here. He caught Selina's attention. She stared back from her striking unearthly eyes as if amused, and then her gaze grew cold. Through his informal politeness to her and his affection towards Brooke he had made it plain he was no longer interested in her. She had seemed not to care, but perhaps she really did. Recalling her unfeeling games with him, he felt a shudder ride up his back.

He said, 'You must all come over to us for dinner next.'

'Oh, yes, please do,' Brooke echoed, but like Ben she was hoping the Boswelds would decline. She had loathed Selina at first sight. She reminded her of a prairie cat, predatory and merciless to domestic stock and lesser prey. *You're dangerous somehow,* she thought.

Selina saw that Reggie was about to pounce on her. She rose and tapped Emilia on the shoulder. 'Could I have a drink of ice-cold water, please? I'll come with you to the kitchen.' When she and Emilia were at the door she called through the hubbub of conversation to Alec. 'Your dairymaid has such a sweet voice. Couldn't you persuade her to sing for us tonight?'

Alec looked up from the gramophone. 'I'll find her and ask but I won't insist. Her free time's her own.'

In the warm empty kitchen, Selina sipped from a tall glass. 'You do realize the Hetherton woman has got designs on Alec, don't you?'

Emilia's eyes widened. 'That's a ridiculous idea.' She fell silent. It was not an unthinkable notion. There was no reason why another woman, a whole drove of them, should not find Alec desirable. She didn't want to think about the possibility that Alec might find other women attractive, not now, while knowing, with guilt and a heady excitement, that if it was Perry who was here with her now and if he tried to hold her and kiss her she would almost certainly respond with enthusiasm. How could that be? She loved Alec and did not doubt his love for her. To hide her bewilderment, and, because Selina, the troublemaking witch, was boring her beautiful knowing eyes into her, she retaliated, 'How did you end it with Jim? He's so miserable. You've led the poor boy a cruel dance.'

'Don't worry about Jim. We all have to go through the bitter-sweet experience of having our hearts broken for the first time.'

'I don't believe that's ever happened to you.'

Selina made a wry face. 'Oh, I've upset you, Emilia. Forgive me, and let me tell you that you've no need to worry about Alec. He'd never stray with someone like Polly

Hetherton. He relates to those who are vulnerable. It's why he's so close to his motherless nephew, Jonny. And Tristan, whose wife betrayed him and who suffered in the war. I bet he was wonderful with Ben when he was growing up but the minute Ben became confident, and was looking forward to becoming an Army officer and making his own way in the world, the two of them lost any special closeness. Alec probably never realized it, but I'm sure he resented it. Am I right?'

Emilia nodded thoughtfully. 'I never realized it myself until now, why there was a gradual friction between them.'

'And you, Emilia, you're a strong woman and you always will be, but I bet you had something worrying you when Alec first wanted you.'

Emilia's mind went back in time, to the struggles of the war and shortage of labour on the farm, her worries for Billy's safety. 'It seems you know how people think, Selina.'

'I've always studied the human condition,' Selina smiled, thrilled and delighted to be getting a little adulation from Emilia. 'You think me rather a bitch, don't you?'

'Sometimes. It would be good to see your nicer ways more often. Are you unhappy?'

Selina reached forward and stroked her hand. 'Yes. Quite often I am, Emilia. Do you know, it's good to have someone in which to confide. The thing is that I get so very angry at all the opportunities and rewards there are for men and not for women. When I was a little girl I would lay awake for hours and wish and wish I'd turn into a boy. Well, I've never been one to mope and I'm thinking of changing my whole way of life to train as a doctor. I haven't even told Perry yet.'

'Will he approve?'

'Oh, yes. Perry's the most understanding man in the world. I suppose we ought to get back to him and your other guests. Thank you for listening to me, Emilia, and I'd like you to know that if you ever need anyone to confide in you can always turn to me. You and I should go shopping together or something. Or take a long walk, yes, I think I'd like that better. Somewhere quiet and private, and away from our busy lives. Come along then.'

Emilia allowed herself to be ushered out of her own kitchen. 'Selina, could you be careful about some of the remarks you make.'

'Such as, my dear?'

With an effort Emilia stopped herself turning a culpable red. 'Well, the things you said about me and Perry could be misconstrued.'

'Oh, I see what you mean.' Selina dropped her voice to a tone that carried soft consideration in it. She slipped an arm round Emilia's waist. 'Anything you say, my dear.'

Sara was lying on her bed in the partitioned space that was her room up in the attics. There was only enough floor area for the single bed, a small wardrobe, a washstand and a solid old chair, but it was her own private realm, and Mrs Em had ensured she had soft bedding, gaily patterned cushions with matching curtains at the tiny window. Carpet was on the floorboards and a floral china chamber pot was under the bed. There were pictures of children playing in meadows on the boarded walls and an embroidered Bible text Sara had made in the workhouse; the only thing left of her childhood, except for odd moments of insecurity when she felt worthless.

Finding no pleasure in her comforts, Sara had her head stuffed against the pillows and she was weeping bitter tears, never more miserable in her life. She had spent the day preparing, with Tilda, Mrs Rowse and Mrs Em, the food for the dinner party. Then she had helped wait on the table and afterwards wash and dry the mountain of dishes. And all the time Alec had looked so handsome, her dream, her fantasy, with all those beautiful, fashionably dressed ladies, not noticing she existed, except for a touch of fatherly kindness when he had thanked her for all her hard work and pressed two shillings into her hand.

'It was my pleasure, Alec.' That's what she had said, instead of, '*When will you share a meal with me? Dance with me? Touch me? Kiss me? Show me how to give you pleasure?'* She knew nothing about the pleasures he was used to. She wanted him to introduce them to her, do them with her. At times her longing for him made her body burn in its secret little place. *Oh, Alec, why don't you notice me? I wish I was dead.*

'Sara? Sara, sweetheart, what is it?'

Now she was imagining his voice.

There was a gentle touch on her back and she jerked her face to look up. He was there! Come to relieve her of her misery. Come like a prince. A lover. A hero. He had come to rescue her and to take her away and to be hers forever more. Oh, no, he was looking at her in that fatherly way, as usual. She sobbed even more bitterly and covered her face with her hands.

'I did knock but when I heard you crying, I came in. My dear, tell me what's upsetting you?' His warm rough hands, made wonderfully brown by the sun and wind were tugging on hers, bringing her out of her concealment.

'Sara, do you want me to fetch Tilda or Emilia?' He was thinking she might be suffering the distinctly feminine thing.

'N-no,' she gulped. 'It-it's nothing.'

'It has to be something. Have you hurt yourself? There's a bruise on your wrist.'

'Oh that?' She sat up, gathering her strength, for his sudden presence was making her feel wobbly all over. She could not find a hanky so he handed over his. She dried her eyes with it. 'It's nothing. I'm . . .' He was leaning forward, smiling right into her eyes, and she had to think of a reason to keep him here, to claim a little bit of him. 'I'm worried about Jim.'

'Are you sure that's all it is?'

'Yes. I can't get through to him. He's so unhappy, so angry with everyone. He was even rude to Miss Bosweld this evening.'

'Well, she's the sort to take anything in her stride, so don't you worry about that particular instance, my love,' Alec sighed. He had tried to talk to Jim again and again, something warning him not to mention Selina Bosweld's name on each occasion, but Jim had refused to listen to comfort or advice and had even sworn at him. 'But of course, it's worse for you.'

'He's never spoken about the girl that broke his heart and he gets angry when I try. He's so bitter about it.'

'Did he do this to you?' Alec encircled her forearm so he could view her wrist.

Sara nodded. Then, with a daring born out of the longing to hold on to him, she pushed her dress down off her shoulder. 'And this. He said he was going down the pub to get drunk and when I tried to stop him he squeezed me here.'

Alec stared, appalled, at the imprint of a large hand left on her otherwise flawless skin. Crouching, he took both her hands into his. 'I can't allow Jim to carry on the way he is, you know that, don't you? And I certainly won't have him upsetting you like this, Sara. Don't worry, I'll sort this out somehow. Now, my dear –' and his grip on her hands tightened and she pressed back on his, hardly breathing, her heart thundering like the stormiest waves on the wildest sea – 'can I encourage you to take a few minutes to compose yourself then to come downstairs and sing for us? Your wonderful voice is highly sought after, you know.'

She would do anything for him. If only she could tell him so. 'Well, yes, but . . .'

'But what?'

He smiled in a way that sent her soul shooting up to the heavens. 'But I haven't really got anything to wear. Only my best dress but it's too plain and I've no shoes with heels.'

'What?' He was puzzled for a moment. 'Oh, I see, I quite forget you're a woman now. Of course, it's important for you to look your best. Let me think. Yes, that's it. How about you come with me and choose something of Emilia's? She'll be glad to lend you anything that takes your fancy.'

He led the way down the short flight of stairs, then through the older part of the house and into the Victorian extension where the bedrooms were fine and grandly furnished. He tapped the bathroom door; the room inside was larger than

Sara's and done out in exquisite porcelain and highly polished brass. 'Change in here, take your time, but first come with me. I've thought of the very thing you'd look lovely in.'

Lovely, he thinks I can look lovely.

Sara waited in his bedroom, her arms twisted together in a state of bliss and anticipation while he searched through her mistress's wardrobe until he laid a filmy ice-blue creation over the bed. She let out an excited breath. She had only worn frumpy plain or pale colours or girlish floral patterns before. The evening dress was delicately feminine, with diamanté swirls all the way down from the low neckline to the short hemline. It must have cost a fortune.

'Are you sure Mrs Em won't mind? She's only worn it once.'

'No, she'll be pleased to lend it to you. It will match your eyes. Now, you're not to sing without payment tonight, Sara. I'm going to start off a collection for you and you'll deserve every penny. Take this to begin with.'

She was gazing at him, not really taking in his words, and she felt him press something cylindrical into her hand. 'What is it?'

'Just a little something so you can buy some new clothes. Go to a proper dress shop and kit yourself out properly. I'll tell the others you'll be down in a little while.'

Her tender mouth sagged open. He must have given her at least five pounds. 'Thanks Alec. You're so good and kind.'

'You're part of my family, Sara.' He kissed her cheek and left.

She lifted her middle fingertip to that hallowed spot. It was some moments before she recovered enough wits to make herself ready to follow him downstairs.

'That was a lovely thing that you did for Sara. The little concert she gave rounded off the evening.' Emilia was in bed, waiting for Alec to get in with her so she could turn off the last lantern. 'Is Jim back yet?'

'Yes, the constable brought him home. He was causing a disturbance at the pub and smashed some glasses. I've ordered the boy to see me in the den first thing in the morning.'

Emilia chewed her lip. 'Poor Jim. I was hoping he'd feel better about himself after the Reverend Rawley's visit to thank him again for his help over Elena's accident. Hope he'll listen to you this time. We must think of something to take his mind off his misery.'

'No, we mustn't. Jim's got to learn to grow up. There's no use in him running away from his problems. It's time he got the Bosweld woman out of his head. I shall confine him to the yard for as long as I see fit. And why should he get special consideration and not Sara? She's perfectly obedient, an asset to us, it wouldn't be fair on that sweet soul.'

Alec had put on his pyjamas. Normally a scintillating evening – and the occasion had been lifted for him by Polly's sparkling company and Sara's delightful singing – would leave him in the mood for making love, but he wanted only to go straight to sleep. He was tired. Strange for him – he being in the habit of thriving on only four to six hours of rest at night, when his endless mulling and considering usually made him rise in the small hours. For some strange reason he was suddenly bone-weary tonight.

In the dark, Emilia moved towards him and he wrapped her in, as he always did, close to his body. She was relieved he did not seek to make love. Not so soon after having Perry in the house. Not after she had contrived to sit next to him while Sara had sung.

She sensed Alec's tiredness. He had an early start, the next stage of the haymaking ahead, loading the pooks on to the wains and building the ricks in the mowhay, but she felt compelled to talk to him. *To keep her mind safely off someone else.* 'I'm so pleased you and Ben have made up. He's thinking of holding a barn dance.'

'Oh? When?'

'Sometime later in the year, perhaps after the harvesting, he said.'

'Good idea.'

'Alec?'

'Mmmm?'

'You know I love you, don't you?'

'Of course, darling. I love you.'

Long after Alec fell into the deep rhythm of dreamless sleep, she lay enfolded in his arms, telling him in whispers that she loved him and no one else. But the image of Perry's handsome smiling face was with her throughout, refusing to shift from inside her head. She ran her hands over Alec's strong slumbering frame, thought about waking him and making love to him. But it wouldn't be fair – not because he needed to sleep; it just wasn't right to take advantage of him even in a way that would delight him, to rid herself of the guilt of having eagerly given and received intimate attention from another man.

She must keep far away from Perry from now on. Refuse to speak to him unless it was absolutely necessary, and then only when they were not alone. Hours passed in which she instructed herself, aggressively, on what she must and mustn't do to stay true to Alec. But what if she failed in these resolves?

Really afraid for the future, she clung to Alec, clung so tight. When he awoke, soon after she had finally closed her eyes and sunk into a fitful sleep, she awoke too and wouldn't let him go for some time.

Twenty-One

Emilia was on her knees tending Jenna's grave. Her baby would rest alone in a new Harvey plot, until joined by the next family member. For now the small granite headstone declared who Jenna had been and whom she had belonged to for such a short time. It was long after Emilia had relinquished the last white lily and the bunch of forgetmenots Tom had picked, that she said a reluctant goodbye.

Someone was there, a walking stick in one hand, holding out the other to help her up. 'Hello, Em. I went to the farm, Tilda told me where you were. I hope you don't mind. I haven't seen you alone for a while and it's getting more difficult now Selina's forging a friendship with you. I was hoping you might like some company on the way home.'

'Hello, Perry.' She rose without his aid. 'I don't mind you coming here. You've got the right to remember my little girl. I've been trying to imagine her smiling. Jenna would have had a beautiful smile.'

'Yes, she would have, very beautiful. Are you all right, Em?'

She dried her eyes. 'I'll never get used to it, but then I don't want to.' On the way out of the churchyard she adjusted her steps to the slight roll of his. She paused near the church entrance, before a towering Celtic cross raised as a monument to the village war dead. 'There's my brother Billy's name. Jenna's with him now. How did you get here, Perry?'

'I rode. You don't have to hurry home, do you, Em? The children are at Tremore on a picnic. Can we spend some time together?'

Emilia felt compelled to leave the hallowed ground before

answering. Her agonizing of a few nights ago had been for nothing. She still wanted to be with Perry more than anyone else. He was with her in every way, through memories of his kindness and compassion and every word he had spoken to her, and the feel of his touch and the kiss of his mouth. She had missed him even before he had left the room on the night of the dinner, and she knew nothing she could do or say would fill the empty place left inside her. Over and over she had asked herself why she had these feelings, this need for him. She loved Alec. It was a love that had grown soon after her estrangement from Ben, and it was a strong love, an enduring love, yet different to the love she felt for Perry. She was *in* love with him. God forbid it, she was, but God couldn't forbid now, it was too late, it had already happened. Her heart was with Perry, in him, his for ever. Not counting the deep, indestructible maternal love she felt for Tom and Will, and Jenna, somehow Perry *was* the largest part of her life.

This was dangerous. She moved out of his reach. Safely out of his reach. 'Perry, I'm married . . .'

'I know,' he pleaded with eloquent turns of his gentle hands, 'and I like and respect Alec. But, and I'm not the least bit sorry about this, Em, I'm in love with you. Em, darling, I love you. I love you with everything I have inside me and I can't help it. It's happened. I won't, I can't deny it another moment.'

She swung her head away. She mustn't look at him. 'Don't say anything more, Perry. Please, don't . . . I'm going home. Don't follow me. My children need me, and there's Alec . . .'

'Stay, Em, don't go. Talk to me. Darling, don't leave me like this.'

She made the mistake of glancing at him. The pained expression etched in his dark handsome face made her spring towards him, but she still kept out of his reach.

His pony was tethered next to the hipping stock, a few yards behind him. 'I'll fetch Sparkie for you. You should ride away from me.'

'No!' He reached out and gripped her hand. 'Come with

me somewhere quiet. Take me somewhere where we won't be discovered. At least give me this afternoon. Don't waste these precious moments, Em. They might be all we'll ever have. Please don't do that.'

She stared into his passionate blue eyes for some time. Finally, she bit her lip. 'All right. There is a place, we'll need to follow the old track that runs along the side of the churchyard. It leads to a patch of moorland, there's a little secluded place there. Few people know of it and those who do won't go near it because it's rumoured to be haunted.'

Once off the lane, they rode double, she behind him, keeping her hands, and as much of herself as possible away from his body. It was hard, it felt unnatural not to fling her arms around him and press her face against him. With the churchyard left behind, they were now hemmed in on either side by close hedges of dark ominous-looking thorn bushes, having to duck their heads and keep their arms in to avoid being scratched. She explained more about their destination. 'Jonny discovered the spot ages ago but it doesn't appeal to him because there isn't a stream or anything much to climb.'

'Sounds the perfect place where we won't be disturbed and Jonny certainly won't be there with his gang today.'

With thoughts of Jonny and her sons enjoying games on Ben's property, she tried to work up enough guilt to insist that when she and Perry had made the end of the narrow track, where there would be just enough room to turn the pony round, that they go back.

But when they had squeezed past the last barbarous bush, she said, 'To the left now.'

Soon the pony's hooves began to sink into less firm ground and banks of creeping willow, gorse, bramble and a few birch trees took over to hide them from view as they picked a way through spiky purple moor-grass and reeds. Spotted-orchids gave beautiful dashes of rose pink.

Shortly the way ahead was blocked by tall growth and she said, 'We'll have to get down and secure Sparkie here. I'll have to make a path through. Give me your stick, Perry, then hold on to me.'

'Well, I won't argue with that,' he smiled into her eyes.

It was a slow difficult passage for Perry, for they had to avoid patches of deep black mud and small boulders of granite, while ducking under low straggling branches and climbing over those that were lower still.

'Just a little further on,' Emilia encouraged him. 'Then there'll be a pleasant place where we can sit.'

Clinging to her hand, keeping himself upright by the aid of a roughly barked lichen-covered limb, he breathed a long restorative sigh. She freed her hand from his and held up a leafy bough for him to pass under.

Then he was whistling in elation. 'This is amazing.' They were in a small circle of open air, on soft spongy ground, surrounded by tall dense foliage. The sky overhead seemed a magical blue and sweeps of marsh flowers of purple, pink, cream and yellow gave the impression of an enchanted paradise. It seemed a place of gentle warmth and purity, even the multitudes of insects, which had been nipping at his exposed skin, kept at bay.

He eased himself down on the green floor, which felt, to his mesmerized mind, as smooth as velvet. He pulled off his muddy riding boots and Emilia took off her spoiled shoes. She sat close, not too close, yet not too far away, facing him. Looking everywhere but at him.

'We mustn't stay long, Perry.'

'You don't mean that.' He put a hand gently on her face, turned it until she was looking at him then leaned forward to kiss her lips.

She grasped his hand. 'No, this is wrong.'

'Yes, it is, but . . .'

'What?'

'We're here, my darling Em. We met, we needed each other and now we're here.'

He held her face in both hands and she closed her eyes and let him kiss her. And she kissed him in return, with eagerness, with passion, with soaring pleasure. With love. So much love. She did not know where all her love for him came from. It was filling her to the very edges of her being, and the more she was kissing him, she knew that he was feeding off her love, being filled with it to the brim of his soul.

They went on kissing, caressing each other's faces, necks and shoulders, gazing adoringly into each other's eyes, his so deeply blue and gentle, hers so softly brown and tender. Finally he let his hands fall away. 'I need to stretch out. Lay down with me, darling, Em. Talk to me.'

They lay down but did not talk. Or think. Simply enjoying the 'now' of being with each other. They lay face to face, hers resting in the crook of his arm. He smiled. And she imprinted his smile on her heart. For ever. He reached down to rub out the soreness in the muscles above the missing part of his leg. 'Let me ease that for you,' she said. And she placed her hand where his had been and she worked lightly, with a feather-light touch, but with exactly the right pressure to rid him of the pain in the slightly ruined temple of his wonderful body.

'How do you feel about me, Em?'

She clung to him. She trickled her fingers through his thick black hair. 'I don't ever want to let you go. Not ever, Perry.'

'You love me then?' He made it sound as if it was incredible to him that she could love him.

'Yes, Perry, I'm in love with you. And since we've been here, more than ever.'

He held her tight, with his eyes shut. Smiling, so happy. Then he was quiet. His gorgeous face a little shadowed. 'I must tell you something.'

'Perry? You can't tell me anything that would make any difference.'

'Shush, darling.' He kissed her fingers, gripped them firmly. He enfolded her in his arms, so closely, so intimately. 'I want us to have no secrets. I've already told you that my late wife wasn't Libby's mother, the thing is, I'm not her father.' He was staring at her intently.

Emilia thought and considered. 'Is she Selina's child? From the times I've seen them together, they obviously share a very close bond.'

'Yes, she is.'

'Well, it made sense for you to take on Libby as yours, it gives her stability and it protects Selina's reputation, although the way she behaves she's seriously risking it.'

'Selina's always been reckless. She's nearly brought us down more than once. But we've always been close and I owe her a lot. It was Selina who nursed me back to health, and she's determined to stay with me and Libby even though it rather stifles her. And, ironically, it was her promiscuity that brought us to Ford House, and you into my life, darling Em. I've never been in love before and once I'd settled into my new life with Libby, I didn't ever expect to be. But now I am in love. It happened when I first saw you. That sweet, sweet moment of time. I love you so much, Em, so completely, so desperately.'

She ran a finger along the length of the full wide mouth she had been kissing so ardently. 'I should take you back right now. Demand you and Selina give notice on the house.'

'Yes, you should.' He brought his fingers up to her lips, traced their soft outline. 'Will you?'

'No. Nothing could happen to change how I feel about you, darling, Perry.' She was in deep with him, too deep for anything to change that.

There were more kisses, lots of loving kisses. Smothering and giving, and hoping and longing. They fell into another world. Their world and theirs alone.

'Love me, Em. Love with me.' He had regained his strength, was using it tenderly, breeding sensations in her that were indescribably fine, devastating to the beginnings of her being. She was lost to everything except him.

With desire rising in her veins she responded with kisses of fiery devotion, crooning in bliss when his fine hands tenderly began to explore her. Gentle fingers, gentle thumbs. He was searching her, reaching her and carrying her with him.

She felt herself growing inside for him. Sighed against his mouth. And he knew it was time. He arranged her and entered her and held her against him. Taking possession of her depths while she moulded herself around him, to begin a perfect partnership in the exquisite motions of love. In total loving union, in a world filled with new and wonderful things they were lost in moments unfathomable and intense and complete, lost in each other on a golden mystical journey so huge and deep was the pleasure. Until at last, she felt the wondrous sweet release, and then he was crying out too. Both shuddering, both sighing. Ever so gently, they sighed together.

And then they were still, in peace, looking into each other's love-burned faces. Smiling, smiling, smiling. How could a man own such a tender divine smile? She let her head fall dreamily against his neck, kissing him there, and he kissed her hair, softly. He placed little tender touches of love on her with his mouth. And they stayed and they held on. And lived and loved again through more precious stolen moments.

Twenty-Two

A loud humming and brumming, interspersed with whooshes and rat-a-tat-tats and finally a high-pitched wailing, reached Brooke and Vera Rose at the top of Tremore valley, where they were laying out the picnic.

From the shade of a solitary beech tree, Brooke looked all the way down to the ancient Tremore manor house ruins and saw Jonny running with his arms extended, dipping and rolling in the manner of an aeroplane. He climbed up on top a chunk of manor wall, then dived off, shouting, 'Mayday, Mayday!' A war hero going down in glory, but not until after he'd shot down the legendary Bosch ace-pilot Baron Richthofen.

'Goodness, what imagination the boy's got and so much energy. I hope my baby turns out the same.' Brooke's gaze shot round to Vera Rose, who was kneeling on the tartan rug, setting out the inedible things from a large wicker hamper. 'Please don't say anything to Emilia. We're waiting for the right moment to tell her.'

'Congratulations,' Vera Rose said, her young eyes gleefully alight from learning a 'grown-up' secret. She liked Brooke a lot because she treated her as a grown-up: she didn't have to use the honorary title of aunt when addressing her. 'I promise I won't tell. Actually, it's good to see Jonny back to being noisy and daring again. He was so quiet for a while, Aunty Em was worried he was sickening for something. You can go ahead and tell her your good news, you know. She'll be delighted for you, Brooke.'

'Thanks for the advice. I'll talk to Ben about it.' Brooke could almost hear the excited new note that would be in

Vera Rose's vigorous voice when she learned her mother was pregnant too.

Vera Rose loved to impart the adult sayings she had heard. 'It's news that can't be kept a secret for ever. Aunty Em will be fine about it, honestly. Mrs Rowse was only saying the other day to Tilda that she's quite well and content now.' She also had a morsel of her own insight to pass on. 'Isn't Eliza a dark one? She thinks Mr Bosweld's got the looks of a film star and that she'd set her cap for him, only she isn't the type, of course, he'd be likely to take a fancy to. Eliza says he doesn't seem to be looking for anyone and that perhaps his wife was the great love of his life.'

'Yes, perhaps she was.' Deep in thought, Brooke took several steps away from the picnic rug. 'I'll call the others before the insects start to gather round the food.'

The response to Brooke's shout was immediate. Jonny believed in feeding his troops and he had a whole garrison, it seemed, under his command today, made up of Will, Tom, Libby, and eight boys and girls from the village. Also tearing up the thistle-strewn hill were Casper, Bertie and Hope from Ford Farm and a border collie from Tremore.

'Right, you lot,' he yelled in military tones, foot up on the hamper. 'Sit in an orderly circle. Let the little ones eat first. After this we'll have a sing-song. And then us bigger ones are going to eat a prickly roll. You too, Vee.'

'If I must,' Vera Rose replied with resigned patience over his euphemism and his intention, reconciled to the fact she would have to roll down the valley over the thistles and afterwards display the scratches to prove she didn't cheat. She distributed the plates and the ham and pickle sandwiches, the hunks of cheese, the apples and fruit cake to the ring of grasping raised hands with the care and devotion that spoke of her maternal side.

Brooke poured the lemonade – the children having to take turns with the cups – and water for the dogs, and all the while her mind was on Perry Bosweld. And Emilia.

Brooke had noticed how broodingly peaceful Emilia was after being in his company. For a while, she was like a stranger, oblivious, as if she had redefined her position. Could it be Emilia was falling in love with him? No, she didn't want to dwell on that notion. Perry was simply a good friend to Emilia, someone who was part of her grief, who understood it. But Emilia was vulnerable because of her grief and perhaps all the more appealing to the man she had a soul-rending connection with.

Brooke recalled the meeting in Mrs Frayne's front room. She saw a good-natured, stunning-looking man, radiating kindness, a willingness to serve the community, but more so, she saw his smiling eyes settle repeatedly on Emilia, the eagerness to hang on to her every word. She saw his vibrancy of being with Emilia afterwards at Tremore Farmhouse, how light and vital she was at him being there.

Brooke had taken Libby and Casper for a walk round the farmyard and on their return to the parlour, Perry and Emilia had been at the piano, he preparing to play, she standing at his side, very close, her hand near his shoulder, he bringing his hand down from his brow. Brooke saw now that Perry had been bringing his hand down off Emilia's.

She had been blind to their attachment, their empathy, and tender warmth. A ghastly chill clenched at her innards. If her belief was right Emilia's closeness to Perry could rock the entire Harvey family. It could wreck the lives of everyone at Ford Farm. Send shock waves through the village. She hated this: Ben had asked her immediately before their wedding never to keep secrets from him. But what if she was wrong? As a newcomer, not knowing Emilia particularly well, hardly knowing Perry at all, she wasn't absolutely sure of there being something inappropriate between them. If Ben felt he should talk to Emilia it might lead to unnecessary distress, and she, herself, might be seen as a troublemaker and it might lead to another estrangement between those at Tremore and Ford Farm. Brooke was in an impossible position. Risking recriminations if she spoke to Ben or not.

She massaged her ribs to help her to breathe, to regain some calm. She had never had a foolish tongue. It made best sense to keep her fears to herself. She would avoid being in the company of Emilia and Perry together, and then no one need ever know she had suspected anything. Then there would be no risk to her happy marriage.

'Is something the matter, Brooke?' Vera Rose was offering her a sandwich, her frank fairness darkened by a deep frown.

'What? Oh, no, Vera, of course not.' Brooke forced a bright smile. 'I was just wondering if we've got enough supplies to satisfy this hungry lot.'

'So, Ben, my son, you're now a married man. How're you finding it?'

'Never been happier, Dougie.' Ben produced a photograph, a particularly good study of Brooke smiling naturally, taken by Alec on the beach below Roskerne, and he passed it to the man across the casually untidy desk.

'Mmmm. Mmmm. She's a corker. You've done all right there.'

Dougie Blend handed the photograph back and Ben carefully returned it to his wallet. He leaned back in the chair opposite his business associate, business not involved in Tremore's concerns, some of which was conducted unknown to Customs and Excise when ships unloaded certain cargo on Truro's wharves. He always felt comfortable in this office, in St Mary's Street, Truro, where the typist in the next room could be heard merrily tapping out correspondence and the clerk-cum-tea boy could be heard singing as he lit the gas under the kettle. In the legitimate field, Dougie Blend was a fine wines' merchant and he sold the highest quality ladies' hats, gloves and lingerie from a string of shops throughout West Cornwall. Ben had shares in the wine venture. 'I'm going to be a father. Keep it to yourself, will you, please? Alec doesn't know yet. We'd like to give him and Emilia more time to come to terms with their grief.'

Dougie Blend, greasy-lipped, a sagging paunch kept under control by his artful tailor, tossed a fat cigar across to Ben. 'Never understood this need to be buried in the bosom of the family thing. Congrats on the kid, hope it's a son and heir. You'd like that, eh? You're a good boy, Ben. If I were family-minded, I'd have liked a son just like you. Good looking, intelligent, smart, not afraid to take a risk. Discreet. I take it the little woman doesn't know about our other bit of business? Good, good. Time you brought her along to Eugenie's. Eugenie was only saying the other night she hasn't seen you in ages. Well, I said, neither have I. He's too tied up in his little love nest,' Dougie hee-hawed. 'Yank, your little missus, isn't she? Any interesting contacts to be made over and above her dear little head?'

'Not at all.' Ben trimmed and lit his cigar, then leaned across the desk with his lighter for Dougie to light up.

'Shame, shame.'

'I liked France when I was over there. I'm planning to take Brooke to Paris someday soon. I could take a look around then. Wines, in particular, should be interesting.'

'Excellent. Good boy. Never rest on your backside when there's money to be made, that's what I say. When's your garage and petrol station to be opened?'

'Should be finished by the end of September. I'm looking to reap a good harvest this year and to put another one into operation.'

'Well done! Hope you're planning a tremendously huge party to celebrate. Just a thought, my son, your little Brooke's not likely to go poking about in the hiding place we have on your property, is she?' Dougie puffed on his cigar like one satiated with pleasure but one eye was sharp, snappy, no-nonsense.

'I've told her it houses the chemicals for sheep dipping, that I keep the outhouse padlocked in case my nephews or my foreman's imbecile brother wanders in there.'

'Good for you. You must take home my latest range in luxury sheer stockings for her, my son. You'll enjoy them as much as her, I guarantee.' Dougie grinned. Ben knew what was on his mind. 'How much does she have you under her thumb?'

'I'm in love, Dougie.' Ben smiled sweetly. Life with Brooke was sweet. There wasn't a room in Tremore House, a barn or a shed, except for the padlocked one, or a field of his they hadn't made love in. They had made love in the small woods on his land, the ruins of the old manor house had recently borne witness to a sudden, loving, thrusting, jubilant coupling of theirs. And how Brooke loved, how joyful and unrestrained she was. They must have tried everything there was to try by now. Ben smiled again, secretly. He didn't want to stray, and he didn't have the energy to anyway.

'Good for you, my son. Envy you: never known that. On the other hand, what a shame. I had an afternoon of fun and games lined up for you and I and two others. Oh, never mind.' Dougie laughed, coughed on cigar smoke, spluttered, laughed again and jangled with himself below desk level. 'Poor old me, got no choice but to play jollities with the both of 'em, all on me own.'

Twenty-Three

Alec arrived home from the cattle market and came across Sara sitting on the back kitchen doorstep, shelling a large bowl of peas into a colander for the evening meal. He smiled down on her, 'Don't get up, there's plenty of room to get past you. Everything seems quiet. Has Emilia not come back from the churchyard yet?'

'No, she hasn't.' To protect her flawless complexion she was wearing a wide-brimmed sunhat. She stared up at the masterful figure before her – even though the sun was stabbing directly into her eyes; she tried not to squint. 'The children won't be back for ages either. Tilda and Mrs Rowse are down in the village, at the Sewing Guild.'

'And you're alone, Sara?'

'Yes, Alec.' She gazed up at him in the hope, the faint hope, burning hope, silly hope but she could not help herself, that he would suggest something wonderful, anything that would be a way for them to spend time alone together. Mucking out the cowhouse would do.

He frowned. 'Have you been left to do all the work?'

'Well, no. I've just got to finish off this and feed the hens. Mrs Em is going to do the dairy work for the evening milking.'

'Yes, I know. You be sure to take off all the time you're owed. I don't want to see you turning into a drudge. Is Jim behaving himself today?'

'He's with Mr Rowse. He's a bit moody but otherwise he's staying in line.'

'Good. I'm off out again in a minute. To take a few more photographs. Bye, Sara.'

'Bye, Alec.'

She heard him going out the front door, so she did not have the pleasure of him squeezing back past her. *He'll never notice me*, she thought, sighing, puffing despondence. *It was hopeless, a waste of time*, she thought, chin down to her chest, *having my hair cut short and shingled like the movie stars. He might have agreed with all the others that it looked lovely, made me look more grown up, but . . .* but nothing. She had no right to her hopes, her fantasies. Alec was married to Mrs Em, who was as kind as he was, kind enough to have given her a whole day off to make her transformation, to buy new clothes. And Alec and Mrs Em loved each other, were proud to show their love in open affection.

She swept up the colander of peas and dumped it down on the draining board, set aside the pods to be boiled later for the swill bucket, then marched off to feed the hens and the rest of the poultry, collected the second laying of eggs, washed the eggs quickly in the washhouse, then – what she was longing to do – made to stamp up to her room, her divided-off little bit of space. Where she would throw herself on the bed and weep until suppertime. She wanted to scream in frustration.

It was all very well for others to say it was time she thought of getting herself a young man. There were few young men anywhere, thanks to the war, but it didn't stop insensitive rotten people from pointing out all the male interest she regularly received, and no wonder, they said, because you're so lovely. You'd make a good farmer's wife, they said, and even Mrs Em had got excited the other day when Wally Eathorne, the heir of nearby Druzel Farm, had turned up unexpectedly to talk to Alec about black spot on cattle. 'His ruse,' Mrs Em had said, 'to show an interest in you, Sara.' Wally Eathorne wasn't bad looking, he was the same age as herself, and polite and hard working, and, everybody had stressed, owned a wonderful tenor voice, so he had something in common with her, and Farmer and Mrs Eathorne obviously approved of her son's intention; Mrs Eathorne had hinted that Sara would be welcome if she ever felt like 'popping over for tea'. Wally Eathorne would make a good catch for her, coming as she did from the humblest of backgrounds, but she didn't want anything to do with him or any other of the hopeful suitors. Her hope lay in a different direction, one she shouldn't be looking in. Only Jim seemed happy for her to stay resolutely single. 'We only need each other,' he said, and he said it nearly every day, not looking at another girl since he'd been thrown over – Sara knew who by now.

Instead of dashing up the back stairs, she went, as she knew she would, straight to the den, the place where Alec would have gone to fetch his photographic apparatus. She often did this. To be where he had been. To touch his things. Feel his presence. The job she enjoyed most was washing his clothes, when she could hold a shirt of his up to her nose and make the divine smell of him cause those secret wonderful, intense, shivery sensations to rise and spread throughout her body. And she enjoyed making his bed or changing the linen, when she imagined it was she who laid her head on the next pillow and was the one who gave all of herself to him. After this visit to the den she'd lie on her bed and close her eyes and imagine him making love to her. She could at least indulge herself to some moments of forbidden pleasure. Before the tears came again.

In the den her heart leapt. Alec's silver cigarette case and lighter were sitting on the desk. He had forgotten them.

An old saying went through her head. *Faint heart never won fair lady.* She reversed it. *Faint heart never won the fine-looking man you desire more than anything in the world.* She would put on the most stylish of her new dresses (bought from his generosity) and take his cigarettes and lighter to him. He would probably be in Long Meadow, but she would find him if it meant searching all afternoon and getting back late, and she would win him for herself. She would. She'd have a damned good try.

Carrying his possessions as if they were made of brittle priceless china, yet with a vigilant grip, she kept to the lanes to keep her low-heeled shoes in best order. When she arrived at the granite stile that led into the field, which in turn led into the meadow, she climbed over it cautiously, fearful for her dropped-waisted dress. The haymaking had left the ground rough and earthy and golden stalked, but she kept close to the hedge, and where there was a break in the wild growth of brambles and a handful of long grasses to be found, she ripped some off and wiped over the soft blue leather of her shoes. The field sloped gently upwards and at the top, in a long meandering hedge, there was another high stile to climb over. This one was of massive, oddly angled granite blocks and was almost swamped by blackthorn shrubs and she was sweating a little when she finally landed safely on firm ground.

The meadow stretched on and on either side of her, and down at the bottom was the stream emerging from the woods. It was a long descent, a bit hazardous in her heels for it was made up of wide ridges at the top and littered with dried sheep droppings all the way down but it would be worth it. Alec was there by the stream, near the entrance to the woods. His back was towards her and he was repositioning the camera and tripod.

The collywobbles were playing havoc inside her tummy now, but no matter. She must concentrate on getting down there to him and arrive with decorum. Looking confident, nonchalant. It wasn't as if he'd mind, she was certain of that. She was doing him a kindness and he was too kind to mind anyway.

She was over halfway down when he turned round and was looking up the meadow. Her heart thudded to a halt and she stopped her sideways downward steps, fearing for her balance.

'Sara!' he called and waved to her.

She waved back, sure her face was on fire, but continued on down. He began the journey up to her, and her heart and spirit and soul lifted and flew higher and higher for he was smiling, pleased to see her. On his long legs he reached her quickly.

'Oh, you are a dear. How sweet of you.' He motioned towards the silver things clutched in her hands. 'I'd reached here before realizing I'd left them behind. I'll be glad to have a cigarette before I leave.'

'I didn't want you having to come back early.' Sara felt she was slowly sinking inside with nervousness but she kept her eyes fixed on him. He was standing just below her, his height putting their faces on the same level, the sleeves of his shirt rolled up and the buttons unfastened at the top, exposing his magnificent muscles and slightly hairy chest.

'You're kind to give up part of your afternoon for my sake. You're all dressed up, looking lovely. Are you on your way somewhere?' A moment passed in which he was thinking. 'Has Wally Eathorne asked you to meet him?'

'No! I mean no, he hasn't. I'm not . . . I just wanted to . . . to . . .'

'To take the opportunity to look your best. And why not? You get little chance to. I'm sorry you had such a long tramp in your lovely things to reach me. Now you're here, why not let me capture you for posterity? You'll look perfect against this natural background.'

'Yes, I'd love to!'

'A stunning portrait of you will make a pleasant surprise for Jim.'

'Yes, it would. Thank you.' And perhaps Alec would enjoy looking at the picture he took of her.

'Good. Now let me see.' He stared all around. 'Down there by the tree on the bank. Yes, we'll make a start down there.'

It was easier to walk now the worry of keeping his cigarette case and lighter safe had been taken away from her, and now his hand was in under her elbow to steady her descent. Sara thought she knew what it felt like to be in paradise.

She let him take over completely. To position her, with her hat off, against the trunk of an oak tree, to suggest she let her arms drift backwards and tilt them downwards and to turn her face to the side. 'That's it, you look mystical, innocent but with just a hint of being a siren.' She thrilled to that description. He photographed her from three different angles. Then he asked her to put her hat back on and lower herself down on the bank of the stream. He chose a demure pose, asking her to tuck her legs to the side and smile straight into the camera. 'That's it. That was beautiful. Jim will love that smile. I'll give you a copy of all of them to put in your room.'

'Thanks Alec,' she said shyly, although not as shyly as she might have done. What now? She prayed he wouldn't send her home.

'Would you like some ginger beer? I grabbed a bottle on my way through the kitchen just now.'

'Yes, please.'

He fetched the bottle from out of the stream where it had been keeping cool, under the shade thrown out by the tree. He opened the balled mechanism on the top. Offered her the full bottle; it was of Tilda's making, a favourite in the household. 'Sorry I can't conjure up a glass.'

She drank some of the sweet, strong-tasting liquid carefully so as not to spill a drop and look like a child. 'Thank you. It's so hot, my throat was getting dry.' She thought that sounded fine and conversational as she handed the bottle over to him, where he had dropped down, not too far away from her. She watched as he gulped down a long pull, then wiped the heel of his hand across his mouth, in an unconscious masculine, but not disgusting, way. She gazed at his mouth.

'I can't get enough of this stuff,' he said, closing the top of the bottle, then letting it fall gently to the sun-baked ground. He lit a cigarette. 'Tilda's been at the farm, what? About five years, I employed her just before I hired you and Jim. I couldn't imagine life without her or you there.'

'Well, I'm not planning on ever going anywhere else.'

'Good, I'd hate that. I hate things changing. That makes me selfish, doesn't it? I suppose I will have to let you go one day when you get married.'

'I shan't get married.'

'Of course you will. Everyone gets married, almost everyone.'

'Selina Bosweld doesn't seem to want to get married. I loathe her for what she did to Jim.'

'Ah, so you know it was her Jim was seeing.'

'I overheard you and Jim talking about it in the den after

the last occasion you told him off. Jim was cross when I mentioned her, he said it wasn't a subject for my ears. I think I should have been told, I'm not a baby. I wish she'd stop coming to the farm.'

'I don't like her either, Sara. And Jonny's set against her, he keeps wishing she would leave Ford House. I'm afraid it would be difficult to tell her to keep away, she and Perry are my tenants. Sometimes I hate that house, it's brought a lot of unhappiness since my father built it.'

'Why don't you sell it?'

'If the Boswelds suddenly decide to leave I might very well do that.' He smiled, his eyes glinting mischievous fun. 'We might get an axe murderer in there next.'

Sara laughed and laughed. 'Can I have one of those?' She nodded at his cigarette, which he had forgotten to smoke.

'I'm going to say no to that. Some advise against it and you're too perfect to be spoiled in any way.'

She smiled, rapt at how he considered her.

'You chose well.' He was gazing at her closely. 'The clothes you bought, if I may say so.'

Delighted to the roots of her being that he should notice this and comment on something so personal, she lifted the scalloped hemline of her dress between finger and thumb. 'I bought this in Webb's, and this –' her hand went up to her hat, and his eyes followed the movement – 'in the West End Stores, after I'd had my hair done, so I must have looked older because the assistants in the shops called me madam. I'd never been called madam before. They even carried my parcels to the door. It made me feel very grand.'

He took a puff, then tossed the cigarette into the clear chuckling water. Returned his intense grey gaze straight back to her. 'You're not at all grand, Sara.'

'I'm not?'

'Oh, don't be dejected. What I'm trying to say is you're simply natural and lovely. Grand describes someone with affected airs or someone older.'

Sara had dropped her eyes but now when she looked at

him they were shining with delight. With adoration. 'You say such nice things.'

He smiled at her, very softly, and whispered, 'Precious girl.'

She held her breath. Alec gave those he was close to particular endearments. Had he just made up one for her?

'I must get back. Will you walk with me or stay?'

'I'll come with you.'

He helped her up, gathered together his camera gear and the bottle of ginger beer. They didn't speak on the way up to the top of the meadow, just climbed up in an easy quietness. At the stile, he said, 'I'll go over first then help you down.'

On the other side of the mismatched granite stones, he put the things he was carrying safely against the hedge then held up his hands to her. Sara paused at the top of the stile, to experience all the more the warm rough feel of his strong fingers. She smiled straight into his eyes and he smiled back. When she took the last step down the hem of her dress caught on a branch of wicked blackthorn and the fine material tore.

'Oh, no!' She felt she had been slapped back into line somehow and it was all too much for her hopes and emotions that had been so tossed about this afternoon, and she burst into tears.

Suddenly Alec had her in his arms and was rubbing her back and smoothing at her hair and caressing her face. 'Don't cry, Sara. Don't be upset, precious girl. I'll buy you another dress. I'll buy you another ten. I'll give you anything you want.'

Moments passed, then he let her go, and she searched for her hanky tucked away in one short sleeve and dried her eyes. 'I'm sorry. You must think I'm a baby.'

He watched a tiny trickle of perspiration run down the creamy hollow of her throat. 'Not that,' his voice came out in a soft husky tone. From the moment he had stationed her against the tree he had been trying not to think about how much he was enjoying her company. Trying not to notice just how stunningly beautiful she was. How precious. How luscious.

Despite her lack of experience with men, Sara noticed the subtle shift in his expression, and she gloried in the fact that he wasn't running from whatever he might be feeling for her now. 'Thanks for taking the photos of me, Alec.'

'You're welcome, Sara. Thanks for a wonderful afternoon.'

Twenty-Four

Emilia, Dolly, Sara and Tilda were taking a pause from their work to listen to *Woman's Hour* on the wireless.

Emilia had her eyes closed, and with Tom snuggled up on her lap she was enjoying a blissful state of motherly devotion. Soothing him, soothing her. Spreading her fingertips through his soft reddish-brown hair. Stroking his smooth warm cheek, his small strong nose, his cosy little chin, delightful ears. How she loved her child, and wished Will had not grown so quickly out of wanting this kind of attention. While the other women listened to a talk about flower arranging, and the other children got down to Scrabble in the playroom next door, Jonny helping Will with the spelling, she just drifted. Dreamy. Content. Satisfied.

It was raining hard, the wind throwing heavy probing drops of water against the windows and shifting the older timbers of the house in lazy creaks and groans. A sudden exclamation from Vera Rose made her smile. 'Oh, Jonny that's not fair! I won't have it. *Rejouir* is a French word. You're not allowed foreign words in this game.' The next noises were indistinct but it was easy to gather that Jonny had scoffed at her and Vera Rose had threatened not to play, and Jonny, while capitulating to her demands, had scoffed at her again.

Thinking about French words made Emilia think about the French housekeeper employed by a certain wonderful, outrageously good-looking man who lived close by. She smiled and from her depths came the sort of sigh that he alone could wring from her. She didn't realize she had stopped petting Tom until he pushed on her hand to continue. She kissed his tender crown and started the threading of his hair again. Her dear, darling Tom, her baby again, he having almost forgotten there had been a Jenna.

She stayed with the sweetly sad memories of Jenna for a while, then inevitably they brought her back to Perry. He was always there inside her mind. His love for her and hers for him was written on her heart, the loving stamp of his body within her body. How in tune his gentle nature was with her more lively one. Although aching to be alone again they were being careful not to hold any more meetings alone yet. They had agreed never to pass lingering looks, or secret touches, or hidden messages. Soon, they were to meet in Reggie Rule's house on the outskirts of Truro, take advantage of the trip Reggie was to make up to London to study some new scientific advance, he believing Perry would be there alone looking through his medical books.

She was pleased to be this wise. There was something different in the way Brooke looked at her now, as if she was watching her. She may have noticed the connection between her and Perry. And the last thing Emilia wanted was to hurt anyone, specially Alec. Her love for him had in no way lessened. She had formed a way of putting her feelings for him and Perry into two separate compartments. She knew the terrible risk she was taking. She knew how unforgiving Alec could be when he was hurt, and that he might even become vengeful. But she couldn't give Perry up. She couldn't!

Recalling the mere touch of his hand brought a blissful smile to her lips. Anticipating making love with him again made her sink into an idyll of time and space. 'Em. My Em,' he had said, in such a special all-possessing way when they had travelled back from the little secret place on the moor.

'Em. Em! Wake up.' Her mother was shaking her knee. 'Someone's coming in by the front door.'

Perry! She came to without reluctance because it might be Perry, braving the downpour, bringing Libby to play, just so he could lounge in her kitchen with a bunch of nattering women, just to be where she was for a while. Like Dolly, Sara and Tilda, she stared expectantly at the door.

There was a polite tap, but it was Selina Bosweld who came in, dripping in her nurse's cape, her shoes and lower legs splattered with mud. 'Hello. Didn't expect the weather to turn so awful so suddenly. Gosh, you all look cosy in here. Practically half asleep.'

'We were.' Dolly deliberately made it sound like an accusation of them being disturbed. Nevertheless, as the one who presided over the teapot she motioned to Sara to fetch another cup from the dresser. Sara did so, ungraciously. Hating Jim's cruel seducer, wishing her all manner of ills.

Tilda, who had an unbreakable sense of servitude was already relieving Selina of her cape. Selina took the seat nearest to Emilia, then pulled off her soaking nurse's cap. She joined in with the pampering of Tom, who was now sleeping. 'Dear little fellow. He's so much more like you, Em, than Alec.'

Emilia wasn't sure if she liked Selina calling her Em. Aware of Selina's shifts she was puzzled. 'You're back early, aren't you?'

Selina's beautiful eyes grew astonishingly large and bright. 'It was my last actually. I've resigned. I intend to take the plunge.'

'What? You mean you're getting married?' It was so unusual for Sara to speak in Selina Bosweld's presence, let alone to blurt out a scathing question, and everyone peered at her.

'No, my dear,' Selina replied as coldly as an icy draught, without looking at her. 'To study medicine. I'm going to be a doctor.'

'You're really going through with it?' Emilia said. This was wonderful! To be rid of Selina and the unease she always brought with her, but most of all to be able to see Perry more effortlessly.

'I am indeed.' Selina beamed before sipping the strong stewed brew put in front of her. 'Got any of your delicious ginger fairings, Tilda? I'm ravenous.'

'When are you going?' Dolly interjected. 'There's nowhere local to train for something like that, is there?'

'No, you're absolutely correct, Mrs Rowse. I intend to leave before the end of the year.'

'You must feel sad to have left the Infirmary though?' Emilia said.

'Sort of,' Selina replied in an end-of-discussion tone. 'We'll finally have time to shop and lunch and walk together, Em. And I'll be able to contribute more to my one and only sports day here.'

Jonny suddenly pushed the door open. 'Aunty Em, can we all have some—' He had not expected the caller to be Selina Bosweld. He started to close the door. 'It doesn't matter.'

'I'll take some milk and biscuits into the children,' Dolly said, brisk, pursed-lipped. Normally she refused to wait on anyone capable of collecting something on their own good legs, but it pleased her the way Jonny showed his contempt at the Bosweld woman being here.

Selina pretended not to notice Dolly's disapproval. Emilia knew Selina didn't care about it anyway. Selina glanced at Sara. 'I like the way that girl does her hair now. It's time I had a change. Why don't I make an appointment for us at a hairdresser's in town, Em? We want to look our best when we step out together.'

Tom stirred, woke up and stretched himself out like a lazy kitten on Emilia's lap, then cuddled down into her again.

'Hello, Tommy. How are you, dear fellow?' Selina patted his tousled hair.

He scowled at her. 'I hate being called Tommy!'

'Tom, don't be rude to Miss Bosweld,' Emilia chided him, but she couldn't help being amused. 'Sorry, Selina.'

'Oh, he's only copying his cousin's fighting spirit.' Selina demolished one of the crunchy biscuits and gazed intently at Tom, who rebelliously hardened his scowl. 'Although, I don't expect Jonny is quite as brave as he likes to think he is.'

'You come with Granny, Tom, my handsome,' Dolly said gaily to him, while glaring sternly at Selina. 'Join the others for a little feast.'

Selina pulled at her uniform. 'God, this wet cloth has chafed me all over and my feet are clammy in these wet stockings. I know I've only got to whizz on down the lane but could you lend me something dry to wear, Em, my dear?'

'I'll see what I can find,' Emilia said doubtfully. 'You'd better come with me.'

'Any old thing will do.' Selina started undressing the instant they reached the master bedroom, dropping her clothes on the floor. 'Gosh, you have such pretty things in here, Em, darling. The room is immaculate.'

'Sara keeps it like this. She spends ages in here every day.' Emilia opened her wardrobe, chose an ordinary white linen blouse and a loose-fitting skirt for Selina.

'Well, that's hardly surprising,' Selina said in a voice that purred.

'What do you mean?' Emilia swung round and blinked, taken aback to see Selina standing, waiting, quite close to her, in just a pair of oyster-coloured silk French knickers. Her armpits had indeed been chafed by her wet clothes, but there were also livid red marks on both her large hanging breasts. So she had another lover, one who was, at least, a little rough with her. Something, Emilia guessed, Selina liked, probably demanded.

'Thank you, darling.' Selina took the skirt and climbed into it, fastening the pretty glass buttons at the waist. 'What I meant about Sara was that before her years in the workhouse she lived with her impoverished widowed mother, didn't she? She must have had nothing, poor little thing.' Selina homed in on the masculine side of the room. 'Everything she longs for must be found in here. Can you spare a spray of perfume?'

'Help yourself.'

'Gosh, look at all these bottles. Alec does love to spoil you.' Emilia watched, with a troubled yet compelling fascination, as Selina sat, bare-breasted at her dressing table, fingering and sniffing at her perfume bottles. Selina rolled a tall tapering blue crystal bottle between her palms. '*Parfait Amour.* Perry bought me some perfume when we were in France. I haven't come across this one before. Do you think there's such a thing as perfect love, darling?'

Emilia wasn't going to play any silly game with Selina. 'Probably not.'

Selina laughed, long and deep, like a man. 'Oh, don't be cross with me. I'm bored. I've been bored for so long now. I amuse myself with a little psychology.'

'That's not what you do, Selina. You enjoy baiting people and you don't care if you make them suffer.'

Selina pulled out the stopper of the bottle, then dabbed the sensuous perfume on the pulses at her wrists and neck, then inside her cleavage. Smiling at Emilia's stern reflection in the mirror, she replaced the stopper, put the perfume bottle carefully back in its place. 'You know me only too well, darling. I like that. But I'm only a little bit cruel, really I am. And only to people who deserve it. Take Jim for instance. Right from the start I told him there wouldn't be anything permanent between us, but he didn't listen. Thought that because we were having sex he had the right to lay a claim on me. Men can be so stupid.' She glanced at a photograph of Alec up on the tallboy, then looked out of the window that overlooked the back fields and the woods and her own home. 'They rarely see what's right in under their noses. You're the only person I've ever really admired, did you know that, Emilia Harvey? You're so wise and strong and lovely. It's why so many people love you, why so many desire you. Oh, good, the rain's stopped. The sun will break through the clouds any moment. Pass me that blouse please. I must run along home.'

Emilia did as she was bidden, silently, with a horrible crawling feeling in her stomach. Had Selina just been hinting that she knew about her and Perry? She had to respond to Selina's remarks, even though afraid of the rejoinder. 'You do say strange things, Selina. Who is it that you think desire me?'

'Ben for a start.'

'What?'

'Oh, he loves his bride, but I've seen the way he looks at you. I know men, remember? He doesn't quite realize it himself, but he'd give anything to make love to you again –

I take it your first time was with him? And Tristan, he adores you, he'd be easily tempted to take you to bed.'

Emilia couldn't believe this. 'What nonsense!'

After a pause of meaningful silence, something indefinable filtered into Selina's solemnly beautiful eyes. 'And Perry. But we really shouldn't talk about him, should we? It's dangerous. I hope you and he are being sensible. I don't want you having his child, it would complicate all our lives.'

There was no point in Emilia protesting there wasn't something between her and Perry, not to this woman, so worldly wise and astute. 'You needn't concern yourself about that. What sort of danger?' Emilia dropped her voice.

'Emilia, I beg you to be very careful. You must make sure that Alec never finds out, never suspects. He's full of secret passion and dark, dark moods, more so than even you, as close as you are to him, may realize. Never forget how long it took him to come to terms with what Ben did to him. I don't think he'd stop at anything to protect his marriage. If he thought that you, whom he loves so very much, was betraying him, well . . . and what would he do to Perry? I'm sorry, Em, that this isn't what you want to hear. I just thought, as your friend, that I should give you a gentle warning. Can you go on risking everything you have? Can you, darling?'

Climbing aboard her bicycle, the nurse's uniform, no longer of any use to her, stuffed into the basket in front of the handlebars, Selina set off whistling cheerfully, 'Hello! Hello! Who's your lady friend?'

When she reached the exit for the lane, she stayed close to the hedge to allow a taxi-cab to turn in for the farmhouse. Winifred Harvey was the fare in the back. Selina offered her a sunny smile. Then she went triumphantly on her way. Partly triumphantly. For there was also a terrible rage building up inside her.

'Mrs Em!' Tilda called up the stairs. 'Can you come down please? Mrs Tristan Harvey is here.'

Emilia put down the photograph of Alec she was clutching

to her body and pressed out the anguish and guilt in her face. It was the photograph she had noticed that had caught Selina's eye. One she, herself, had taken of him, lounging against a field gate, smiling, smiling so handsomely, taken after he with great patience had shown her how to use the camera. Selina's warning had focussed her mind on Alec and all that he meant to her, and she hadn't had the time yet to think over what her feelings, in the light of this, were about Perry now. 'Just coming!'

'Winnie, this is a lovely surprise,' Emilia said, in the sitting room. 'But are you well? You look all flushed.'

'Hello, Emilia, dear. Tilda's bringing me a glass of water,' Winifred smiled from an armchair, while fanning her burning face. 'Sorry about this.'

'Don't be silly. What is it?'

'Tris and I were in Truro. He's there to see some chap, about some more war memorabilia for his own private collection. We were going to spring a surprise on Vera Rose and Jonny on the way home. They'd said hello to me, by the way, then Tilda felt it best to shoo them out so I could recover. Well, I suddenly came over all hot and bothered and it was too much and Tris suggested I come on ahead. Oh, Emilia, you see, I really have to tell you this now, and don't be upset. Please don't be upset, but well, I'm going to have a baby.'

'Good heavens!' came an unexpected male voice, a voice that made Emilia's heart lurch in self-reproach, but filled her also with warmth and pride, because the voice, as usual, was steeped in understanding, its owner delighted with the news. 'But that's brilliant. Isn't it, Emilia, angel?'

'Yes, Alec, it's wonderful. Congratulations Winnie,' she said. After Alec had squeezed her hand and she had squeezed back on his, he went to kiss Winnie. Then she hugged Winnie, and gently pulled off her hat and gloves and started unwrapping the wreaths of silk scarf around her neck. 'Oh, you are silly. Of course I'm not upset. Alec and I have been sure for ages that Brooke is pregnant too. It's time she and Ben announced it to us. They must be dying to tell the rest of the world. Here's Tilda with the water. Take a sip, you'll soon feel better.'

A short time later, Winnie, a comely pink now, her feet up on an upholstered stool, said, 'When Tris arrives, we'll be able to tell the children. Hope Jonny won't hate the thought of the baby.'

The door had been left open and there was a lot of stifled whispers and giggling coming from the passage. Alec grinned. 'The little blighter's been listening in on us. Come inside, Jonny Harvey and the rest of you.'

Jonny, unusually for him, entered slowly, embarrassed to have been caught eavesdropping. He approached his honorary Aunt Winnie, his stepmother, on uncertain feet. She met his bold dark eyes anxiously. 'Does this mean I'll be an uncle?'

'No, Jonny, an elder brother. And you, Vera Rose, darling will be a big sister. Are you both pleased?'

'Oh, Mummy, I'm ecstatic!' Vera Rose squealed in joy, and ran and swept her long gangly arms round her mother's neck. 'A baby in the house. I can hardly wait.'

Alec nudged Jonny. He was as still as a granite cross. 'Well, old chap, what do you think?'

Jonny put his hands in his shorts pockets, grown-up style. 'I suppose it's all right. Of course I'll be a brother, how did I think otherwise? I never thought I would be, not after my baby sister died with Mummy.' Later, when he was alone with Alec and they were having one of their private pals talks, he confided, 'I wish my little sister had lived even for a few hours. I wish I'd seen her. It hurts me so much that I'll never know what she looked like.'

Alec took his empty mug – Emilia had made fresh tea for him – out to Sara, in the back kitchen, where she was washing up. 'Sorry, hope you don't mind a late one.'

'Not at all.' She took the mug from him. Set it down on the draining board. When he had gone she would lift the mug to her lips, put her mouth where his mouth had been.

He didn't go straightaway. 'Jim seems happier today. He

was even whistling cheerfully a short while ago. Do you think he could have a new girl?'

Sara took pleasure in him being confidentially close to her. And pleasure in smiling up at him. 'Well, he might have. I found him writing something the other night and he went red in the face and quickly covered it up. I joked that it was a love letter. He told me to go away, but he wasn't angry or anything.'

'Well, I'm glad he's more cheerful anyway. When you've finished here come to the den. I've developed the photos I took of you. I'd like you to see them.'

She smiled again, deeper, making it last longer. 'I'll be there in just a minute. Alec.'

He left on speedy steps. The way she now said his name, in a sentence on its own, somehow intimate, somehow possessive, disturbed him, because he liked it. A lot. So did the way she looked at him. And moved past him, always close. Sometimes a little bit too close, not touching him, but he'd feel the shadow of her warm young body. He had been going to give her some money for a new dress, to compensate for the one torn at the stile, but he had changed his mind. Somehow, doing that would have seemed like an intimate gesture. He felt that, for some silly reason, his intention might be misconstrued by Sara, and others. Yet he felt bad about not keeping to his promise to her. He wanted to promise her a lot of things. He tore himself away.

Emilia was on her way to the back kitchen, to put on her outdoor shoes before going to the dairy. He swept a strong insistent arm round her waist, carried her along with him. 'Got a moment, darling angel? There's something I'm longing for you to see.'

Sara choked back her disappointment to find her mistress in the den with Alec. Looking over the photographs of her by the stream in Long Meadow. It wasn't right. Mrs Em had no right. The photographs were *hers*.

'Oh, Sara, I had no idea Alec had taken these. They're lovely.' Emilia held one up to her, of her sitting down. 'Jim will love this one of you. You look so lovely. We'll get it framed for you to give to him. Alec's thinking of entering the others in a competition. They fully deserve a prize, they're about the best thing he's ever done.' Emilia smiled proudly at Alec and stretched up and kissed his face. 'You're so clever.'

Sara looked at each study of herself, taking her time, proud to see the love that she had for the photographer shining out of her whole being. She held up one of those of her lounging on the bank of the stream for ages.

Emilia thought she knew what was on her mind. 'Yes, it's a pity that one is slightly blurred. You must go out with Sara when you've got time, Alec, and take something like it again. You can borrow my silk stole, Sara, if you promise to be careful with it. Look, I really must get on with the goat's cheese. Sara, mind you take your break before supper.' To Alec, 'I'll see you later, darling.' She didn't glance at him before leaving, not with Perry's image once more streaming into her mind, bringing with it the terrible new conflict that Selina's advice had plunged her into.

Alec could only smile briefly at Sara. He had never been at a loss about what to say to a woman before. He mustn't think of Sara as being a woman. She was a girl. Sweet and innocent and vulnerable, but now it seemed she also had beguiling strengths, a combination he was drawn to. He had tried to end the business of these wretched, beautiful, haunting pictures, but now Emilia, of all people, had opened a way for him and Sara to get fully involved with them again, and not secretly this time.

Twenty-Five

Selina threw her bicycle down outside the stable at Ford House. She turned the ponies out into the little paddock and leaned on the fence; keeping still and expressionless, she watched them trot away, tossing their proud heads as if they were investigating the washed-through air. Then ripping her wet uniform from the fallen bicycle, she tore it to shreds.

She entered the house by the kitchen. Mirelle saw the darkness in her, and with it something akin to the look Libby got when hurt or afraid after a bad dream. The old French woman left the bread she was making and invited Selina to come to her by patting her tiny sloping shoulder. Selina came, and leant forward and pressed her face against the bony ridge. Mirelle felt her trembling, her upset, her rage. Then Selina mouthed slowly, so she could lip read, 'I'll tell you later, *cherie*.'

Libby had been taking a geography lesson with her father. A relaxed affair, with her sitting on his lap on the settee while looking through a book on the British Empire, and he had told her how India had become Queen Victoria's 'jewel in the crown'. Libby had thought the Queen, large and imposing in her wide black clothes, ugly, awesome and fascinating, putting her on par with Florence Nightingale, Grace Darling and Lady Astor, the first woman member of parliament to take her seat in the House of Commons, whom her Aunt Selina had told her about. 'They were women who strove for higher things, who got things done, who were an example to the rest of us,' Aunt Selina had said, and they were great and sensational in Libby's young mind, these hard-working adventuresses, whom her aunt thoroughly approved of, and her aunt approved of few women.

Perry closed the book. 'That's enough for one day, darling. The sun's come out to play. Why not put your old shoes on and take Casper out to run about the garden?'

Automatically they hugged, then Libby slipped down to the floor. 'If I have a daughter when I grow up, Daddy, I'll call her Victoria.'

'Not Florence? Not Grace? Not Nancy?' he laughed.

Libby thought for a moment. 'I might choose Emilia. Aunt Selina likes her a lot. She's nice, isn't she, Daddy?'

'I think she's very nice, Libby,' Perry smiled. When alone he'd indulge in his memories of Emilia, *his Em*, every memory pleasant, wonderful, unique, precious.

But Selina crept in and sat down close to him, and curled her bare feet up in under her, and roped her arms round his body and leaned her head against his neck. He knew her every mood; all being in the extreme. This time, however, something had distressed her on an unprecedented level. He could feel the violent buzz of the wrath barely contained inside her. She could so easily explode into bad temper of terrible proportions, but she also needed his care and reassurance and he gladly gave it to her. Enfolding her in his arms, lending her his strength.

He let long moments pass. Wondering why she was wearing Emilia's clothes. He put his nose to the blouse and could smell the sweet, divine essence of Emilia there. Selina must have got soaked to the skin on the way home. But why go to the farm first?

Mirelle came in silently with a tray of coffee. Perry thanked her soundlessly. The maid caressed Selina's unruly hair and withdrew. Perry waited another minute, then said, 'Want some?'

She shook her head.

'Can you tell me what's happened?' He employed his voice as softly as when comforting Libby.

She clung to him a little bit more. 'They threw me out.'

'Who? Surely not—?'

'Yes, the hospital authorities, blast them!' It was as if some malevolent spirit was only just being checked inside her. Perry held her tighter, hoping he could forestall an outburst. 'Someone informed Murray Sadler's wife of our affair and she turned up at the office and caused a scene! She said she suspected there was something going on between us for some time, but now she'd got the proof. They promised the wretched bitch they would sort things out entirely to her satisfaction. The words were put very carefully to me, of course. They couldn't risk a scandal. I was offered a sum of money as compensation to resign quietly and immediately. A generous sum, actually. I got the impression most of the money's coming out of Murray's pocket. He's staying on, of course. It's not fair!' She clamped Perry's neck until it hurt, then suddenly she flung her arms high in the air, then she beat on a cushion.

'I'm sorry, but in the circumstances, Selina, well, don't you think you've come out of it, pretty well? Sadler's usually a skinflint. It'll hurt him where he'll hate it most, and that wife of his – I know of Mavis Sadler – she'll make his life a misery.'

Selina's eyes were blazing. 'Don't you see what this looks like? That without news of the affair getting out it will be thought I was bustled out because of incompetence or something. I saw Murray later in the corridor. He walked past me as if I didn't exist. And while I was packing up my things, one of those sanctimonious wretches had the nerve to come to my office, and he said he knew there were others on the premises who'd had the pleasure of me. Junior doctors and porters, and another important member of staff. Lying swine! It was exaggeration. He propositioned me, Perry. He said our needs were the same. And he asked me to meet him in some poky lodging room that he keeps just for that purpose. I told him to go to hell! Hypocrite! They're all bloody hypocrites and I hate them! I hate them to death!' She hurled the cushion against the mantelpiece. A china ornament of a fairy, bought for Libby's fourth birthday, fell off and broke into several pieces.

Perry puffed in irritation. 'Selina, try to calm down.'

'God, I hate this world! It's a playground for men, where you get to make all the decisions and get off scot free for your indiscretions. I wish I knew who it was who caused this trouble for me. I'd rip them to pieces.' Suddenly she went limp and leaned against her brother again. 'Those wretches.' She muttered those same two words, with hate and hurt for some time.

Perry no longer wanted to give her comfort. Wanted instead to say a great many things to her. That she deserved her 'roundabout' dismissal. That he'd be furious if this brought embarrassment to their door. Then he thought of her being at home all the time. It would make it harder for him to see Emilia alone. Selina had latched on to Em, wanting her as a bosom friend. It would be close to impossible to be with Em in the way he ached for.

'Try to think on the bright side, Selina. You're free to start a new life now you've got a good sum of money of your own. Think about what you'd like to do.' Please God, make it something that would put her at a distance for several hours every day.

'Yes, that's true, but I know already what I want to do. I'm going to get even in a way that'll please me most. The medical profession needs more women in it, to break the stranglehold of pompous men, many with antiquated ideas and no ambition for progress in medicine. I'm going to train as a doctor. You've got contacts, Perry. With your recommendation, I could easily get into one of the best colleges, couldn't I?'

Selina leaving here for good and all the benefits it would bring was a thrilling prospect. 'I'll write to one of my old professors tonight. I think I know the very one who would be sympathetic towards your aims, Selina.'

'You do that, you darling.' Selina's agitation was decreasing. 'I'm in no particular hurry to leave here. I want to spend some time relaxing and lots of time with Libby. Pour the coffee, will you, before it gets cold.'

Perry did so and when he passed a cup to Selina he felt the

throbbing emotion still there in her hand. It would take hours, perhaps days, before her upset and anger fully dissipated.

She drank the coffee down, helped herself to a second cup. Eyed Perry in the direct way that put him on his guard. What now? He realized then just how little his sister could be trusted and what a trouble she was to him, a drain on his peace of mind. 'This will be the first time in ages I've been without a lover. As for you, Perry, I'm glad she provides you with all that you need . . . Emilia.'

In one terrible second all the colour drained from his face. From the way Selina had mouthed her last sentences there was no point in him denying he loved Emilia or how far their love had gone.

Selina stroked his cold stricken face. 'Don't worry. I won't make it hard for you to meet her. In fact, with me about more to be with Libby it will make it easier for you both. I'll cover for you. Em can say she's meeting me when in fact she'll be meeting you. We've both got a fresh start, Perry. Come on, smile. I promise I'll make things work out for us. I'll go up now and change, then take Libby and Casper for a long walk. It will be wonderful being a proper family for a while. Won't it?'

'Yes, Selina,' Perry gave the answer she wanted to hear. There was no hope of them ever being a proper family. She must have confronted Emilia too, it was why she had gone to the farm. He should have denied it, but that would have made Selina angry. In her current state of emotion he must use all his wits to avoid that or Selina might do something rash, or even deliberately cruel, to make both him and Emilia suffer.

While Selina and Libby went laughingly off with the puppy, he was left alone with his fears and dejection. And despair. It had seemed so simple, loving Emilia, wanting her, winning her. But their affair couldn't last. He had always known it, of course, but the mind was weaker than the heart, and a marvellous vehicle at not facing up to cold honest truths. Libby could end up being hurt beyond measure, and Emilia had more to lose than he did. She may have already made up her mind to end it with him. If she had not, because he loved her so much, because he would never do anything to risk her getting hurt, he must disentangle himself from her life. If he could ever find the strength to do it.

Tris had finished his business with Mr Harrison Arscott, an elderly gentleman who lived in a small grey house in Quay Street. Mr Arscott had read his advertisement in the *West Briton*, and now that he was tragically left with no one to inherit his worldly goods he wanted to part with the few poignant effects of his grandson, sent home after he had fallen at the Somme.

In a large box, meticulously wrapped in brown paper and knotted with new string, Tristan carried a biplane made out of a 75mm shell case, French in origin, skilfully sculpted from scrap metal, the propellers made from cigar box wood. Mr Arscott had no idea how his grandson had come by it, but he had been happy and satisfied that it was going to a dedicated collector who would carefully catalogue its origins and previous owners. Tristan could hardly wait to show it to Jonny. He would be fascinated by this worthy addition to his inheritance. Which, hopefully, would make him feel special and a much wanted son.

Now to treat him with something he could play with today. Tristan popped into a toy shop and bought a red kite, aptly and cleverly shaped like an aeroplane. He chose a skipping rope for Vera Rose, a football for Will, and for Tom, a sweet little brown teddy bear. He was coming out of the florists, next door, armed with a wealth of yellow roses for Winifred – they were a particular favourite of hers. The roses in her garden, growing so close to the coast, didn't always do so well. Now he was anxious to reach Ford Farm to see how she was faring. He never mentioned it to anyone, but after losing one wife in childbirth, he was so afraid Winnie might die during labour and every day, in spite of longing for the child, he berated himself for not taking precautions.

He was suddenly pulled up sharp on his feet, making an old war wound in his ankle bite painfully. He gasped, not so much from pain but irritation. A lady, tall, refined and fair, holding the hand of a shy little girl with a noticeable red mark on her face was there in his path.

Tristan shifted his purchases into one arm and lifted his trilby. 'Good afternoon, Polly.'

Sombrely, Polly inclined her head in its velvet cloche, with a tiny blue feather. 'Tristan. It's not often you're in this neck of the woods.'

'No, not usually. I'm in rather a hurry. If you'll excuse me . . .'

Polly's cool demeanour was replaced by flame-fuelled indignation. 'I've no wish to speak to you either, not ever in fact, but no, I'll not excuse your belligerence towards someone very dear to me. I find your attitude a disgrace.'

'Aunt Polly, what's the matter?' Louisa hid behind her.

Polly propelled her towards the adjoining shop. 'It's a grown-up thing, darling. Nothing you need be concerned about. You go on into the toy shop. Ask Miss Trewoon if the furniture we ordered for your doll's house has arrived. Tell her I'll be along directly.'

Louisa stared nervously up at the tall thin man as she edged past him. Jonny Harvey's father wasn't nice and full of fun like Jonny himself. 'Don't be long, Aunt Polly.'

'I can't think what we could possibly have to say to each other.' Tristan chose attack rather than defence.

'Oh, can't you? People often say you are the most pleasant of the Harvey brothers. I don't see how. Would you mind explaining why you treat Louisa with such obvious contempt? She's noticed it, it upsets her, and I won't go on putting up with it. Do you understand?'

People were staring. She had been steadily raising her voice, getting more and more angry with him. 'We can hardly talk about this in the street, Polly.'

'Where then?'

'I don't want to talk about it at all.'

The determined switching off in his dark eyes was reminiscent of Alec's habit of drifting off, and the stubborn set in his narrow jaw was so like the stubbornness in Ben, and with his anger and distaste evident in the very stamp of him, Polly wanted to smash a hand across his face. 'How dare you be so offensive! I would make a scene here and now if not for Louisa waiting for me. You've never stayed at your homes long enough to know what it's like to be a parent, Tristan Harvey. I love Louisa as if she was my own flesh and blood. Alec, Emilia and Ben have included her in their lives and if you don't like it then it's too bad. If you don't change your attitude towards her – and it isn't as if you actually see her often, is it? I'll complain to them about your beastliness. Your son will then see he has good reason to prefer Alec to you!'

As if hit by a wave of freezing hostile water, Tristan was beset with the wretched hopelessness he'd felt on the night Ursula had bled to death. 'Polly, you're right. We do need to talk. I need to explain why I regret your late brother talking me into letting him take my late wife's child.'

'Good, that's something, I suppose. If I fetch Louisa out of the toy shop will you come to my house?'

He thought of Winifred, feeling faint and frail, waiting for him at Ford Farm, but this needed to be dealt with first. He knew where Polly lived, and arrived at her house after allowing her time to dispose of her young ward to the nursery.

He refused a drink, refused to sit down. In her well-lit drawing room, the summer sun streaming in and laying a golden glow on her fine possessions, he stared down at Polly, in an armchair. Her ankles were neatly crossed, her hands in her lap, as if she was interviewing a tradesman.

'You're right about my son and I not being close, and I don't suppose we ever will be, not lovingly close, not on his part. And if, as I fear, that one day, he somehow finds out I lied about his half-sister, that she did not die and is in fact one of his playmates, well, Jonny will hate me and who could blame him? I'm sorry I've been cold towards the girl, but she is a constant reminder of my dead wife and the wretched cowardly cad who was her lover, whose resemblance, in some ways, she bears. I loved Ursula so much, but twice she chose Bruce Ashley over me.

'That child –' when Polly winced at the way he had said it, he softened his voice – 'Louisa, her birth, took Ursula away from me. Emilia had only just pointed out to me that very day how harsh I was being towards Ursula over her first betrayal. I'd agreed and I was going to give her my wholehearted support throughout her confinement and during the horrible moment, when as previously agreed, the district nurse was to take the baby away to its adoptive parents. It was a terrific blow to discover Ursula was about to go off with Ashley again and take Jonny with them. As you know, when confronted with my presence Ashley ran out on her and by this time Ursula was in labour. I told Ursula she could keep her child, that I'd set her up somewhere with it, but that I never wanted to see her again. After her death, Polly, I realized I still loved her. I might have come round to her. I believe I would have done. I loved her so much. I haven't told anyone but you about this last part of the whole sorry business.'

'So what you're saying, and let us be clear about this, is that you believe you might have taken Ursula back, her and her child, but now you hate her child because her birth led to Ursula's death? Have I got it right?'

He raked his hand down over his face, distorting his harrowed features. 'Put as cold-bloodedly as that it makes me sound like a monster, doesn't it? But I don't hate Louisa. I don't hate anyone, except for Bruce Ashley. I just can't stand her near me. Oh, God, that does make me a monster, saying something like that about a child. Look I . . .'

Polly moved over to him, appealed to him with open hands. 'Tristan, I'm worried too about Jonny or Louisa discovering the truth of her origins. It's why I keep her away from Ford Farm when Jonny's there. But when I think about it rationally, I realize it's virtually impossible. Perhaps we've been worrying unnecessarily, don't you think? Can't you forget the past and try to like Louisa, just a little bit? She's a delightful bright little girl. Please, for her sake, give her a chance.'

Tristan couldn't get the pain, the anxiety out of his mind. 'But surely she's bound to wonder where she came from, who her mother was. One day she'll start asking questions. What are you going to tell her?'

'The truth, but not the whole truth. How her mother fell into temptation, like so many other women did during the war, and that tragically she died giving birth to her. The district nurse travelled here that night with Julian, so I'll tell her that was it she who brought her here. The nurse refused to utter a word to me, so I shall be able to say truthfully that she refused to divulge anything about the baby she carried into the house.'

'And her birth certificate?'

'It's safely locked away at the solicitor's. Now does that reassure you?'

'I suppose so.'

Tristan realized that he had picked up the parcel with the biplane in it from the car seat, was holding it so tightly it was hurting his hands. In some ways he was clinging to his new, happy, uncomplicated life with Winifred. 'Look, I really must go. I promise I'll make the effort to be more sociable when I see Louisa again.'

'Thank you, Tristan. I'm so pleased we've had this talk.'

When Polly saw him to the door, he found himself telling her, 'I'm to become a father again. God willing, Jonny will accept it, and I'm going to do everything in my power to make a better job of raising this next child. I wish you good fortune, Polly.'

'Tristan, I apologize for what I said about you and Jonny. Please don't go on blaming yourself, it was the war that came between you and him, just as it did between you and Ursula. I'm sure Jonny will love the new baby.'

She watched him drive away, satisfied with what she had accomplished for Louisa's sake. Envying him for having so many people in his life, a spouse, hope for the future. Now all she had to do was to get rid of her appalling loneliness. She was well travelled and had already set into motion a cruise around the world for herself and Louisa. It would boost Louisa's confidence, broaden her outlook and stimulate her mind. She was taking Ivy with them, and she would order her to pack now for Southampton rather than next week.

Brooke was out riding round the village boundaries. Before going home, she reined in at Ford House. She had argued with herself about whether she should come here or not, but she had to, there was too much at stake for Emilia, and the Harvey family if things went on as they were. The more she thought about the possibility of her sister-in-law growing rather too close to Perry Bosweld the more she had come to realize that there truly was a distinctive intimate connection between them.

Let in by the maid, she took a seat at the side of Perry's desk, and he explained he was writing a letter to a former soldier about the benefits of joining the Royal British Legion, when in fact it was a letter aimed at obtaining the education and training Selina desired, and getting her started in it as soon as possible. Once it was settled, she was unlikely to baulk at the arrangement, she was always impatient to experience something new.

Brooke did not speak. She gazed and gazed at him.

Perry had put his pen down. He picked it up and clenched it tightly in his fist. 'Well, Mrs Harvey? Brooke?' His voice was firm but his heart was frozen through. He knew why she was here.

'I've not known Emilia long enough to say this to her but I can to you, Perry. You can't have her. She belongs to Alec, and to her family and the farm more than she realizes. She's linked to Alec in every way. By the baby they lost. By the children they will have in the future. If you don't get out of their way they may never reach each other again as closely as they once were. From now on you must keep away from her, you must. If Alec ever found out about your feelings towards Emilia, and that she's attracted to you, it would bring chaos, heartbreak to everyone. Is that what you want for Libby?

'You must give notice on this house. Leave as soon as you can. You must see that you've no right to Emilia. What she would lose with Alec is far more than what she would gain with you. I believe you're a fine and noble man, Perry Bosweld. If you really love her and want what's best for her then I'm sure you'll do the right thing. I'm sorry. I know it's hard for you, but there it is. I shall expect to hear soon that you, your daughter and your sister are planning to go away. Goodbye, Perry.'

After she had left, her words echoed revoltingly round and round inside his head, for they had given him the strength to do what he must, to protect the woman he loved. He finished the letter to the professor. As soon as Selina's new position was put into place he would give Alec Harvey a month's notice on the house. No other explanation to their landlord would be needed. He would do the right thing, move away with Selina, make a clean break from Emilia, but there would still be some time left to spend with her, his Em. Surely there would be still some precious moments left for them.

That night in bed Emilia laid herself in Alec's arms and held on to him very tight.

'This is nice,' he said, hugging her, reaching for her hand and bringing it up to his lips to kiss. 'You've been distracted all evening. Are you worrying about something, angel?'

The way he cherished her made her want to cry. In a choked whisper, she said, 'I want you to know that I love you, Alec. More than ever. Perhaps it's time we thought about having another baby. Alec?'

He was quiet for a while, holding her, caressing her. 'What's brought this on, darling? You sound as if you're in a bit of a panic.'

'I just think it's time, that's all. Don't you?'

With gentle force he unlocked the hands around his neck. They were hurting him. 'Tell me what's wrong, Emilia. Is it because Jonny and Vera Rose are soon to go home? Are you frightened of the house suddenly seeming too empty?'

How could she tell him she was frightened, had never been more frightened in all her life of losing him and everything that was involved in their life together. 'Yes,

I suppose I am.' She was crying softly. Crying over every terrible and wonderful event that had happened since Jenna's birth. Crying because she was safe, here in Alec's strength and gentleness. 'Sorry if I alarmed you.'

He wrapped her up close. 'There's no need to say sorry. Darling, I hate to see you so unhappy. We'll get through this, I promise. She'll always be a part of us, our little Jenna. We'll have another baby, but not now. Not until the time is right. I love you so much, Emilia. More than anything. More than anyone.'

They lay quietly. It wasn't until he was asleep, his arms around her, protecting her, that she allowed herself to think again about the precious someone she was about to let loose from her life.

She had to let Perry go. But not abruptly. She couldn't do that. She needed more time with him. To see him again, alone. Whatever the risk.

Twenty-Six

The terrible moments of ending her association with Perry were looming in front of her. Emilia wouldn't think about that now. It was enough to be seeing glimpses of him. To be with him when the children played together.

Two days ago he had invited her and Alec to Ford House to demonstrate the use of the archery gear. Perry had hit the inner gold zone several times and they, and Selina and Libby had applauded his skill. Alec, who had a deadly aim with the shotgun was a good shot and Emilia had cheered him on enthusiastically. No one thought it odd or inappropriate when Perry, leaning forward from behind had physically helped her to position her hands on the longbow and sight the arrow. By terrific luck she had nearly hit the outer gold zone. Recoiling from the force of the shot, she had tumbled back against Perry's chest. 'I love you,' he had whispered, touching her momentarily with his gentle steadying hands.

Selina had invited Alec to take a turn round the front garden with her and Libby, leaving Emilia to help Perry gather up the equipment and stow it back in the garden shed.

He had caressed her hair. She had pressed down on his hand. 'Selina knows about us, darling Em. We must talk.'

'I know, but not yet.' Perry was to tell her the same dreadful news, that they couldn't go on with their secret love and somehow she knew he would say something even worse. That he was going away, for ever. Perry was too honourable, too sensitive to stay on here, so agonizingly close to her, where without the slightest doubt they would keep on with their love affair.

It was enough to know for today that he was to come

to where she now was, in Higher Cross field to set up his archery gear for the sports day.

'I love you so much,' she told the image of him she had fashioned in her mind. Soon, images and beautiful memories would be all she had left of him.

'Don't cry, Em. Someone might see,' Selina's voice whispered in her ear and her arm came to rest heavily round her shoulders.

'What? Sorry, we'll never finish setting up these archery lanes, will we?' Emilia gazed at the rope hanging limply in her hands. She shrugged Selina's arm off her, ill at ease in her company after her so-called friendly advice about her and Perry. Emilia saw Selina as a habitual liar, a complicated misfit, and if not for her close connection to Perry, as someone she could talk to about him, hear about him, even the little mundane things like what he ate for supper last night, so she could feel she had been with him, she would allow Selina very little time.

'Life's not fair sometimes, is it?' Selina took the rope and measured out a short lane of fifty-six yards for the men, then placed another rope down for a shorter one of thirty-four and a half yards for the women.

In a state of numbness, at an aloof distance, Emilia watched her making the swift efficient movements.

Selina, an imposing figure in a shirt and trousers and walking boots, rejoined her. 'I can't see what difference the size of the lanes are really for in something like this but Perry wants everything just right. Come on, try to smile. You know what we need, don't you?'

'What's that?'

'A drink. Ruby Brokenshaw's offering a bottle of ale to the chaps working here. Can't see why we should miss out. The crate's sitting over there in the shade behind the platform, where Daphne Dowling's unlikely to see it. Come on, we're due for a break, let's shock the honourable Daphne by leaning against the hedge and swigging straight out of a bottle like a man. Not scared, are you?'

The proceedings were to start at four o'clock in the

afternoon, eight hours away, with the children's races, and the field was already bustling with activity. The lorry had arrived with the marquee and a host of brawny arms were erecting it. Mrs Dowling, carefully hatted although the early morning sun was only just finding its wings, and followed by an anxious, cotton-frocked Mrs Frayne, was striding through the scratchy yellow stalks of the cut grass, making sure everything was being accomplished to her perfectionist requirements. She had taken no care to avoid showing her disapproval of Selina's presence and had actually been curt and rude to her.

Selina had laughed into her impatient taut face, and said later to Emilia, 'I suppose Perry and I would have to live here for at least ten years to be considered bona fide residents of Hennaford. Stupid mare. How dare she object to me helping out! I despise her type, narrow-minded and hypocritical.' Emilia had thought Mrs Dowling had come across as indignant and angry and strangely disquieted.

Emilia cast her eyes up and down the long, broad field, shimmering silver in the sunlight. The marquee bunting was up. Edwin, Jim and Midge Roach had erected the poles for the sheaf-pitching. Alec and Jonny had brought over a cartload of sheaves, then had left to get on with the everyday chores of the farm. Jonny had an important air about him today – Alec had asked him to be a member of his tug-of-war team and the boy had insisted he would, even though Emilia had pointed out he should, as Ben's nephew too, be impartial.

Other Ford Farm labourers were working on the greasy pole for the pillow fight. The wooden bowling run, the small hard balls and the skittles had been carried up from the pub, as had the rope for the tug of war; the red and yellow and blue flags were already in situation on it. Elena Rawley and her father were supervising the positioning of the trestle tabling brought up from the Wesleyan hall. All was fitting into place as on every other year, but Emilia had been given no warning that this year her emotions would be in tatters, stretched to their limits.

'Are we having a drink or not?' Selina's eager-to-please tones broke off her latest musings.

Emilia wanted to go off on her own but Selina would only follow her. 'I'll take a bottle but I'll not offend anyone here. We must drink discreetly.'

'Fine by me. Let's stroll down the field. Too bad if virtuous old Daphne doesn't like it. I was never such a slave driver on the wards.'

Jim was now beside the dancing platform, near old Mr Quick, who had parked his creaking bones down on it, while Ben, Brooke, Eliza Shore and Cyril Trewin were admiring their handiwork. All except Brooke were quaffing ale, and old Mr Quick was telling tales about the days when he was 'light on his feet'. They were answering his deaf ears with indulgent nods. He saw Emilia and Selina approaching. 'Now here comes a couple of maidens I could've whirled round any dance floor in my day. Should've seen me then. I was a good-looking man, I'll have 'ee know. Had me pick of the local girls, I did.'

'Hello, Mr Quick.' Emilia smiled down on his gaily squinting, upturned, antiquated countenance. She chatted a while with the Tremore contingent, noting, while dampening down her reawakened feelings of raw maternal loss, that Brooke's pregnancy was beginning to show.

Brooke eyed Emilia and Selina, wishing her sister-in-law was not at all friendly with the other woman.

Selina yanked the stoppers off two ale bottles. She met Jim's steady stare at her with direct uncompromising aloofness. There wasn't the usual hateful snarl on his outstanding lush fair features. He was watchful, quiet almost, except she saw the naked raw energy of hate driving through him. Jim would always be overrun by passion of some sort – it was this that had prompted her without hesitation or remorse to seduce him. He wasn't a man to be trusted, but she reckoned he was no threat to her.

'How are you, Jim?' Her question was short, to the point, interested, almost soothing, as it might be to a patient under her care.

'Very well as it happens, Selina.' He smiled. Sort of smiled, it even reached his eyes.

'Glad to hear it.'

Jim was still smiling when the two women walked away. The Tremore contingent also left. Jim stood alone, his cap off, the sun making his hair shine like polished gold. He fished for a smoke. Held his head high, proud, satisfied. Selina Bosweld had said he ought to believe he was good enough for anyone. He did now. No longer was he workhouse scum. One day he would make something of himself. He wanted to move on, move up, to a better life. And his route, and for Sara was through Sara. Through Wally Eathorne of Druzel Farm. He was hers for the taking. Wally's parents had acknowledged it. It was time Sara thought differently too and considered the future. She would be a farmer's wife instead of a farmer's skivvy. Mrs Eathorne was ailing, was consumptive, so it was said, and wanted to see grandchildren playing at her hearth before she died.

He and Sara would not sleep in the attics at Druzel Farm. He would make decisions on the farm; Wally and his father were easy going, pliable sorts. Jim's mind was made up. He would see his sister married within the year.

From a backwards glance he spied the approach of Myrna Eathorne. Doubtless, the nosy shopkeeper was intent on inspecting the dancing platform. He was pleased to see this particular busybody bearing his way. Anything Myrna Eathorne was told or overheard would be all over Hennaford in an hour, and would make for many a tasty reworking, and, if this second part of his plan for revenge on Selina Bosweld worked, many an exclamation of disgust would be issued before the sports day got underway, to resurface, when it did, in public indignation. How he would like to have been in the Infirmary when the seductress had been given her marching orders, but, he grinned maliciously to himself, he'd not miss witnessing the village unceremoniously giving her the boot!

He sat down close to old Mr Quick. Waited. Made his voice loud and clear. 'Poor Mrs Dowling, she's some upset, you know, Mr Quick. I heard her telling Mrs Frayne that

Miss Bosweld's gone and ruined her cousin's life. The cousin found out, you see, that her husband, who's a doctor at the Infirmary, was up to no good with some nurse. Well, turned out that this nurse was Miss Bosweld, and she was sacked the very same day. You wouldn't think it to look at her, would you? She's a bit modern, a bit eccentric, I suppose, but I always thought she was *respectable*. But you never know about someone, do you? Who'd have thought that she was a marriage wrecker?'

'Eh? What?' Old Mr Quick prodded Jim's arm. 'What'd you say, boy? You'll have to speak up. Never heard a word you just said.'

A gasp of shock came from behind the two men. Mr Quick did not hear this either, but Jim smiled all the way down the field to where his former lover was walking in the distance. 'Never mind, Mr Quick. Sadly, word'll get round soon enough, I suppose. Well, must get on. Have to build a pen for the piglet. Here, you have this last bottle of ale.'

He dropped his own empty ale bottle back in the crate. When he turned round he saw Mrs Eathorne hurrying off, beckoning to a group of neighbours.

Emilia and Selina were making their way along the side of the tall hedgerow, out of sight now and no longer hiding the filched bottles in front of their bodies. Emilia intended to turn back soon.

Selina took off her cardigan and flung it over her shoulder, to enjoy the gilding of the hot sun. 'Jim seems quite content now. I'm curious over what's brought about the change in him.'

'I suppose Sara finally got through to him. I spoke to him myself yesterday. He says he's finally got everything sorted out in his mind.'

'I feel quite bad about upsetting him. I should have behaved with more feeling, he was just an ordinary chap, a boy really, when I took up with him.'

'Yes, he was.'

'Don't you believe I'm sorry?'

Emilia did not. 'I hope you'll be more careful in future.'

'Well, I don't think you need worry about any lasting effects on Jim. From the steely look in him just now I'm sure he'll be fine.' After her defensive remark Selina allowed a pause of silence, then she grew jolly, buoyant, and Emilia knew she was trying to change the mood. 'This is nice. Spending time with a friend. I hope you like me, Em, darling. Really like me.'

'Haven't you had many friends?'

'Women friends? Oh, lots, from time to time. Some I've been especially close to. As for male friends, lovers, I'm not seeing anyone now. I think I've had enough of men for a while.' At the lack of sympathetic response she was getting she went on in a rather pitiful tone, 'I know you're distracted at the moment, Em, but you do like me, don't you?'

Emilia hated this, she had more urgent, more disheartening things to consider and she had no real choice in her answer. 'Of course I do.'

'Oh, I'm so glad!' Selina leaned across and hugged her round the waist and pecked her cheek. 'I like you lots. I want us to get very close before I leave.'

Twenty-Seven

Sara had been in Alec's thoughts day and night. He was thinking about her now while taking a bath before getting dressed for the big village event, his favourite for it was held entirely out of doors. The end of the evening was best: after the fun of the events, as darkness crept comfortingly down from the skies and the music turned to softer, quieter tones, the young and old alike would be lulled into a sleepy other-world, when all, even though not realizing it, would be at one with those who had gone on before them, and perhaps even somewhere deep in their hearts they would be touched by those who were to come. It was how Alec saw it – a vision conjured long since from his deepest thoughts. Usually saw it. Today he was thinking about Sara.

So disturbed had he become over his attraction to her, the lust breeding in him for her, that he had turned to his long-standing mentor. Eugenie Bawden, the glamorous, town-dwelling hostess and long-time widow, who before his first marriage and before her own had been his intended wife. They had remained devoted friends, had become lovers until he'd taken charge of Jonathan. He had consulted her over his feelings for Emilia. Now he needed advice over his desire for the naive young work-maid he should be keeping only a paternal care for.

'I don't know what to do, Eugenie!' he had paced her drawing room floor like a great, threatened beast. 'I can't fathom out why I feel like this towards Sara Killigrew. I know I must send her away. But I'm responsible for encouraging the infatuation she's developed for me. She's going to feel so hurt and rejected.'

'Sit down, Alec, you'll wear yourself out.' Eugenie, renowned for her wit, benevolence, youthful spirit, chain-smoking and raven-black dyed hair, had pushed him down on the nearest chair, which had taken considerable strength for he had resisted her. Then perching on the embroidered padded arm, she had taken his hand and brushed the tumbling dark hair back from his sweating forehead. She'd lit two cigarettes, hers clasped in a ridiculously-long jade holder and placed his between his lips. 'Now, dear-heart, take a deep breath on this.'

She had held his head in the crook of her arm, stroking his hair, and he had leaned gladly against her breast, somewhat flattened in her chic tubular dress, but he was comfortably aware of the feminine bolstering against his throbbing temple. He smoked and waited. If anyone knew what he should do, it was Eugenie.

Now, while he got out of the bath, rubbed his body rapidly and harshly dry, and dressed in a casual shirt, black tie, trousers and dark sports jacket, and dashed a comb through his thick black locks, he was wording and rewording how to translate Eugenie's advice into the right approach to Sara, to spare her feelings. And then to Jim, for this involved him too. He would offer them a cottage of their own to live in, to form a distance from Sara. It was the best he could do, he couldn't bring himself to sack her or find her a new position – what explanation could he give anyway? God, he prayed, please let this come out right.

He nearly let out an oath to find Sara on the other side of the bedroom door. Looking at this shining, tender, provocative young creature he felt a betrayer, and not a little bereft at what his good intentions would deprive him of. She was stunning. Perfect. Matchless. More promising than the clearest sunrise. She smelled of pure woman. And she could be his. The way she was looking at him now, her desire for him was transparent and so blatant it tempted his flesh like nothing ever had before.

He clenched his fists, forced his voice to sound something

in the way of normal. 'Oh, Sara. I thought you'd gone with the others after the milking was over.'

'I got held up. I thought I could ride with you.'

'I see.' Afraid he might lean forward and kiss her and be totally lost, he turned on his heel and headed for the front stairs. She hastened after him and with each step down he fought with himself. He cleared his throat. Angry with himself for now he must be cruel. 'You shouldn't take things for granted, Sara. It was silly of you. There won't be any room in the car. I'm only taking it to pick up some of the elderly and infirm. Mrs Dowling asked for volunteers to collect those who couldn't cope with being there for the whole event.'

'Oh, I didn't know,' she said, halting halfway down the stairs.

His insides were as crushed as her tiny voice had sounded. 'I must get on. The boys will be desperate to tell me if they've won any of the races. Borrow Mrs Harvey's bicycle, if you like. I'll . . . I'll see you there.' He snatched up his hat and was out of the front door, locking it behind him.

Stunned, desolate, Sara slid down on the bottom step of the stairs, hardly believing what had just happened. Since the wonderful afternoon in Long Meadow she had kept introducing herself to him whenever she could, wherever he was, and at times he'd responded to her with interest and pleasure, calling her 'precious girl'. But she had been blind! Taken for a fool. She had thought the times he had not been warm and friendly were because he was being careful in case someone else was about. She could see now why her unsuccessful pleas about the retaking of the photographs that Mrs Em had suggested had been met with his excuses of being too busy.

One time, to try to get more reaction out of him she had tried to make him jealous. 'Wally Eathorne was here not long ago.'

'Oh, really?' Alec had frowned. 'Not a crisis over his mother's health, I hope.'

'Wasn't nothing to do with her.' She had tried to sound mysterious.

'I take it then he didn't want to see me?'

'No, it was me.'

Alec had stared at her, through jealousy, she had hoped. 'And?'

'And nothing.'

He had given a heavy sigh at that. Impatience with Wally Eathorne, she had thought. But she knew better now. It had been impatience with her! He had lost interest in her, interest, even in her inexperience, she was sure had been there. Damn it, he was too much in love with Mrs Em to want love from anyone else. He adored Mrs Em, had been petting her more than usual lately. Sara's face sunk into her arms. Lately he had referred to Mrs Em as Mrs Harvey, not Emilia, when speaking about her.

On the bottom step Sara stayed and stayed. Steeped in misery, feeling lost, abandoned, foolish. The sun moved more and more to the west and no longer shone through the passage window.

Was Alec, was *Mr Harvey* – she would call him that from now on and keep her distance – wondering why she had not shown herself at the sports? He might come back and see if she was all right. The thought lifted her wallowing heart. Just for a minute. No, he wouldn't. His wife and children were there. He didn't want his servant girl for anything but skivvying.

Damn him. Damn him! How dare he trifle with her! How dare the wretched man set her hopes so high and stamp on them so unfeelingly. He'd want to be rid of her next. Masters were all alike. They didn't really care about their staff. Jim often reminded her of that. 'There's them and there's us, 'tis the way of things and there's no good us wishing it otherwise.'

Jim was right when he said, 'We've got to stay on our guard. Always look out for ourselves. Never forget it, Sara.' Just before he had left for the sports, all spruced up and in a strange quiet mood, he had looked her straight in the eye. 'Be nice if we got away from here and had a place of our own, wouldn't it?'

'But I'm happy here!' she had wailed, thinking she would hate her brother if he did anything to upset her dreams.

'All I'm saying is that it would be nice. Take Druzel Farm, for instance. I've been against it before but if you were to consider Wally Eathorne, the farm could be more or less ours one day. Wally and his father are easygoing sorts. We'd fit in all right there. Don't look like that, Sara. If you married Wally you'd become an Eathorne, and they've got standing in the village. Don't you ever want to be more than next to nothing? 'Cause that's what we are, and no mistake. Well, I'm going to make something of myself. I'm going to see myself proud, make the buggers round here speak to me with respect, you see if I don't.'

Sara shot to her feet, ignoring the aches and stiffness of staying crumpled for so long. What had Jim meant? He would never have spoken like that if he didn't already have something put in motion. He might already have a way out of her terrible predicament, for one thing was certain, she couldn't bear to go on living and working here.

She seethed aloud, 'Leave me as next to nothing would you, Alec Harvey? We'll see about that!'

The dogs out in the yard started up an excited barking, yapping each in their distinctive voice. It wasn't Jim come back to check up on her, they would not have made a sound. The terriers were not sounding aggressive, so it was someone they knew. There was many a kindly villager who might walk here to see what was holding her up. Or, quite likely, because he had said he was going to ask her to dance with him tonight it was Wally Eathorne.

Wally Eathorne grinned a little shyly when she opened the back kitchen door to his determined knocking. 'Jim was getting worried about you, Sara. Me too. Not been taken poorly, have you?'

He was not great in height and with her up on the doorstep their eyes were on the same level. It was different from when she had faced her master in a similar way on the slope in Long Meadow. Wally wasn't the source of her girlish fantasies and this time she was in charge. She watched him blanch, his ruddy face drop in disappointment at her hard stare until she said, 'Come in, Wally.'

A glance in the hall mirror on the way here had shown her eyes were tinged red from unshed tears, her cheeks white from fury. 'I had a headache,' she said when they were in the kitchen.

'I'm sorry. Anything I can do for you?' Wally had taken off his best tweed cap and he was passing it from hand to hand. A more ordinary man would have been hard to find. Wally wasn't good looking, nor was he ugly. He had the usual sturdy build of a hardworking farmer, the usual wrinkles creasing the corner of his eyes and mouth from constantly grimacing into the wind and rain. Just turned twenty, he was teetotal, likeable, had a joking nature, was clean in his habits and treated his mother with respect. All positive aspects when a girl considered a man as a husband. Sara looked him over in the way Jim had suggested she should.

Under her penetrating gaze, Wally was treading the carpet square under his best boots, risking a viciously scratched ankle if he stepped on one of the sleeping house cats. 'Have you taken an aspirin?' he said at last.

'Yes,' she replied quickly. 'I'll fetch my hat.'

'You're coming to the sports then?'

'Yes. Just give me a minute.'

'Oh, that's . . . that's . . .'

She didn't allow Wally time to make up his mind over his sentiment. She went through to the hall, to the front stairs where she had left her new cloche hat. She used the mirror to set it at the best angle.

Wally Eathorne had an inquisitive streak. He went after Sara and in between giving her admiring glances, peered into the sitting room and the den, the doors left slightly ajar. 'Grand place.'

'Do you want to see something really grand?' she snapped, suddenly furious with Alec again, this time for taking her for granted as a loyal servant.

Wally looked unsure but straight away, he said, 'All right then.'

'Follow me.' She started up the thickly carpeted stairs.

'Is this all right?' Wally asked doubtfully, but did as he was bidden anyway.

At the top Sara led the way down the wide corridor to the master bedroom. She pushed open the door, went inside. It was in pristine order, as she had left it that morning, except for where Alec had dumped his work clothes, left his wardrobe door open and carelessly tossed down his comb. The place reeked of his aftershave, a smell she had once found intoxicating. Now she hated it. She had no right to be in here, but she didn't care! 'Can you imagine sleeping in a room like this, Wally?'

He whistled through his teeth. Sara noticed he had straight white teeth. 'Never.'

'Never?'

'Well, I . . . Sara, what's upset you?'

'I'm just sick and tired of cleaning and tidying up after others, that's all!'

She saw herself shaking in rage in the long mirror on the inside of the wardrobe door. Saw Wally come up behind her. Place his rough stocky hands firmly on her shoulders. 'Sara?'

'What?' she asked his resolute reflection.

He spoke in one rapid breath. 'Marry me, and although I can't give you all this, I promise I'll do everything in my power to make Druzel farmhouse a home as grand as possible for you. I'll build more rooms on to it. Father wouldn't mind. I'd do anything for you, Sara.'

It was a tempting proposition, but she did not answer. Overwhelmed by all the emotions she had suffered during the last couple of hours, she did not even think for a while. Then she felt Wally's mouth on her neck, behind her ear, kissing her. Felt his hot breath making her skin tingle. So he wasn't backward in coming forward, as the older people said about those who quickly reached out for what they wanted.

Wally came round her, put her hands on her face and gazed into her eyes. 'I think I love you, Sara. You're the most beautiful, most special girl that ever there was.'

She looked at Wally's lips. How many times had she looked at Alec's and longed for him to kiss her. To make love to her, fully, doing everything, and doing it in this very room. She had known she could only have ever been his mistress, but she would have gloried in that distinction. He might have taken her away from here, set her up in a little house somewhere, where they could have loved and dreamed two or three times a week. She had even been prepared to have his children. She looked closer at Wally's lips. They weren't full and dark red and sensuous like Alec's, but they did not repulse her either.

Wally brought his face close and after hesitating, he kissed her dry lonely mouth. Comforted by the contact, needing someone, she responded. Wally had courted a girl or two before, so he knew how to kiss. It felt warm and pleasant. And because she had rehearsed what she would do if Alec finally kissed her, she automatically moved her lips under Wally's and let her body fall against his. With her arms hanging on to him they kissed, rocking slightly, and this brought them into each other ever more intimately.

'You're beautiful. I do love you,' Wally moaned against her mouth, before sliding his lips down over her chin and her neck.

Just as she had done in her fantasies, she crooned back, 'I love you too.'

'You do?' Wally's head shot up, he looked into her eyes, his own warmly grey and smoky. 'Oh, Sara, that's wonderful! This means we're engaged. Just a minute.'

'Why?'

He kept hold of her waist while he rummaged in his inside jacket pocket. 'I was hoping to give you this tonight. Can't believe I'm actually doing it now. It belonged to mother. She wanted you to have it, if you'd have me. She's going to be so pleased.'

Sara took the ring he held up between his thumb and forefinger, a diamond solitaire on a decorated gold band. 'Father had it made specially for her. It's in perfect condition because she's only ever worn it on special occasions.'

For a moment Sara thought she was under a spell, which was making her behave foolishly out of character. In a flash of panic she made to push Wally away from her, to order him out of the house, out of her life. Then she saw the great Victorian bed, and remembering Alec didn't want her on it with him, she decided she knew exactly what she was doing. She gave the ring back to Wally.

'Don't you want it?'

'Put it on for me.'

She felt Wally's great sigh of relief ripple through her own body. She studied the ring. 'It's beautiful.'

Wally kissed her. He turned the kiss into a long, deep happening, in which he explored the sweetness inside her mouth. Then he pounced on her neck, pushing down the soft filmy material of her best dress to taste and kiss her shoulder. Sara felt him unfasten the tiny pearly button at the back of the dress.

Wally began to breathe noisily. He put a hand over her breast. She pushed it off. ''Tis all right, isn't it?' he breathed against her ear, nibbling the lobe. 'We're engaged.' He made it sound like a wondrous achievement, and for an orphan from the workhouse it was. So she let him put his hand back and keep it there and move it to her other breast.

Somehow they had shifted towards the bed and suddenly they were tumbling down on it. Sara let him keep on kissing her. When his hands strayed, taking the most daring of liberties, she didn't stop him – instead she shifted her limbs to allow him freer access. For he was a gentle soul, tormenting her slowly, and then quickly, and she was filling up with heat, a heat a hundredfold more intense than what she had conjured up alone, when dreaming, when aspiring, and the maddening heat was burning its way through her and seemed to have a need of its own.

Wally reared over her. Sara lay still but breathing greatly, willing him to progress before the timidity in her, the fear for her self-respect, the fear of consequences, became stronger in force than the desire to have her fiery needs fulfilled.

Wally threw off his jacket, snatched at his bootlaces and

wriggled off his boots. He looked down on her. He spent a brief time kissing and touching her then he mounted her. She felt his heavy bones sticking into her. 'Don't be afraid.' His voice came raw and husky.

'I'm not.' She wasn't afraid but she had grown chilled, all desire and mysteries had come to a sickening halt for her and she did not want this now. But she was not going to stop it happening.

She reached up and gripped the brass rails behind her head and took Wally's weight, his closeness, and the pain of his urgency. He was a little rough, through lack of know-how, she guessed, but he went on instinctively. And instinctively, she moaned and knotted her face, pretending to enjoy the wildness as much as he was. Looking up at the ceiling, then casting her sight downwards and sideways, taking in the opulent satin bedcover, wrinkled and rucked under its illicit use, she didn't care how long Wally laboured away inside her. This submission was her gift to him.

He fell suddenly and lay on her, panting softly, needing her differently, needing comfort from her, and her forgiveness for hurting and sullying her, and she held his cheek tenderly against her breast.

'I love you, Sara,' he gasped, as if in dread and wonder, as if he had discovered some awesome secret. 'That was, that was . . .'

'Yes, it was, Wally. Because we're in love.' Of course she didn't love him, not yet anyway, perhaps she never would, but she would try to, in gratitude for everything he was to give her. She caressed Wally's commonplace, damp hair and smiled. She had just assured her own and Jim's future and that was something to be joyful about. Wasn't it? She was a proper grown-up woman now. She had achieved a measure of freedom and from now on she would strive always to make decisions for herself.

I don't need counterfeit love from you, Alec Harvey. Mr Harvey! I don't need your employment and I don't need your roof.

But behind her smile, urgent tears were building up. 'I'll

straighten the bed, Wally. I know exactly how it goes. Can you give me a minute?'

Wally placed one last kiss on her hot moist face, eased himself off her and gathered up his jacket and shoes. 'I'll um, I'll wait for you downstairs, my love.'

After the minute she had asked for, the loneliest minute of her life, Sara saw to the bed then slipped up to her own room to change her dress.

Twenty-Eight

This was the first year of her life that Emilia had not shared in the excited buzz of the sports day. She was trying to enjoy being with those she loved and the greater village family, but she felt no part in the intimacy of friends and neighbours as they mingled gaily in carefree summer clothes, while buying cakes to take home, or sweets and ice cream, or roamed to and from the beer tent or refreshment marquee.

She had cheered and exclaimed throughout the children's races, called congratulations to the winners and encouragement to the runners-up. But in her trim black skirt, black shoes and stockings, her square-necked white blouse, a black silk scarf round her neck, her coppery-brown hair pinned up, her eyes kept wandering to the banner raised up above the platform after she had left the morning's preparations. THE JENNA HARVEY MEMORIAL SPORTS DAY.

It was time for tea and there was a break in the events to allow for the workers to arrive. Emilia was sitting on a bale of straw at a good vantage point to watch the races, in the welcome shade of a row of towering elms which were incorporated in the high natural hedge behind, beyond which were the school premises. Tom was curled up on her lap, tucking into his lemonade and face-sized, yellow, thickly-fruited saffron bun, making crumbs on her lap and all over his delighted little face, tugging off pieces of bun and offering them to her, which she nibbled off his thumb and forefinger and thanked him for and kissed him every time.

Will was devouring his bun on the rug at her feet, Libby beside him, grasping hers timidly, uninterested in it. Selina was on the bale, very close to her, coaxing Libby to eat, and Perry was next to Selina, in his wheeled chair for ease of comfort. Edwin, Dolly and Winifred were close by on chairs, drinking tea fetched for them by Jonny, who had since disappeared. Vera Rose was with Tristan, looking grown up, pleased and important on the arm of her second-cousin-cum-stepfather, basking in the mutual affection that was theirs, as they chatted to Ben and Brooke beside the dancing platform.

Everyone was there except Alec, and Emilia felt lost without him – yet, setting aside the guilt of having an affair, of loving someone more than she did him, her sadness was cut deeper by the reality of having to end it very soon with Perry, and by the fact that he knew it without her having to tell him. His bearing was slung low, brimming with hurt. And the inexplicable shunning of his archery set-up exacerbated his hurt. Few people had taken part in it, and Emilia had watched in horror when children who had come near out of curiosity had been pulled away smartly by their parents and scolded. Some people had been offhand towards Perry, many more had been downright rude to Selina, and Libby, it seemed, was now not welcome to mix with most of the children.

Only Mrs Chellow had offered Selina a half-hearted, 'Good afternoon.'

'What's going on? What have we done?' Selina had demanded from the woman.

Mrs Chellow had shaken her head and would only say, 'It don't matter to me, Miss Bosweld.'

Burning with hurt and indignation on the Boswelds' behalf, Emilia had helped them pack the archery gear into the trap. Perry had wanted to leave, but Selina insisted they stay, laughing as if she didn't care about the snubs, while muttering something acid under her breath.

She had returned the curious glances of Dolly and Winifred, and Tilda when she came by, with blunt brush-offs. She was quiet now. The music, a spirited mix of brass instruments, fiddles, accordions and drums, started up again, people became even more animated, and she was taking it all in, smoking in curt puffs and strident exhalations, her eyes turning a vicious violet. When Libby passed the unwanted saffron bun up to her, she tossed it behind the bale.

Wishing Selina would show more restraint for Libby's sake, Emilia shifted away from her, but Selina shuffled up, closing the gap. The strength of the sun had waned and the atmosphere was fresh and light yet Emilia felt she could hardly breathe. She was finding the sweet strong smells of cut grass, the rich earth and wild foliage almost stifling, and she longed for the cool evening air and refuge of a darkening sky.

Jim sauntered up to them. ''Scuse me, Mrs Em, how much longer do you think Sara'll be? Milking should've been over ages ago.'

'Well, she ought to be here any minute then, Jim. Don't worry. You know how Sara takes ages getting ready to go out nowadays. You look very smart. How did you get on bowling for the piglet?'

Jim beamed and squared his shoulders manfully. 'Scored most points so far. I'll be taking that little beauty back home, if old Mr Quick and Hector Skewes don't raise an edge to their bowling.'

He grinned wickedly straight at Selina and she took an angry intake of breath. Emilia caught her own breath. It was easy to see Jim was enjoying his former lover's rejection and Selina was trembling, so Emilia thought, with fury, and Emilia feared she might issue an unladylike retaliation.

'Alec's taking his time too, isn't he?' The impatience, almost an accusation, in Selina's accent was all too evident.

Dismissed, but jubilant, Jim swaggered off.

'We're going, Selina,' Perry said suddenly, sucking in his breath.

'We are not!'

'You're about to blow your top. I don't want Libby to witness a scene.'

'No one, absolutely no one is going to force me to skulk

away from here. You don't have to stay, Perry. I'm not leaving until I find out what's going on.'

'Why don't you ask someone, particularly Daphne Dowling?' Perry, confrontational, offended, asked his sister. 'All this has something to do with her, and with you probably.'

He cast Emilia an apologetic look steeped in hopelessness, then reached over Selina's knee and tapped gently on Libby's head. She had gone stiff all over, and Will and Tom were staring at the adults, nonplussed. 'Libby, darling, come to Daddy. We're going home.'

Alec drove his reliable Ford Coupe into the field just then and Perry stayed put. The motor car jolted over the dried-earth ruts at the entrance and swayed like some refined chugging monster down the field. Alec stopped the car as near as he could to the spectators' seats. With the help of Elena, he offloaded his elderly and infirm passengers. Two men in shiny-worn suits and wing collars, retired brothers, former employees of Ford Farm, dwellers in one of his rented cottages, were grinning broadly, feeling their conveyance here by the squire had upped them to a position of some esteem. Jim, hovering near by, shot out his arm to escort a petite, bent, dark-clad, bonneted nonagenarian, wielding a fearsome walking stick and a moth-eaten handbag to a chair cleared in her honour. While Elena attempted conversation with the hard-of-hearing Widow Bennett, who was trembling a little due to her very first journey in a motor car, he dashed off to buy, at his own expense, a tray of three cream teas.

Will ran to his father and Alec swung him up on his shoulders. 'Well, son, how did you get on in the races? Daddy's sorry he had to miss yours and Tom's events but the beasts had to be seen to. You know that, don't you?' Although the scar from the dog bite on Will's leg had healed ages ago Alec glanced at it as if to reassure himself of the fact.

Will held on proudly to his father's upraised hands. 'I know, and I know you like for the workers to come as early as they can. I came second in the egg and spoon race and joint third with Tom in the three-legged. Tom couldn't get his legs to work with mine, even though we'd practised hard.

But, Daddy, I've won a first! I ran faster than anyone else in the fifty yards. I won my first sixpence all to myself. Tom fell in the sack race, he's so clumsy.'

Alec grinned, proud and satisfied to the ends of his soul over his sons' achievements. 'I don't suppose Tom was in the least bit concerned about the fall.'

'No, he just got up and stood there and giggled and giggled. Like a girl,' Will finished in disgust.

Alec searched and found his younger son, so good-humoured and simplistic, where he expected him to be, joined to his mother, the mother he adored and was so proud to be with. Tom's mother, his wife, lovely, courageous Emilia. Alec's love for her took on a new depth in that moment. Emilia had saved him from a life of loneliness and misery, and he had come so close to betraying her. A part of him, the base nature in him recognized that he still wanted Sara Killigrew. He put the matter of having to move her out of the farm aside for now.

His eyes fell on Perry Bosweld. Why was he so down in the dumps? There had been something about the Boswelds in the back of his mind for some time, like an itch in his subconscious, which he had been meaning to scratch, to explore. Something was wrong. Something was going on. Perry seemed a fine, decent chap, he made good company, he had been a rock to Emilia; a Godsend to them both, diagnosing Jenna's problems, giving them the chance to spend her last moments with her. But his sister . . . there was something insidious and dark about that woman. He would keep watchful for now, but the days of the Boswelds living in his property were numbered. Having them there was unsettling and all he wanted for his family was to know peace and security.

Will leaned down to Alec's ear and said cajolingly, 'Daddy?'

'I know what's coming, son.' Alec was nothing but indulgent.

'How much can we have? Me, Tom and Jonny and the girls too.'

Bringing Will down to the ground with such an exaggerated swing that it made an exciting whooshing, Alec placed a pound note in Will's hand and closed his fist round it. 'Equal shares for all now, and don't tell your mother how much I've given you. Where's Jonny? I suppose he won every race he entered?' Alec hoped he had not sneaked off for a smoke.

'Of course he did. He's got a trophy. He's about somewhere.' And Will tore off to find him, clasping the pound note as tightly as if it was precious gold.

Alec joined the rest of his family. He parked himself closely on Emilia's other side, kissed her, hugging her tightly, keeping his arm round her. Selina was up so far to her he felt the back of his hand resting against her fuller body. He did not like the woman monopolizing Emilia, being so familiar. He ruffled Tom's hair and Tom patted his large rough hand. 'Well done, son, on coming third in the three-legged race.'

'Where's Will gone?'

'Where do you think? You'd better be quick.'

The promise of sweets and the fear of his brother scoffing some of his share made Tom abandon his beloved mother and hare off to the shop stall. 'Come on, Libby!'

Alec laughed. 'Now if Tom applied himself to the races in the same way he'd come out a winner every time.'

Emilia shivered inside. Her lap felt cold with Tom gone.

Unsettled by the antagonism shown to her and her family, Libby stayed with her father, whispering to him that she wanted to go home. Emilia leaned round Selina to give her a reassuring smile but her little face was pressed into Perry's neck.

Alec gazed up at the banner bearing his daughter's name and stayed silent awhile, his thoughts his own. 'Are you all right, darling?'

'I'm fine, Alec.'

'You're looking lovely, Winnie. You're blooming like a huge beautiful flower.'

'I'll take that as a compliment, cousin.' Winifred's answer was restrained due to the awkward situation. 'I'm looking forward to the tug-of-war.'

'Ben and his team don't stand a chance.' Alec was a little aggressive in his boast. He glanced at the Bosweld brother and sister. 'Hello. Why the long faces? Libby's doesn't look happy either.'

'We don't feel welcome here,' Perry replied, and he sounded so miserable, so hurt and offended it was an effort for Emilia not to jump up and go to him. In turn, he was thinking wretchedly that if not for Emilia, he would pack up and leave Hennaford tonight. His despair plunged to an even deeper level, for part of him for one terrible moment wished he had already endured the final parting with her.

Emilia explained why the archery gear had been taken down early, indignant anger making her shake.

Alec held her firmly. 'How strange. I wonder why.'

'That's what I intend to discover and what I already would have done if this event was not partly a solemn occasion.' Selina crossly lit another cigarette. 'Come for a walk with me, Em?'

'Sorry.' Alec put a note of curtness in his tone. 'I haven't seen my wife all day.' Then tender and kind, 'Let me take you to the marquee, darling. I'm hungry and thirsty and you look like you need some attentive care.'

Emilia went with him, glad to get away from Selina's clinging company, trying to convey love and encouragement to Perry in one short look.

'So that's Ben's famous dancing platform, is it? He's made a good effort, even had the timber varnished. I suppose he and Brooke will start off the dancing,' Alec said, a gentle grip on Emilia's hand that was tucked through the crook of his arm. He could not help feeling rankled to see Ben, with Brooke, beside his creation, receiving acclaim like some benevolent lord. Then it amused him to see Ben and his bride were exchanging vexed words.

Glancing back over her shoulder, Emilia saw Perry heading towards the trap, pushed over the uneven ground by her father, with a mournful Libby trotting at the side of the wheeled chair, clutching Perry's hand. Selina had stayed put, staring ahead, jerking a cigarette up to her lips. 'What? I suppose they will. Mrs Dowling asked me if you and I would like to do the honours, after you'd given a short speech about this being a memorial day for Jenna this year. I said no to the dancing, but I thought you could say a few words, Alec. That was all right, wasn't it?'

'Yes . . . yes, I'll think of something appropriate.' Alec took Emilia to Ben and Brooke. 'Not interrupting your first quarrel, I hope.'

'Not at all,' Brooke replied, while Ben's darkened eyes settled uneasily on Emilia. 'I've been urging Ben to tell you both something you really ought to know.'

'I'm sorry, Emilia,' Ben said, 'I thought it could wait until the evening was over, but now you're here I believe Brooke is right.'

'This has got to be about Selina Bosweld.' Emilia raised her head, bracing herself, willing it not to be anything too terrible for Perry's sake. 'Well, what is it?'

Emilia listened, furious over the hurt Perry was already suffering, the humiliation he had to bear, the distress for Libby at the scandal Selina had caused. 'The despicable creature! I'd better get my mother and Winnie away from her.'

'Where's Tris?' Alec scanned the crowds. 'He doesn't seem to be anywhere.'

'I've no idea,' Emilia said. 'I'd assumed he'd gone to fetch something for Winnie.'

Tristan was on the school premises, creeping close along the side of the hedge, having scrambled over it silently and unseen. He was soon climbing again, under cover of the trees and foxgloves and tall greenery, and there was his quarry, his son, flat on his front, his long legs dangling against grasses, dock leaves and cow parsley. He was directly in line behind Selina Bosweld and aiming a slingshot at her.

With military skill Tristan leaned forward, swiped the slingshot out of Jonny's hand and smothered his mouth, cutting off an exclamation of surprise and sudden fright. 'Don't speak, son. Slip down on to your feet. You and I need a little talk.'

Red-faced, nervous sweat sparkling all over his dark skin, Jonny plodded tensely at his father's side, a heavy paternal hand on his shoulder, until they reached a corner of the girls' playground, where there was no chance of them being overheard.

'She deserved what she was going to get, Dad.' Jonny shivered despite the fever he was in, his head hung over.

Tristan lifted Jonny's chin and was alarmed to see the panic in his generally fearless son. 'Why so, Jonny? Surely you've not got anything to do with what I've just been hearing about her, why she was dismissed from the Infirmary?'

'I know nothing about that.'

'What then? You're scared half out of your wits. If you were so worried about getting into trouble over what you planned to do, why go ahead with it?'

'Revenge. I hate her!'

'Jonny, what over?' Tristan was disturbed by the vehemence, the contortion in his young face. 'Did she do something to you? Don't be afraid to speak up. You can tell me anything. I'm your father.'

'I saw her with Jim, doing things.' Jonny mumbled, embarrassed now. 'You know, grown-up things. I mentioned it to her. I thought she was nice, you see, and I wanted to warn her before she got found out and people turned against her. But she got angry.' Jonny's lower lip wobbled at the fearful memory. 'She said if I told anyone she would . . . would cut off my privates with a surgeon's knife. She meant it, Dad. She really did. She looked like an ogress when she said it.'

'Right!' Tristan grew grim. He took some time to hug his son, allowing Jonny's tears to fall. 'Jonny, I want you to know that I'd never let anyone hurt you. I'm going to sort this out. I'll have a word with Miss Selina Bosweld.'

'But Dad—'

'Don't worry, Jonny. No one on God's earth is going to threaten my son!'

Tristan reached Selina Bosweld at the same time as Emilia, Alec, Ben and Brooke arrived to extricate Dolly and Winifred from her company. Jonny trailed a little behind, eyes confidently on his father's upright back. His father had gone far up in his estimation now. 'I want a word with you, woman. Now! Alone.'

Selina gazed at him, unblinking, as if bored and annoyed. She took in the boy, keeping behind his father. 'I'm going nowhere. If it's about what I said to your Jonny a little while ago, I didn't mean it, of course.'

'He believes you did. You frightened him very badly, and it's a contemptible thing to say to a child anyway, let alone issuing it as a threat. You'd best leave here immediately. The whole village knows you for what you really are. Mrs Dowling is baying for your blood. The unfortunate innocent wife was her cousin and Mrs Dowling's furious that there's now a public scandal.' It was a rarity to see Selina blush, to gulp in unease. 'As I thought, you didn't know about that.'

Selina looked pleadingly at Emilia. 'Let me explain.'

Emilia wanted to say, 'Don't seek comfort from me, Selina Bosweld. You ruin people's lives,' but to spare further pain to Perry and Libby, she said stiffly, 'It would be better if you go, Selina.'

Springing to her feet, Selina made to hurtle away.

Daphne Dowling was in her path. The rector's wife swung back her prim white-gloved hand and slapped her hard across the face. 'Harlot! You'll burn in hell for what you've done and none will deserve it more.'

Selina held her seared cheek then she pushed past her accusers and ran. A volley of jeers followed after her. Near the piglet pen, she yelped, fell with a resounding thud sprawled forward, then was reaching down to a sprained ankle. Jim was there, but not wanting the village to know he had been this woman's lover too, he stepped away as if in quiet distaste. There were a lot of people about. No one offered to help Selina up.

Emilia started towards her. Perry had witnessed the fall and was leaning forward, beckoning to Selina. For his sake, she couldn't stand by and watch Selina flounder.

Alec grabbed her elbow. 'Leave her. We'll collect the children together and enjoy the rest of the day.'

'But Perry and Libby—'

'He probably knew what she was up to. He should have stopped it.' Alec was stern, uncompromising. 'I'm not allowing you to go to that family, Emilia. This is our community and they don't belong in it. Tomorrow I'll give them notice to leave my house.'

Her heart rent over Perry's feelings and the sound of Libby's gasping sobs, Emilia had no choice in allowing Alec to turn her away from the spectacle of Selina hobbling in humiliation towards them. 'You can't turn the family out of their home, Alec,' she argued. 'I won't let you. Perry and Libby aren't responsible for what Selina's done. You know how headstrong, how independent she is. It would be like trying to turn back the tide.'

'Why do you like the family so much?' Alec was curious and demanding, piqued. He wanted his way over this. 'You spend a lot of time with them. You didn't like Selina Bosweld at all at first.'

'You're forgetting how good even Selina was to me over Jenna. She will be leaving here soon anyway. She wants to be a doctor. I don't see why Perry and Libby deserved to be punished over her failings.'

Alec was thoughtful. 'It would mean a lot to you if I went easy on them then?'

'Yes,' she clasped his hand. 'Please Alec. At least don't do anything in haste.'

During the confusion, Sara and Wally Eathorne had arrived, arms linked, unmistakably a couple. Wally was talking enthusiastically to his parents and Jim. The frail, wasted Mrs Eathorne, who was about to be taken home to rest, beckoned to Sara to bend her head and Sara received a welcoming kiss. Eustace Eathorne was shaking his son's hand, slapping him on the back. Jim was hugging Sara. Sara had got herself engaged! Alec wasn't pleased about this. She might have just made a terrible mistake. It would be his fault. He had encouraged her and pushed her away. He would be responsible for any future unhappiness that came her way. This would solve his problem over Sara's accommodation and it was better still that she would be leaving the farm altogether, but his irresponsibility, his selfishness made his insides squirm, for even now he didn't like the thought of her going away, of leaving him. Who am I, he was thinking, to pass judgement on others?

'Alec?' Maddened, Emilia shook his arm to regain his attention. This was not the time for him to retreat into meditation.

He gave her a conciliatory smile. 'You're right, darling. It isn't Perry and Libby's fault. I won't ask the Boswelds to leave but I hope Selina moves out very soon. Perry's been a good tenant. He's a good man. You may do all you can to make him and Libby feel wanted.'

Twenty-Nine

Libby Bosweld lifted her chin to the window in the back of the taxi-cab and gazed out at Ford Farm. The only signs of life were Bertie and Hope sniffing about the hedge and a fat straying hen. 'No one's come out to wave goodbye to Mirelle and me, Daddy. I hate the Harveys. I hate Hennaford. I never want to come back here again!'

Perry reached out to her but she clamped her arms round Casper's neck; the dog was fretting on the seat between them. 'You must never hate, darling. Don't be cross with the Harveys, they're still good friends of ours, remember? They probably thought the cab would be driving through the village.'

'Tell me again about our new house,' Libby said, still looking fierce, anxious, rejected.

Perry stroked her tawny curls and rattled off the details of the terraced house Selina was renting in a quiet suburb of South London. 'She's going to meet you and Mirelle off the train and I shall follow on in a couple of days.'

'But I want you to come with us now!'

'I know darling, but we'll soon be all together again. I've to finish packing up the house and there are people I need to say goodbye to.' One in particular, and after waving his daughter off at Truro railway station he was to spend the rest of the day with her.

Libby, a little pacified, a little brighter when Hennaford was completely left behind, began playing with Casper's ears. 'I still never want to go back there.'

I do, Perry said to himself, holding the perfect image of Emilia in his mind. One day I shall come back. That I swear.

* * *

She wanted to run to him. She made herself walk instead, at a normal pace, a dark figure, hidden in the shade of a sunhat and parasol. She had got out of the taxi-cab shortly after it had branched off from Highertown into Penweathers Lane. Reggie Rule's secluded, stone-fronted little house was now in sight and Perry should be inside waiting for her.

She rolled up the parasol and put her hand out to the door the same instant he opened it. She stepped inside quickly, through the porch into the hall, taking no notice of the simple decor, the basic surroundings, while Perry locked and drew the bolt on the door. All she saw was Perry. All she knew was Perry. All she felt was for Perry.

'I was so afraid something would happen to prevent you from coming, darling.' He carefully lifted off her hat and peeled off her gloves. 'I watched you approaching from the window. You looked so small and uncertain. You don't regret it do you, Em? Having to steal the time to come here to see me? Having to be circumspect?'

She went to him, gathered his body into hers, settling into him as he brought his arms around her. 'All I care about is just being with you, Perry, darling.'

'Let's forget about everything but us, darling Em, and not think about the dreadful words that we must say until the very last minute.'

She nodded. Smiled, sending all her love to him in that one smile. A smile he would hold in his heart for ever. She reached for his mouth, wanting to kiss him all day, to turn these few hours, this last encounter into a lifetime of loving. To make enough memories that she could store and cherish for a lifetime. His lips felt blissfully familiar yet new and fresh to her. The way he kissed filled her with fierce, raw, rapturous sensations that were almost painful to bear.

Just one touch from her was enough to rend from him a sacred sigh of love. His whole being was flooded with life. He had never really been alive until the moment he had first met her, and after today he would return to a state of semi-being, half-alive, a soul without its mate. It was how he would be until he felt it was time to return. Secretly he would come back, and see if there was a chance he could have her for himself. Selfish it might be, but he had to allow himself this vestige of hope if he was to endure the lonely years ahead.

The progress of their love moved them, with her aid on the stairs, up to the bedroom at the back of the building, overlooking the spacious garden. The room was light and pretty, the bed covered with bright cushions of Eastern silk and design. Roses of red, white, purple and gold were in a glass vase on a little round table. 'I've no idea what colour rose is supposed to be the most romantic, so I got you some of every colour I could find,' Perry said, holding her, kissing her. 'Think of me every time you see or breathe the scent of a rose, darling.'

'I will. I'll keep roses in the house all summer long.'

'I will too. I brought some food and wine. We have everything we need here.'

'We do.'

He looked and looked at her, smiling a little sadly, loving her. Seeing her love smiling back at him. He put his hands on her, began unfastening her clothes. 'I want more than anything to lie down with you, Em. I want to hold you until I feel you'll always be with me. I want to look at you until your face is always before me. I want to know you and see all of you.' Then he stopped, a little uncertain. 'You won't be put off by my disablement?'

She caressed his gorgeous face. 'Darling Perry, I love you exactly as you are and I will never, ever, stop loving you.'

And so they grew familiar in every infinitesimal way, knowing the finest, the beautiful, and the superb. She looked into his eyes until she felt her own eyes were the same precious-gem blue of his. She kissed his mouth until she felt the exquisite touch of his would be on hers for ever. She touched his handsome face until her fingertips were left with the everlasting impression of his beauty and nobility. Sometimes there were tears in their eyes and the other would kiss them away.

They held on lovingly, expressing their love in utter

tenderness, in wild passion, in gentle touches and silken caresses. Again and again they loved as close as a man and a woman could get. Sometimes a near desperation lent an edge to their pleasure, he taking her with him and she taking him with her. They flew, they soared, and they knew glories. They knew love. They knew things even beyond love. Experiences so profound, so extraordinary, it left them sweetly disturbed, clinging in heart, in body, in soul. They knew a sweet dark peace, a golden peace. And stayed in it. Making time last, until it would no longer be swayed by their desperate spirits or the completeness of their love. Until time no longer allowed them to stretch out its moments.

Her steps echoed bare, lost and heavy as she wandered through the empty house. Everything Perry, Selina, Libby and the tiny French housemaid had brought to Ford House with them was gone. But a sense of each personality lingered still, in a fleeting shadow, a snatch of whisper, a brooding hush, a resonance of laughter. Or even the scratch of a puppy's paws.

In the kitchen she could almost smell Mirelle's alarmingly strong coffee and taste her mouth-watering Continental bread, almost hear the tireless blackbird of a woman jabbering as she scolded Casper, or sang in a strange evocative pitch in her own language; times when she'd paused to dry away a tear. Once Mirelle had stared at her, shaking her peasant-scarfed old head, lifting her scrawny shoulders high while making a doomed-to-failure gesture, conveying, so Emilia had believed, that she knew about the impossible future of the love that had begun in this house. Then she had turned away, apologetic and crying. Crying for Perry, Emilia had silently acknowledged.

Please don't be too lonely, Perry. Find someone else. You have so much love to give and you deserve to be loved every day of your life.

Slowly, for her legs would go no faster, she mounted the stairs. Little Libby's bedroom, so abandoned, so forlorn, the saddest room of all. Jonny and Vera Rose had spent the last day of their stay here with her, returning to report that she was both excited and afraid of the move to London, but glad to be getting away from those who had been so beastly towards her adored Aunt Selina, her daddy and herself.

It took courage to venture where Selina had slept. Where, Emilia imagined, she had gloried in her seductions and affairs and where she had planned the next, her greatest coup.

The morning after the sports day, Emilia had come to Ford House to find out how the family were. Not unexpectedly, Libby was fretful, keeping attached to Perry. They had been poring over a photograph album.

'I'm trying to distract her,' Perry had smiled bravely, his smile as usual, wholly beautiful, and Emilia's love for him, infinite and ageless as it was, had burned even more intensely and her pain was nearly unbearable.

She could not keep at a careful distance, a proper distance, and sat beside him on the sofa. Secretly they had held hands, so tightly. 'Perry . . . ?'

'We're going to be fine, Em. I'm fine, honestly. Here's a photo of Libby and I, taken just before we came here. It's one of our favourites but you must have it.' The underlying intention in the gift was plain in the sadness of his voice. It was a studio study, a non-intimate gift to everyone except her. 'Perhaps, I could have one of you . . . ?'

'Of course.'

There had been a moment when neither had known what to say, in which he had almost crushed her fingers.

'Could I . . . could I ask you to go up to Selina? She's in a bit of a state.' His look had conveyed this to be a watered-down description for Libby's sake. 'She won't come out of her room, or eat or drink. She might listen to you.'

It had been hard to leave him then, nearly as painful as the anguish at the very last time. 'I'll see what I can do.'

She had found Selina a shadowy figure, curled up, hugging a pillow on the big double bed. Her impious eyes closed. The curtains were closed. She was in the same clothes as the day before, her ankle bandaged. She babbled something viciously in French; ordering the maid to leave her alone, Emilia had guessed.

'It's me, Selina.' Emilia quietly closed the door.

Selina gazed up but did not make a movement or show any emotion. 'Why have you come?'

'To see how Perry and Libby are.'

Easing herself up stiffly due to lengthy immobility, Selina had settled herself against the headboard. The violet hue of her eyes had gleamed in the dimness, strangely active. 'You'll be glad to learn I'm leaving on the overnight train for London. My brother and niece will be following me as soon as I've found somewhere for *all* of us to live.'

Determined not to reveal the appalling effects of actually hearing for the first time that Perry was going away, Emilia had flung back the curtains, wishing the brilliant sunlight would blot out the other woman's eyes. 'You're a cruel heartless woman, Selina Bosweld.'

'But you don't wish you'd never met me, do you, Emilia? Or it would mean you'd never have met Perry. You'll never regret that, will you? Even though you're about to lose him, even though when you started with him you must have known you could never really keep him.'

Emilia had darted up to her, leaning forward, on fire. 'Think you know something about how it feels to love and lose someone, do you?'

'Yes! Yes, I do.'

'How? How could you possibly know?'

'Because I too am about to leave behind for ever someone I love. A love that could never be reciprocated, and it's even worse now because the person concerned despises me.'

Emilia regarded her disbelievingly. Selina's returning stare had softened, full of meaning, and Emilia had thought hard to grasp what it was. 'You don't mean Alec? Do you think you've fallen in love with him?'

'Not Alec, Emilia. You, Em . . .' Reaching out, Selina had grabbed her hand. Began to cry softly. 'I've always wanted you. If I could have made it happen nothing would have stopped me. I didn't realize until yesterday, when I knew I had no choice but to leave here straight away, how strong my feelings really were for you. I admit I've hurt a lot of people. This time, I've hurt myself too.'

Jerking her hand free, Emilia had stood back from the bed, the shock of the declaration spreading icy rivers through her entire body. 'I . . . I don't know what to say. I had no idea.'

Selina could not meet her astonished, appalled eyes. 'Why should you? The very idea of what's known as ancient love disgusts many, and most aren't even aware it exists. I've explored all kinds of love, never believing I'd ever fall in love. And now that I have, all I will have to show for it is a terrible loneliness that I don't think will ever leave me. It's my punishment. I deserve it. Go downstairs to Perry, Emilia. Spend what time you can with him. He doesn't know about the other side of my life, please spare him that.'

She had looked up, pleading. 'Please don't hate me. Just let me tell you this one time, that I love you, Em. I love you.'

Emilia left behind the echo of Selina's tormented sobs as she went downstairs to Perry's empty bedroom. The room where their association, their love had begun. The language of his love and devotion was whispering to her now as she stood in the space where the bed had been, where she had laid her little girl down, where she and Perry had first kissed. The room was returned to a dining room now and like the rest of the house pristine, ready for prospective owners to view. Emilia was thankful that Ben had no wish to buy it. She would never step over this threshold again.

She went outside and locked the door. Locking away the part of her life she should never have possessed, and never would again.

Going back down the hill, she took the fork in the lane to the ford. It wasn't necessary to use the bridge, there had been no rain for several days and the dip in the ground was dry. As were her eyes. She had already cried herself dry. She'd had her moments with Jenna. And her moments with Perry. Now she must go on with Alec.

She climbed the hill to the farm. Returning to her children.

To the enduring love she shared with Alec, which would see her through the years.